# THE
# LONG
# SUMMER

# THE
# LONG
# SUMMER

## ALAN WHITE

HARCOURT BRACE JOVANOVICH

NEW YORK AND LONDON

Printed in the United States of America

Library of Congress Cataloging in Publication Data

White, Alan.
    The long summer.

    I.  Title.
PZ4.W5827Lrg3   [PR6073.H49]      823'.9'14      75-17601
ISBN 0-15-153079-3

First American edition 1975

B C D E

# 1

When I turned my head round I saw the sergeant major
and behind him the ships sailing across the line of advance,
and I heard the boom of guns and the crack of answering
fire from the land. White pillars of foaming sea were being
drawn up around the navy and some shots from the land
hit and made fire and smoke.

'Eyes front, Tom,' the sergeant major said softly, 'or you
may never know what hit you.'

Sergeant Williams on my right, Chalky beside me, Runty
forward, next to the Bren, Lance Corporal Smith somewhere
at the back. 4732849 Private Wilkins, T. (for Tom), that
was me, and if they caught me that was all I would have
to say.

'Don't worry, lads,' the sergeant had told us, 'the Gestapo
and the SS don't bother with privates.'

'They just cut 'em off,' Runty had said. His was a right
macabre sense of humour.

I was finding it hard to judge distance low down on the
surface of the sea in a landing craft. The coastline was
perhaps half a mile away, long and dark, but not the least
bit sinister. But why should it be? That's all in the mind,
like being frightened. I looked across the sea which glistened
like a polished bald head to where the waves chopped the
edges of the coast. So that was France. I felt disappointed;
it could have been any one of our training beaches. The
landing forces to our left and right weren't having an easy
time, but so far nobody had fired at us. I was sitting half
way along the landing craft on the left side. Chalky, beside
me, had been sick time and time again. Now his face was
grey-green in the strong starlight and shone smooth as rubbed

 1

plasticine. There were tears in his eyes. Poor bugger once said he'd never be able to kill anybody, never be able to bring himself to do it. Soon he'd get a chance to prove that one way or the other, because that wasn't a training beach out there no matter how it looked. It was the north coast of France. And those weren't straw-filled sacks you charged and yelled at, feeling like a prick with your bayonet sticking out. They were real live Germans and they'd been sitting comfortably for a long while, stacking concrete blocks round themselves for bullets to bounce off. We'd be on our feet running or on our knackers crawling, while they took time to aim and fire, placing each shot with precision like Runty going for double top and never ever missing.

When they called me up in 1942 I wanted to go into the Artillery and went before the Selection Board full of confidence. I'd got a distinction in maths in the school cert. But they put me into the Infantry, sent me on a thirteen-week course and posted me to the Royal West Kents at Maidstone. In the camp up the road, the one with barbed wire round it. Not the barracks near the town where you could get a late pass any night of the week and it didn't matter anyway since there were a dozen points on the perimeter you could get out and in again. Life in the camp settled down to a routine. Training every day, weekends off when you weren't on guard duty, long leave every three months, weekend pass every month. The only complaint was the food. I reckon I spent ten bob a week in the NAAFI. I was dead lucky, of course, but then they say I'm the sort who would fall in a cowpat and come out smelling of violets.

I had two birds. One worked in the British Restaurant in Maidstone and was always good for a free meal. The other was the daughter of the adjutant, who'd had a bad leg all her life, and I taught her to dance. Well, it started out like that. One night, at the camp dance in the gymnasium at the barracks, I won the ballroom-dancing prize with a scrubber from the NAAFI who looked like the back-end of a bus but could do the tango a treat. The adjutant, a nice old buffer

2

about fifty-five who'd been brought back onto active duty to run the regimental office, asked me if I'd give his daughter a few lessons. Strictly professional, you understand. He had his quarters in a house near the gate, and the main room, the drawing room I suppose you'd call it, was thirty feet long and twenty wide. We would push back the furniture Tuesdays and Fridays, when I wasn't on guard duty, and I taught Mary the waltz, the foxtrot and the quickstep. At first she was dead awkward, but the Harley Street specialist had said the dancing was good for her muscle development, and we kept at it. Half a crown an hour, and a bloody good supper afterwards.

It was a good life, until we were put on permanent standby in 1944, March, and the dancing had to stop in more ways than one. Almost overnight I had to grow up. Almost overnight I had to forget the little things – like my blistered feet, and the sores on my shoulders where the pack rubbed them, the back-sight scars on the thumb of my right hand. There was no time to bother about things like that. Because now I had to face up to the fact that I was a trained soldier on standby to go to France and fight the enemy; nobody was going to hold my hand any more, and say, 'no, not that way, go back and do it again.' Because my job had suddenly become kill before they could kill me.

Now I had become a soldier, and the only reason for soldiers is to fight wars, to stop people doing what you don't want them to do. The only way to do that, in the long run, is to kill them.

The coast of France was perhaps half a mile away. I'd been told the plan. We'd run as far up the beach as we could. We wouldn't fire from the landing craft, only disembark on orders from Lieutenant Soames. On disembarkation, we'd make our way up the beach keeping a distance of six feet from the next soldier in line. We would not bunch to provide a more easy target for the enemy. We would advance as far as the road at the top of the beach. We would not cross the road until ordered to do so by a responsible officer or NCO.

When we arrived at the road, we would dig in to the best of our ability.

Our target was a gun emplacement sited on a hummock three hundred yards from the water line. We would wait at the side of the road until we received orders to advance. We would then observe normal fire and movement techniques, in the manner in which we had trained, by section and platoon. When we had taken the gun emplacement, Lieutenant Soames, or a responsible officer or NCO, would inform us of the next target. Under no circumstances would we undertake individual and independent action. Our general purpose, given to us for information only, was to advance twelve miles into France where we would make contact with airborne units dropped previously. The contact code word was Jupiter. Once contact had been established we would regroup.

Any moment now, I'd see the gun emplacement. Any moment now, the gun emplacement would see me. Chalky moaned, tried to be sick again. Cutler in front of me was sick over the side. Somebody had gouged the word 'NAPOLI' on the wooden capping of the boat's edge. I traced it again with my finger. The wood of the seat was damp with dew and spray, and my left trouser had pulled out of my gaiter. I bent down and tucked it in as best I could. I eased the pack straps on my shoulders. Cold for June; air smelled of salt spray like a cockles and mussels cart. Guns firing over on the right, a long slow pounding boom, with a lacing of staccato machine-gun fire. Over on the left, black night, deep now the tracer had ended. And ahead of us, silence, dark silence. The chug of the engine of the boat sounded loud, but I could hear other boats making the same sound chugging through the water. Somebody forward of me dropped his rifle clattering into the metal boat and I heard him curse as he bent down.

'Watch it, lad,' came from the sergeant major behind me.

They say you don't feel the pain when a bullet hits you. Only later. They say it's like a thump, like when a friend you haven't seen for a long time, and whose name you can't remember, greets you enthusiastically because he's also forgotten your name, thumps you on the shoulder and says, 'Look who's here, you old sod.'

They say you never feel a landmine. The shock's so great it knocks you unconscious. Corporal Runty lost a toe on a landmine in North Africa, had a bullet in his shoulder. He should know. He told us about it once over a pint of shandy in the NAAFI. Silly bugger got the pox off a nurse in a hospital in Bradford. He should have known about that, too, but he didn't. What if he was wrong about the bullets and the landmines? Lance Corporal Smith took the moral line as usual. 'The Good Lord's taken care of that,' he said, pouting at his shandy like a reluctant virgin. 'Why do you think He makes us faint at moments like that?'

'Faint, you bleeding ponce,' Corporal Runty said, 'I've never fainted in my entire frigging life.'

Lance Corporal Smith looked smug, cast his eyes to the heavens, and said nothing.

We'd been told the beach would be covered in landmines. The boat in front was full of Engineers and Chalky had a mine-detector. Went on a course for it. Sixpence a day extra. He'll be on my right, Lance Corporal Smith on the left. The lance corporal had the signal exchange. Poor bugger, it takes sixty lines and weighs sixty pounds. I had my rifle, five hundred rounds of .303 ammo, six hand-grenades H.G., six two-inch mortar shells for the mortar team, a bayonet and my own two legs.

'Carry you anywhere, your legs will,' Mr Soames had said once after a route march. 'So long as you wash your feet properly and dry between your toes.'

Mary Brassingham had beautiful long toes at the bottom of her bent leg. The bend had something to do with a bone disease – osteo something or other. She was eighteen. The top of her head came level with my eyes. She'd soft fine hair that moved when I blew into it. I noticed it moved when I talked into it to correct her steps. She was very conscious of her leg, had spent a lot of time crying about it, her father told me. Her mother died when Mary was born and she lived alone with her father, Major Brassingham. Plenty of money, servants in the house and all that. The major had retired from the army in 1935 and grew roses in Hampshire, until they brought him back. He sat in the regimental office, dispensing authority and justice from a book he hadn't written. Mary was working at the hospital in Maidstone, and sometimes she'd come home late and the major and I would sit and talk. I was always at ease with him. He called me 'lad' at first, but when I got to know him he called me Tom. I never called him anything but 'Sir.' He'd pour a couple of glasses of whisky from a decanter he kept on the mahogany sideboard. It was all his own furniture; he'd brought it with him, and thrown out the army issue. I felt he'd brought so many things with him I could have the privileged use of – his dignity, his decency, his interest in everything. Especially his concern for Mary. 'I'm too old for her,' he said, 'the girl needs companions her own age. That's why I'm so keen on this dancing. Bring her up to snuff, Tom, and you'll be doing a great service. Build her confidence, make her ready to take her place in the world.'

At first I thought he meant 'prepare her to meet the right sort of blue-blood.' Kind of getting her ready for the cattle auction. And in the early days I resented that. I think he used to enjoy it when she was late from the hospital. Sometimes I'd be able to make him chuckle, and I felt he hadn't had too many chuckles in his life. I'd lay it on a bit thick, say outrageous things, exaggerate a bit. Our worlds were so far apart he had no way of checking up on me. And all the commonplaces of my working-class life in the North fascinated him. 'You don't mean to tell me they actually . . .' but his use of 'they' was not a snobbish separation into us and them. It was a glimpse into a world he knew existed, but the one club from which he was automatically blackballed by birth – the club of the working class. It was a damn pity. He'd have made a marvellous union secretary, or charity organizer for the Salvation Army.

He had grey cropped hair and one of those faces of tanned leather that never changes, winter or summer. When his eyes weren't focused directly on you, you got the feeling he was off in a private world. Don't run away with the idea he was always like that – he could be really angry. I only saw it once and was glad it wasn't directed at me. One evening the telephone rang as we were drinking whisky. He listened quietly then said, 'Have him brought to me.' The look in his eyes made me shudder. 'You'll have to excuse me for a few moments, Tom,' he said. I went into the drawing room and moved the furniture for the dancing class. The door to the major's study wasn't properly shut and I heard 'him' arrive, a young officer who'd returned to camp, drunk. Apparently he'd abused the camp guard and the guard commander had telephoned the major. I'll never forget the tongue-lashing he gave that young officer.

I waited in the drawing room until Mary arrived, not wanting to face the major again.

'Right lads,' the sergeant major said, 'get your heads down.'

The French coastline was seven hundred yards away and the engines had begun to turn over faster. The stink of oil and fuel was suddenly stronger, almost overpowering. Cutler was wiping his face where he'd been sick. Chalky pulled the mine-detector between his feet, held it with his calves and rubbed his hands together. I wouldn't swing a mine-detector for sixpence a day, knowing how many feet were following.

Dank smell of serge uniforms, and, oddly, a sudden whiff of dubbin. No polished boots tonight. And brasses covered with blanco that rubbed off if you weren't careful. I'd painted mine with dull green enamel I bought in Woolworths. It was the last tin; other people had had the same idea. Anybody behind the counter using his loaf would have guessed something was 'on', but I never gave that a thought. We were all supposed to be confined to barracks at the time, but thanks to the dancing lessons I had a special pass. I was

7

just finishing off the reverse turn in the tango.

Dew everywhere in the landing craft, on the gunwales, the seats, the rail. What about the ramp? Would the ramp be slippery? Silly picture of myself falling, going like a skittle ball, knocking 'em down. A smell of shit; somebody had to do it. No disgrace, the MO said, merely a muscular reflex. 'Now, if any of you men should find that in the course of sudden or violent action your muscles should relax and you pass a motion, I don't want you to get the idea that this is a manifestation of cowardice. Quite the reverse. Some of our bravest men . . .' I wanted names. Did Wellington shit himself at Waterloo? Prince Albert on the night of his wedding?

When the sergeant major says *Now*, stand up, take a pace to the right into the aisle and double smartly forward. Practised it many times with chairs in the NAAFI, benches in the ABCA hut. We'd never actually tried it with a landing craft, never even seen a landing craft before last night. And didn't ever want to see one again. We could empty the ABCA hut in one minute flat. The trick is that you all start running together and nobody says 'after you Claude, after you Cecil'. That first step does it; get that right and you'll be off and running before they have time to reload. They did say that Number 3 platoon did it in seventeen seconds. We would have, too, if Chalky hadn't got the pole of his mine-detector stuck between Cutler's legs and brought him down. Only it wasn't a mine-detector, it was a broomstick. The actual Detectors, Mine Mark II, Invading Armies for the Use of, didn't arrive until the day before we left and then they had to be worked over by a guy from REME who had a sour face and bad breath. One of the valves was wrong or something.

'Don't trip anybody this time,' I whispered to Chalky. He looked sideways at me with a crooked smile. 'Like to carry the bloody thing?' he said.

'You're the one getting the tanner a day, mate.'

The sergeant major hissed at us. Silence in the boat now,

8

deliberate ending of noise. Everybody still, holding his breath, everybody cramped, no one moving.

'They probably won't fire until we're six hundred feet from the shoreline,' Mr Soames had said. 'The heavy stuff will go over our heads at the fleet behind us, and the mortars will be working at either side. All we have to worry about is one gun, maximum range seven hundred and fifty feet, but they'll be nervous too and probably start when we're just out of range.' Six hundred feet plus three to the road plus another hundred and fifty: that's a hell of a lot of nervousness. You can forget the quoted range of a weapon. One of the lads had his eye put out by a .22 target rifle at six hundred feet, and any ballistics expert, any armoury man, will tell you that's impossible. The impossible is the thing that's never yet happened. No guarantees.

Like I said, everybody sitting still in the boat and nobody moving, and how I knew was because a star shell went off hanging in the air above us and we were picked out like statues in the game we used to play as kids at birthday parties when we'd eaten the tea. Somebody used to stand by the door to see nobody went out and somebody used to stand on the table with his hand on the chain of the gaslamp, and he'd bring the gaslamp chain down so that the room was in almost total darkness and people used to move about in the gloom, and then the one on the gaslamp would pull the other chain and the lamp would splutter and shine and he'd look to spot if anybody was moving. In that boat with the flare bright above us I felt the same urge to stay absolutely still, in case anybody should see me moving, knowing that they'd tag me. But it would be with a bullet, not a pat on the shoulder.

Hard to remember I was a kid once and played games like statues. We lived in a valley, and I'll always remember it, though I'll never see it again. When I was a kid, that valley was the whole world to me. Ours was what they call a back-to-back house in a terrace stuck on the side of the mill where my dad worked until the night he fell into the

9

race. They picked him out the next morning and had to clean the fat off him before they could know who he was. Lanolin makes the skin smooth, and must have embalmed my dad because when they scraped him clean he looked as if he was asleep, not as if he'd been in the water all night. The dad of one of my pals fell into the water of the mine-workings and in one night bloated to twice his size. I've always had a fear of falling into water. My dad had a deep bass voice and used to sing in the chapel. Every year they gave a kids' outing but you had to attend a minimum of fifty services and they stamped a card when you went in. Arthur Brangsome worked out a way to get into the chapel and steal the stamp, but I never dared.

I never had much courage. The others knew it and dared me to do things I never could. It was a game they played when they were tired of other games. In time I learned to make up by cunning what I lacked in courage. When they'd dare each other to jump across the beck, I'd be working out a more easy way, looking for a rope or something to make a bridge. When I started work at the mill, I became very good at escaping the tough jobs without anybody noticing. That was how and why I used my school certificate maths to get into the pay office, away from the millhouse floor and the trolleys of bobbins that weighed a ton.

I wish I could have used that cunning on the Army Selection Board, but they were used to lads like me and not as easy to impress as the men in the mill.

I thought the army would be a repeat of the mill situation; somebody would soon recognize I had a certain amount of nous, I would never let myself sink into the common rut of people, I was a potential leader. Several of the lads said to me you ought to be a corporal. But nobody gave me the chance, nobody trusted me with that much responsibility. It was a long time before I realized people would never trust me. If you've been cast in the common mould any attempt to break out is automatically suspect. My mam used to say, 'Don't go getting ideas above your station or they'll never trust you.' I was never trusted after I got my clean job at the mill. I took that extra bit of 'push' into the army with me. On the very first day when we were queueing for our kit, the sergeant went along the line giving each of us a complete uniform before moving on to the next one. That meant he had to go ten times to the hairbrush stack, ten times to the comb stack, and so on. I was foolish enough to say, 'Look, Sergeant, why don't you give us each a brush, then each a comb, then each a pair of socks, and so on? Save yourself a lot of walking.' He fixed me with his eye and said, 'When you've got a sergeant major's rank, lad, you get 'em to wheel you back and tell me how to do my job.'

The only man who trusted me, except Major Brassingham, was the sergeant major. 'You could make lance corporal easily,' he said to me; 'even corporal, if only you'd get it into your head that before you can *give* orders, you've got to *take* them without always trying to *bend* them.'

I can remember these thoughts as I sat in that boat, waiting for the flare to die down and the game of statues to end. The flare had drifted to the side and the figures in the boat were silhouettes, cardboard cut-outs like you see at a fairground shooting gallery, with the rim of the land behind them a moving background. Any moment I expected a bull's eye target to appear. To hear the sound of fairground music and smell boiling black peas with vinegar. But all that came to me was the stink of diesel and sweat and the smell of the salt water and the thought that I was floating on a strange sea, lonely and far from home, and the dawn hadn't come yet, and we were just a few men, not the main landing force south of us on a beach called, I think, Arromanches, getting all the shit. North of us I could hear another lot having a rough time; nobody had bothered to tell us who they were.

Monty came to the camp one day in a staff car and they threw packets of cigarettes off the back, stale as Monty's 'rally round the flag, boys' speech. Five minutes throwing out the fags and five minutes talking from his car to the officers who'd been lined up, poor bastards, outside the mess

11

for three hours. Five platoons had been set to line the road from the gate; I suppose they needed somebody to catch the fags and give a spontaneous welcome. I was on cookhouse fatigue in denims and eating a second dinner of liver and bacon by the time he arrived, and if it came to a choice between Monty and liver and bacon, I'll leave you to guess which I'd go for. Even though the fags were free.

'This is an isolated gun,' Mr Soames had said, 'and any guns they might normally use to back it up will be busy elsewhere, so we only have the comparatively simple task of taking this one gun. Of course, there will be mines, and a certain amount of sporadic mortar fire' – Cutler, cheeky, asked him what sporadic meant – 'but that should present no insuperable problem.'

The gun was silent. I hadn't located it because the boat was bobbing about so much, but I wasn't worried yet. I'd know I'd located the damn thing just as soon as it started firing at me.

The first grey light had appeared over the hill ahead, and it picked out clouds like sheep's wool, the colour of oatmeal, moving, really moving fast. There'd been a storm the night before last and rumour was that we'd been supposed to go only the weather was too bad. We'd been told *this is it* six nights in a row and no longer believed it. We hadn't believed it when they took us by lorry to Southampton two weeks previously. When we arrived an army major with a white armband swore at Mr Soames and sent us towards Plymouth. Twenty miles along the road a despatch rider flagged us down looking as if he'd spent all day riding the roads searching for lost lorries. Luckily we were outside a café and had tea and wads while Mr Soames, who by then was bloody angry, got on the telephone. After the break – Chalky and Lance Corporal Smith didn't have time to get their tea and wads and so we shared ours with them – we were ordered back into the lorry and returned to Southampton. The trip felt like a Sunday School outing and we sang all the way. We cheered the major with the white armband when we saw him again and his face went purple and we knew that if the lorry stopped we'd all be on a charge of insubordination.

As it was, they stuck us in a Nissen hut and forgot about us, but we didn't mind. Parade each morning to check for deserters and two 'lessons'. The one taken by Lance Corporal Smith was always full of bull, stripping down the Bren, stoppage in the breech and all that stuff, but Runty's lesson was a skive with him watching the time while we played cards and smoked in our hands and he'd break us early so we could be first in the NAAFI queue which, by the official break time, extended a hundred yards or more. As a full corporal, Runty could have used the other door but he never did. Sometimes, I don't think he even remembered he had privileges of rank. And then, after three days the crafty sod got us put on permanent NAAFI duty and we were behind the counter smiling out and feeling good.

Runty always looked out for our interests. Once we were on a night scheme in Detling Quarry and he was supposed to teach us laying booby traps, and the first night of the three-night scheme he taught us to lay wires all round our perimeter. When the orderly officer came sneaking in about four o'clock with a thunderflash in his hand to give us all a rude awakening he tripped over our wires and set off our thunderflash charges and I bet he damn near shit his pants in fright. He never came back again and every night after that Runty gave us an hour of really good instruction and we all concentrated so that we could learn it quick and then we could really get in the bell tents and off to sleep. Whereas the orderly officer was prowling all night round the other platoons who'd come weary eyed for breakfast to the field kitchen when we'd be fresh and already have eaten. Smithy was pissed off at Runty, and one night he threatened to talk to the sergeant, but Runty took him on one side and I overheard him saying that if Smithy said one word, just one word, Runty would have his knackers for garters. So Smithy was put into a bell tent all his own, and when I'd go to sleep I'd see the faint light from under his canvas and knew he was still reading an army manual.

We were now six hundred yards off a thin black line I took to be the actual coast, and the water was running up on it and breaking along the sand in spume. Six plus three plus one fifty. Bloody close. 'How do you feel?' I whispered to Chalky and he turned and looked and that told me all I wanted to know, and Cutler turned round in the hope, I suppose, of finding somebody feeling worse than he was. I felt the sergeant major's hand on my shoulder but he didn't speak.

One night I was on guard duty and a lad asked me to let him out. No pass. He spun me a yarn about an ATS girl who was leaving and it'd be their last chance. So I let him out. A provost sergeant caught him down the road, and they gave me seven days. Afterwards, the sergeant major saw me in a pub and bought me a beer; 'You'll find there's always somebody who'll ask you to bend a regulation.' He even showed me the scar down his arm where an Indian on the North-West Frontier had asked to be let out of prisoner stockade on some religious pretext, then produced a sliver of glass from under his loincloth and went for the sergeant major's jugular. Only the sergeant major was too quick for him. 'You never know, lad,' the sergeant major said, 'when your time comes you may not be quick enough. Especially if you slip on a bit of that old milk-of-human-kindness.'

The touch of the sergeant major's hand on my shoulder might have been saying the time had come, or the time was coming soon, and don't worry about Chalky and the way he feels, don't be suckered just because some lad is spewing his guts out beside you, think about yourself and your own safety and not about him and his. It was as if the sergeant major was reminding me once again that Chalky and all the rest were his concern not mine, that I should look out for myself.

There'd been a storm during the night, just after we got on the LCI. I thought the boat was going to tip over forward at one point. The bows went down into the trough of a wave

14

and suddenly I was looking all the way down the boat as if I was in a theatre and sitting in the circle and the Bren in the bows was the prop for a play. Water swilled into the bottom of the boat and the bilge pump wasn't working too well and the water started to fill the boat and every time the boat heeled over the water came slopping up the side, up my left leg and once over the gunwales of the boat into my face. I'd been glad of it at the time; my face was hot with sweat and my eyes had been clogged and I'd been about to spew with the rolling motion when that dash of cold salt water washed my face clean and held back the seasick feeling. We'd all been talking then, to keep our spirits up. And we'd told jokes again, remembering every one we'd ever heard and ever told on route marches and exercises. We'd all heard them before but nobody gave away a punch line and we all tried to find a laugh somewhere among the rollers.

In the middle of it all Smithy looked at his watch and decided this was the time to distribute the official ration of biscuit and chocolate and a can of soup per person. I could see Runty was going to argue but he didn't and Smithy worked his way along that heaving boat, climbing the duckboards against the waves all the way to the stern passing out his goodies like an ice cream girl at the pictures. My soup was tomato, cold of course, but I didn't mind that. Chalky had to get down a lump of meat and vegetable which was crusted on the top with some kind of fat and maybe that's what finally did for him, poor bastard. The chocolate was good and the biscuit helped and I was glad we'd put the whisky and tea in our water bottles, Chalky and me, because we had something tasty to wash it all down with, not canteen water that no matter how hard you try always tasted of chlorine. I got the tea-and-whisky tip from Major Brassingham and one of his stories about hunting. You wouldn't believe it, the way he told it. Ordinary stuff to him, of course, about the time he broke his collar bone when a pheasant flew out of a hedge as his horse was starting a jump and the major took the fence but the horse stayed back, then changed its mind and jumped over and on him. All very matter-of-fact stuff to him, but to me it conjured a picture of the sort of thing I'd only seen on chocolate boxes and never thought really existed. He told me about the flask he carried in the inside pocket of his jacket containing coffee and brandy; take it out and swig it anytime, anywhere you wanted. Ever after that, when we went on a night scheme I'd fill my water bottle with tea and whisky since brandy was almost impossible to find and I couldn't afford it anyway.

I told the major about it, once. He laughed. 'You'll go a long way, Tom,' he said. But he didn't mean as a soldier. 'You have all the qualities of success,' he said, 'you're independent, resourceful, proud and courageous. We teach obedience in the army, and that curious and indefinable feeling we refer to as initiative. Yet we reprimand anyone who marches out of step. That's a paradox for you.' I didn't know what a paradox was and told him so, and he laughed again. 'Knowing you,' he said, 'you'll find out what it means by tomorrow.' And I did.

Long line of the beach ahead and I heard them throwing what sounded like a million shells at the men on the north and on the south, but nothing was happening in front of us. Just a long black skyline, now beginning to be haloed by the coming dawn. We were going forward to meet it, with no chance to gauge or assess it. Dammit, I still hadn't found the gun and that was our sole reason for coming. Well, not our sole reason, but our first objective if you like, the first consideration. Get your sequences right. Gun's firing, gun stops. Stoppage in the barrel. You don't strip out the barrel until you've taken off the magazine.

We weren't going to advance to contact the paras until we'd taken that gun. That was the sequence. There was no other possibility. No one had suggested what we could do if we didn't take the gun. There was no contingency plan. At

16

least, nothing I had been told about, and Mr Soames, who was normally a great one for 'contingency plans', had briefed us and made Runty construct a model out of a pile of builders' sand and some stones. So what happens if we don't, if we can't take the gun? The dawn will be here damn soon, but what happens if we can't take the gun? What happens if, for instance, there's no gun there? Okay, that one's easy, we just pass through. In out on guard and pass through. But what if the gun's built solid into concrete, and we can't stop it firing? Simple. We'll all die.

At that moment, waves screwing along the side of the boat in foam, dawn tracing a skyline out of the black, the sergeant major's hand on my shoulder, Chalky still spewing, dammit *still* spewing beside me, it seemed utterly logical that every last one of us was going to be killed by that gun. Nobody's *destined* to do anything. We have the choice in our own two hands. Of course, Lance Corporal Smith wouldn't agree. He would say it's all been decided by the Lord, that He knows what's going to happen to us and He'll make it happen in His own good time. But the good men go and the bad ones stay, the Smiths of this world say it's all according to God's master plan. Well it's my private belief that if there is a master plan, somebody made a balls of compiling it. Because any master plan that had me sitting in a landing craft infantry next to Chalky spewing his guts out, waiting for the dawn to arrive and that gun to start belching at me, was a bloody awful plan so far as I was concerned.

Time to check again. Check, check everything. Loaded magazine on the rifle contains ten rounds, right, and there's one up the spout. Safety catch on. Foresight clean. Backsight clean and set at three hundred. Anything you fire over three hundred yards through a Lee Enfield you can safely forget, the way I shoot. Best I've ever done at three hundred yards is a six-inch group. Not that I'm ashamed of that – some of the lads can't manage better than a twelve-inch group at three hundred yards and some of 'em can't even hit the target, though you're supposed to be able to, to pass the final test.

Runty's a wizard at teaching shooting, and he's also a wizard in the butts and many a lad firing in the air above the target has come home with a neat six-inch group and got a mark in his paybook passing him out. Because, let's face it, we're only fire power, not bloody snipers, and if we shoot enough rounds at 'em, we're bound to hit enough of 'em to stop 'em. At least, that's Runty's philosophy and he should know because he got a mention in despatches somewhere in North Africa, and though he says it was for cleaning out the officers' mess another corporal told us Runty had driven a blazing jeep away from a petrol dump and deserved the bleeding Victoria Cross not a stinking little mention in despatches. But that's all part of the master plan, too, I suppose, and Smithy would say that Runty didn't get the VC because the Good Lord didn't intend him to have it and end of conversation. You can never argue with a bigot, like you can never argue with Cutler over politics and him saying that if only there hadn't been a Chamberlain, we wouldn't be in this mess. But there *was* a Chamberlain, and we *were* in this mess and I needed to check a few more things like if I had put the cork back in my water bottle and had the webbing straps pulled tight and if ever I could keep that sodding trouser leg in my gaiter and pray to God we weren't going to disembark with fixed bayonets because say what you like that would be the ultimate melodrama, charging up the beach with a fixed bayonet towards a gun that hadn't yet decided to fire.

And I hate bloody melodrama. In the early days I used to get that from Mary Brassingham. I'd be showing her a step and she'd bring her foot down in the wrong place time and time again and I'd say 'For God's sake turn your ankle a bit more so that your foot comes down parallel with the one on the ground else how can you step off again in the right direction?' and she'd get all melodramatic and say, 'I can't, I can't.' Her foot had turned about thirty degrees, no doubt because the muscles were twisting it. Well, okay, so she'd

18

had the disease and they'd cured it and it had caused this twist and normally when she'd been standing upright and looking forward her foot would be pointing somewhere out to the left. But what could I do? Major Brassingham wanted me to teach her to dance. That's what he was paying me for, not to stand there listening to her saying 'I can't, I can't possibly,' when any fool would know that if she merely made a bit of a shift with her hip when the foot was going down towards the ground, the foot would wind up parallel with the other.

I suppose I was cruel. I'd say, 'Don't tell me you can't. I'm not interested in what you think you can and can't do. I know damned well it's not impossible, and therefore you can do it, and you will do it if we have to go on practising it for ever.' She'd look at me and her eyes would gleam; 'All right, tell me again, show me again.' That's how we'd conquer it. Until finally she accepted that everything is possible if only you go about it the right way and don't spend half your time telling yourself you can't do it.

Like it was going to be possible to take that gun. One bullet would do it, straight through the slit of that bunker, knock out the man behind the gun. One bullet, well aimed, and we could finish our bit of beach work and take the long soft walk twelve miles inland to where the paras would be waiting on clean ground. Runty had told us. It'll be dead clean ground once we get off the beach. Stands to reason, Runty had said, because how much frigging coastline is there and how many Germans? Only enough to run a thin red line round the coast. Funny to think of the Germans holding a thin red line but it stands to reason, doesn't it? Once we get through that line sweet fanny adams and the maquis waiting for us and all the French dames along the road with the bottles of vino and sloshing out the kisses right left and centre. And boy, Runty said, if you ever had it French the way I did in Oran . . . you'll never want an English girl again. Runty really had it all worked out that once we were through the coastal defences we'd have it cushy on a one way ticket to Berlin. No more foot slogging. They'd be mounting us in trucks and driving us triumphant through the streets with the mayor standing on the balcony in his ribbon shouting 'Vivent les Anglais.'

But first, we had to get the gun. And first, we had to find it. It had to start firing.

The bombardment to our right reached a fresh crescendo, with equal amounts going in each direction, but towering pillars of flame every time the guns firing from behind us hit something big, and a million tracers criss-crossing the sky with the crump of the mortars and the beach explosions that may have been shells but could have been mines. And the same to the left of us. The mere thought of explosions made my foot begin to itch; they would be mines and I knew I'd rather have a mortar drop down the back of my collar than a mine blow under my foot. Why didn't they get us boots with steel plate soles, but who'd be able to run up the beach on a steel plate?

Apparently they'd tried Mary with a steel plate for a while, on steel shafts which ran down the side of her leg. The idea was to try to force the foot gradually to come back into line, ninety degrees with the angle of her body. But apparently the pain had been bad and the minute they took off the plate her foot went back into the crazy sticking out angle. When she walked she put the outside of her heel down first and always wore her shoes out that way until they thought of the idea of nailing Blakey's Boot Protectors on the outside back of her shoe. That was awkward too because the Blakeys became polished by wear and slippery and sometimes she'd fall down. In the end the major clotched that. 'I'd rather her shoes were mended every week,' he said to me, 'than that she should fall down.' Which was saying something because he had her shoes specially made in London, in St James's, and one day he got me a pass and a travel warrant and a meal voucher so's I could collect a new pair for her. I sold the warrant and hitched, and cashed in the meal voucher in a pub where I had a drink, and only thinking about it in the boat did I realize what a rotten thing that had been to do because it made me late coming back with the shoes. And I was suddenly sure that Major Brassingham had known what I'd done but hadn't called me out over it. How many times had he known what I'd done, and said nothing? I felt bile in my mouth, and said to myself that it was because of the motion of the boat, but you can't really hide feelings of shame like that. Or the knowledge of what a bastard I'd been. Over that whole business with Mary.

Look at it this way: I'd been dancing for as long as I could remember once I was grown up enough to go out on my own on Saturday nights. I'd taken my lessons at the Methodist Hall, where they had a class that met every Thursday night, dancing to the piano music thumped out by Miss Arkwright who was better at hymn tunes but at least could keep a steady rhythm. Mary hadn't had that advantage. Nobody had ever taken the trouble to give her dancing lessons. She'd been to a boarding school, and when I asked her about dancing classes she told me they'd taught Greek dancing, whatever that may be. Poor devil, what use was that in a competitive world where you use every skill you can get. Like self-confidence, and chatting people up, or riding a bike, or swimming. I'd managed to learn all those things, but Mary had been protected against them. Of course, she could ride a horse or drive a car and speak French, and presumably she could dance like a Greek so she'd be dead lucky if ever she met one of them – like Andreas, who owned the fish and chip shop in Skelly Lane and was married to a girl from Batley.

I hadn't given Mary a chance. The major had taken me into his home, not just for the half a crown an hour lessons; he'd sat me in a chair and talked to me like a son, and went out of his way to try to fix things for me, to give me a better life, but what did I do? I threw it all back in his face. Look at the money he'd spent on gramophone records for us to dance to, and yet when Runty and I wanted a few records

21

for a social we had in the NAAFI, I borrowed them without even telling him.

The social had been Runty's idea, but we were all dead keen. We borrowed the corporals' mess at the NAAFI. Sold tickets round the platoons for a bob a head, two bob if you brought a girl. The NAAFI sold us the beer at wholesale prices, and the whisky – only one bottle of that, but six bottles of rum. That's what started the trouble because a lot of the girls weren't used to drinking rum, and we ran out of stuff to put in it and so the lads were tipping beer into it. We had about fifty there. Started with a whist drive, all very tame, but it got 'em moving about. And then we had a quick tombola, cards a penny apiece. Runty was rubbing his hands together when I took the card money to him.

'We'll clear five quid apiece on this little lot, Tom,' he said, 'and think what a piss-up we can have on that.'

And then finished the evening off with a bit of dancing. The records the NAAFI lent us were old and scratched to buggery, but I said, 'I think I know where I could borrow some.' So after the dancing lesson, the night before, I cried off staying for supper afterwards, and sneaked out of the major's house with a dozen of the best dance records under my battledress blouse. They were the ones we used for the dancing at the social. But when the rum started to pour out – mind you we were making threepence a tot profit on it – the party got a bit wild, and a bloody great lad from 2 platoon started to get stroppy every time I put on a quick-step because he'd brought a bird and wanted nothing else but waltzes because that was the only dance he could do and smooch. And when I put on a quickstep so I could do a bit of fancy stuff with a girl who'd stayed behind after washing up for the NAAFI, he came over to the record player, pulled the record off, and skimmed it across the room. It hit a bottle of rum, knocked it off the table and broke it and bang went all our rum profit. The record was smashed, too.

Runty wasn't letting him get away with that, and he came across and took off his battledress jacket because it had the stripes on it, and had a go at this lad from 2 platoon. His name as I remember was Bolton or something like that, and he had muscles on him like a blacksmith, but Runty had learned to fight rough. He butted Bolton on the nose with his forehead and kicked his legs from under him, and Bolton crashed down into the pile of records and smashed 'em all. Jesus Christ, I thought, what am I going to tell the major? I put them all back in their sleeves, all the broken pieces, and took them with me. The following night I hid them under my battledress blouse again and while I was getting the room ready for dancing I pretended to fall over and knocked them all to the ground. The major was very understanding. 'Accidents will happen, Tom,' he said, 'even in the best regulated families.'

Runty asked me if I'd got away with it, and I said yes, but he told me all the profit from the social had been eaten up paying for the broken glasses and the spilt rum so we had nothing to show for it.

And, into the bargain, next time we were out on a scheme, a mob from 2 platoon, led by Bolton, broke into our bivouac late at night and wrecked our tents and somebody chipped one of Runty's teeth with the butt of a rifle in the dark and they threw a thunderflash into the ruins of the tent I was in and the damned thing made me deaf for a week and singed off part of one of my eyebrows. So we didn't bother with any more 'socials'.

# 2

The dawn that came over the beach was a lousy dawn, grey and cold and all you could say for it was that the silhouettes were misted by it and everything had three dimensions. Even my own feelings of cold and misery. Four hundred yards to go. I could see every detail of the beach in the cold light. A cove on a segment of the circumference of a circle. The sides came back out to sea. On the right side was what once had been a lighthouse but it now had no top and stood up like a broken ice cream cornet. On the left was a breakwater wall flat on the top and about six feet across. Thirty, forty yards of it sticking out into the sea. Once there would have been boats tied to it, little paddle boats and possibly even boats with sails and I could see the rings set in the concrete, about six or more inches in diameter with long fishtails of rust running down the wall beneath them, brown and yellow. Straight ahead the sand looked hard packed above the water line but soon lightened and softened and I knew it'd be hell to run up.

We'd practised in Morecambe Bay, up and down the sand and along it for hours, first in bare feet and then in socks, developing the muscles of our feet and our legs. The first week had practically crippled me and brought out muscles I never knew I had, but then when we came to do it in boots and with packs on it was a doddle. Though a couple of hours of it could still give you a hell of a cramp between your legs and once I felt as if my balls were going to drop out and thank God I was wearing trousers or they'd have been dragging on the beach.

The first night we were there Runty found a bird and every night, after all day on the beach, he'd go back there to lie with her and every morning we'd be running along and the bastard would show us the stick he'd poked into the sand at the spot where he'd done it and he'd left the frenchie hanging on the stick like a flag of triumph. A right randy bastard was Runty. Mind you, I will say this for him, he was never selfish, and would always find out if his birds had a friend. I think he liked going out in a foursome, or even more, and making a party of it including me and sometimes Cutler. But never Chalky. Because on these occasions Chalky was a liability. Oh, he was all right at the chat, and he could pull his weight at that. He was very good when we were at a dance and say we wanted to pick three up together. But then when it came to getting them huddled down on the beach, something would go wrong with Chalky's bird, and ten to one you'd just be getting to the point when she would loom up behind your back and say, 'Come on, Mavis', or Ethel, or whatever your girl's name was, 'It's time we were getting back.' And no matter how hot you'd got your girl by this time, with another girl standing by watching she wouldn't open her legs. The whole evening would be wasted. So on the occasions when we were stuck with Chalky, we'd arrange to get rid of him and his girl somewhere, to avoid that. But ten to one he'd turn up on his own and find us and no matter how much you told him to piss off, he'd never take the hint. Anyway, what with one thing and the other the exercise on the sand had hardened our muscles in more ways than one.

The sand, above the water line, looked soft as sugar. Very good for sand castles, very good for digging moats and lines down to the water's edge so the water would run up and fill the moat, and little paper flags on sticks, like we did one day on an outing from the mill, ten shillings and for it you got the coach to Blackpool and all your meals and a free apple and orange and a packet of flags.

It took my mam six months to save up for me to go. She couldn't go herself; said riding in a coach made her sick, and I believed her at the time. Ten bob was a quarter of a week's wage for my dad, and mam saved it out of the money he gave her for food, every Friday putting a few coins on the mantelpiece in a tin they gave her for the Jubilee, a square one with photographs of the Queen and the King on it. Nobody ever touched that tin except one time when the gas went out and my dad had no money, and so mam went into the tin and 'lent' it to him. Dad paid for the gas out of his own pocket, but mam bought the new gasmantle when it was needed. Crouched in that landing craft, I could remember the soft warm plop of the gas when dad would light it and suddenly the darkness of that room would be lit by a tender warm glow.

We never lit the gas too early; the fire would be going and mam baking and dad sitting there, fiddling with his paper, holding it up to the window to read by the daylight as long as he could, then sitting in his chair by the oven, using the light of the fire to read by, until mam would get impatient with him, and push him away. 'Get away from my oven,' she'd say, 'and light your gas if you want to read.' He'd move his chair, and sit looking at the fire for at least five minutes before he'd take a paper spill from the mantelpiece, put it in the fire and light 'his' gas. Once I was working on a model on a corner of the table and I asked him if I could have the gas on to see better and he looked at me in surprise. 'Is tha' paying for it, then?' he asked. And I hung my head in shame because I'd spent all my pocket money on the model, and couldn't have paid for anything else for another week. Now, of course, mam has the electric and they send her a bill, but she still puts money for it in the Jubilee tin.

The gun opened fire at three hundred yards to go. The first I knew about it was when a round whanged off the side of the boat in front of my hand which was touching the top of the gunwales. I dropped my hand down quick. More shots, this time a short burst; the sergeant major said, 'Christ'. This was it. The first bullet to come near to me. I should have been shit-scared but I wasn't, not yet, only curious. We all strained to try to locate the machine gun but they must have had some kind of baffle to hide the muzzle

26

blast, or perhaps ammo that doesn't make the flame we'd been led to expect, in our spot-the-gun exercises.

Now I knew why the bastards had waited; the sun was coming up, a red glow along the skyline that hid anything they might be doing. Jesus Christ, we were facing east into the sun; we wouldn't be able to see a thing. They'd be able to see us clearly, picked out as their eyes slowly became accustomed to the improving light. We were looking into the sun and we'd spent the night on the sea, and our eyes were tired, and we wouldn't be able to make anything out. So much for my hope we'd be able to drop one into the slit and knock the gunner off the end of his machine gun. He was picking targets on single round, and we had less than three hundred yards to go. The engine of the boat began to race; we all had our heads down below the level of the gunwales; my tin hat fell forward over my eyes. I had the sudden thought that maybe my neck was exposed, and I eased up my hand and pushed the tin hat as far as it would go on its strap. I had my strap under my chin; most of the lads had the strap behind like you were supposed to wear it so nobody could come up behind you and pull your hat backwards over your head and use the strap to choke you; I still kept my strap long and under my chin because I'd rather run the risk of being strangled one day than have the perpetual fear of the damned thing falling off at the crucial moment. One of our lads, who must have felt the same way I did, jumped off the back of a lorry and his tin hat caught on the iron framework that held the canvas roof and his hat stuck there and he broke his neck. You'd think a thing like that would persuade me, but it never did. I still liked to keep that strap under my chin and finally Runty said, 'It's your own funeral', and left me to do as I wished except on regimental parade when the RSM would have had a blue fit if he'd seen. So I pushed the hat as far back as the chinstrap would allow and leaned forward as we all leaned forward and therefore didn't see the one that got Sergeant Hunter.

It couldn't be a straight shot because we were lower than

the platform, weren't we, so it would have to be a ricochet, wouldn't it? These questions kept running through my mind. It was so incredible that the first casualty was the sergeant, and in the boat, not half way up the beach as we'd all geared ourselves to think. You're running up the beach and they're shooting at you; it stands to reason they're going to get some of you. A mathematical equation, though you never believe you're going to be the one, and you're reassured because even if you get hit by a bullet, well a lot of guys have been hit by bullets and have survived. But not the sergeant. Jesus Christ in heaven above, to get the first one here on the boat.

'Is he dead?'

'We don't know. Cutler says he is, but you know how Cutler panics.'

'Where did it get him?'

'We don't know, but Cutler says . . .'

'Cutler says, Cutler says . . .'

I wanted the real facts, not what Cutler says. So the sergeant's got it and what the hell do we do? Throw him over the side, burial at sea? Carry him ashore, dead on arrival? Or just leave him in the landing craft. Because he's become a problem. Leave him where he is and he'll block our path getting out and we'll be sitting ducks if we have to scramble over a body. So much for the practise, so much for rehearsing how we're going to get out of that damned tin can. Because we never practised stepping over a dead sergeant. How could we have? It was inconceivable he would be killed, he was the one teaching us how to get out. The sergeant major was shuffling forward. I could see his arse out of the top of my eyes as he wriggled down the narrow central corridor, and Runty had come back, and the two of them were pushing and shoving because there was no room. Cutler was wriggling over and they were pushing the body under the bench he'd been sitting on, Runty pushing one foot and the sergeant major the other. God, what a way to have your corpse handled, pushed under the bench of a landing craft. They meant to leave the poor sod there and that

28

seemed all wrong to me.

What did I expect? A full military funeral with Cutler sounding the last post on the mouth organ? And Soames reading out of the Army Manual Bible and Smithy correcting him in the form of service? Is that what I wanted them to do to me if I should get one? But I wanted to *know* how the sergeant got it and where, because we all ought to have that piece of knowledge. The sergeant had spent the last year giving us all the knowledge he had and though he'd been a distant sort of man and we'd never got to know him personally, at least he'd tried hard and sincerely to give us everything he had in the way of knowledge, and it seemed to me he would want us to have this final piece of information, how he died, and what he'd done wrong, or for us to know if he was merely the one sitting in the wrong place, the one whose name was on the bullet. I wasn't going to accept Smithy's talk about God having decided to take the sergeant first as a lesson to us all; I wasn't going to accept that the sergeant's death had been inevitable, I wasn't going to accept any fact other than that he was the first one to die.

The bullets were coming faster, whacking the side of the boat. There are other landing craft, aim at them, why pick on this one? I lifted my head cautiously and now the mortars had started and there were sudden gouts of water coming out of the sea that rose eight, nine, ten feet high and the strump of the underwater explosions and I wondered how strong the bottom of the boat was and if we overran one of those mortars before it exploded would the bottom of the boat be blown in? I had a dreadful feeling between my legs. Serge trousers over cotton underpants and that's the full extent of the protection between my balls and the bottom of that boat. Head down again from instinct, bullets felt rather than seen but where the hell can they be coming from because we're going forward behind the shield of that ramp. Already the pins that stopped the chain had been pulled out and I'd heard a section of the chain rattle, but when I looked along the boat I couldn't see a gap between the ramp and the sides of the boat so it couldn't be from there.

And then I heard the sergeant major's voice, '*Watch left*,' and I saw the sparkle of fire from the end of a short jetty, but at the level of the jetty itself. Hell fire – they've got a gun at the end of the jetty and who the hell would be daft enough to lie on the end of the jetty? Mr Soames was talking into the radio quietly and I could hear his voice though I couldn't make sense of what he was saying. 'Gun on fixed lines at the end of the jetty,' the sergeant major whispered and now I understood. They'd mounted a gun in the stone work, probably given it a long belt of ammo that would feed slowly in as long as there was no stoppage. Working the gun on wires from the shore installation. The gun set to rake the mouth of that beach, the sides of any landing craft where the gunwales are lower than the ramp, and I almost laughed. We hadn't thought of that one, had we? I bet that was how the sergeant got his, in the side of his head from the unexpected quarter.

'Gun on the breakwater, Cutler,' I said, 'pass it on.' The whisper ran electric forward and I saw them turn. To the left the steel plate of the gunwales of the boat came to my shoulder, so I didn't have to lean far to get my head down below the level of it, but then the awful stench of fuel oil and vomit and sea water on leather boots came up at me and I knew that unless I could get my head up again I'd be sick. It seems easy to say – all right, keep your head down, what does it matter if you're sick – but you can't be as sensible as that, and more than anything else I wanted to land on that beach without being sick. I looked to my right. Chalky was sitting up. 'Get down you bloody fool,' I said, and used that as an excuse to lift my head, and then suddenly I saw a fleck of red appear along his cheek, a fleck of red that rapidly swelled and started to run down his face, down past the corner of his mouth. He didn't move, didn't even flinch, just sat there, and I knew he was in a trance of fear, incapable of movement.

This happened to me once, crawling through the barbed

wire mat of the obstacle course knowing they were firing real live bullets because Runty had told me and I could see the tracer, and then feeling my back pocket stick in the barbed wire and not being able to free it and seeing that tracer suddenly dip, knowing in that fraction of a second that the fixed lines gun had slipped its mounting and was firing down into the ground, not three feet above our heads as we had been promised. So you move fast, and my mind had already worked it out that if I twisted hard enough I'd tear that barb out of my trousers, maybe leave the pocket behind with my paybook and a letter from my mam but what the hell and then I froze, unable to move, fixed like Lot's wife. Watching the bullets come closer as they zipped into the ground in front of me, almost as if it was only one bullet and it was walking slowly towards me and within a fraction of a second would reach and consume me with fire. Chalky was set now as I was set then, and I remember I lay there for at least a minute before I realized someone must have grabbed the gun because the bullet was walking away from me and I could take time to clear my arse from the barbed wire.

There was nobody to grab the gun on the end of the French breakwater and Chalky stayed locked, blood pouring down his cheek. I reached out my hand but didn't touch him, because if I touched him he'd come back to his senses and know he'd been hit. The colour had come back to his face and he'd lost the grey-green look; there were beads of either sweat or spray on his forehead and his eyes, opened wide, had the glazed look of a drunk or a man exhausted. The sweat shone with a glint of pearls and I wanted to wipe it away; the blood welled upwards on his cheek and ran into the sweat pale as a port and lemon. Then, almost in slow motion, I saw the sergeant major's hand come forward and in it was a wad of gauze dripping with sulphanilamide powder and the gauze rested on Chalky's cheek. The blood ran out at first through the powder. When the sergeant major took his hand away, Chalky's face was covered in white powder like the woman who played the piano in the

31

Methodist Church Hall who, they said, used flour. Chalky turned to look at me as if I'd been the one to shoot him and he said, 'I've been hit, Tom,' with great reproach, and as his face worked, the powder became caked with blood and cracked.

'It's only a scratch,' the sergeant major said, 'but I'll see they give you a stripe for it.' Rusty had four wound stripes on his arm like four brown caterpillars had crawled there in military line and died. The sergeant major had none even though he'd been on active service. I expect he'd been too busy dishing out the sulphanilamide.

I'll say this for Chalky in his favour. He didn't scream, didn't make a noise, but I could guess he'd been hurt badly because that sweat was squeezed out of his forehead and ran down his face and must have stung like hell. You get used to pain, learn to live with it. It had taken me a long time to see how strong Mary had become, fighting the pain in her leg every time she tried to walk. But then I had to be the one who came along and gave her a whole new set of pains, because dancing isn't like walking and you use different muscles and move your feet and your legs in different ways and that must have been a new vision of pain for her. How little I'd understood about that; how small an allowance I'd made for it.

I can remember one night the major had come into the room while we were dancing and, of course, knowing Mary better than I ever could, appreciating the effort she was making, there were tears in his eyes and I wondered why. When we were having supper afterwards, and Mary had insisted on going out to the kitchen to fetch the mustard, he said, 'Don't push her too hard, will you lad?' and I said, 'No sir', not really understanding what he meant. But now, looking at Chalky, I could see what the major had meant, and thought about the other ways I'd hurt Mary and was ashamed again. So I put out my hand and touched Chalky lightly on his sleeve and said, 'You'll be all right' – as if pledging myself to look after him, which was a bit ambitious because I had nobody to look after me, except the sergeant major.

We were two hundred yards away and Lieutenant Soames had stopped talking to the navy, and I saw the explosion in the sand and water as the gun of our support ship missed the jetty. It took six shots before the end of it was blown off. The mortars that had been bursting in the water were suddenly lifted and I guessed they were being fired up and beyond us, tit-for-tatting the gun of the ship. I didn't care. Anybody who took six shots to hit that jetty deserved all he got in return.

And then I located a gun. Dammit, it was firing from a point at the shore end of the jetty. I found it because it was sweeping from side to side, using a one in ten tracer mix of green and red and yellow. The gunner must have held his finger on the trigger because the coloured tracer spewed out of that gun faster than any gun I'd ever seen. But, dammit, Lieutenant Soames had had an aerial photograph of that beach and the position of the gun we were supposed to assault had been marked with a red ring and Runty had made the sand model based on that information. The gun was supposed to be on the third ridge from the right with the end of the jetty as the start point. Runty had even put a leaf in the sand to show the tree which I could now quite clearly see on that ridge and the gun was supposed to be within twenty feet of that tree. But the gun I could see firing was bang at the shore end of the jetty and at least two hundred yards to the left of where it was supposed to be.

'Second gun, sergeant major,' I called out. Now the noise didn't matter with all that holocaust out there.

'Number 2 gun, number 1 gun right of arc, fifteen degrees ruined hut.' You're supposed to give the range but I was so angry, I forgot.

'Good lad.' He passed the information to Lieutenant Soames, but he'd seen the gun and was already back on the radio. Our support ship was laying a carpet of fire on that upper ridge where the gun was supposed to be and now the

33

carpet was being pulled to the left, but I didn't have any time to think about that because we were no more than a hundred yards out and I heard the rattle of the chains as the ramp started to go down and I thought 'Oh my God they're going to drop us in deep water and we're going to have to swim for it.' The engines of the boat were screaming loud and it sounded to me as if a bearing had gone because one of the screams was too metallic, too high pitched, but it was no concern of mine to run forward with an oil can. A matelot by the side of the door was looking at the clock face of the depth gauge rod and the boat was creating a wave of its own that rode up level with the gunwales and even slopped over into the boat in front of me, but Cutler stopped it dousing me and the sergeant major was shouting, 'Stand by lads,' and we all knew we were coming to the off. I pressed my feet against the rail on the bottom of the boat and took the weight off my arse, lifting myself and flexing my stomach muscles in readiness for the quick up and off and I forgot all about guns and bullets, thinking about the run through the water and were they going to drop us deep so's we'd have to swim. Mary Brassingham couldn't have run through the water though she could run after a fashion.

The ramp went all the way down with a clatter and I thought 'Thank God we weren't trying for a silent landing.' The ramp's end was in only two feet of water and we were up and running, stepping sideways as we'd practised and trained, even Chalky holding his mine-detector the way the sergeant major had shown him, and I was in the narrow aisle and some bloody clown at the back was shouting up two three up two three and I realized the bloody clown was the sergeant major.

# 3

From the training battalion in the camp, I was posted to Number 1 battalion, also in the camp, so I didn't have far to walk with all my kit. When I got there I found I'd been posted to C Company, and when I got *there,* I found myself in Number 1 platoon. Which narked me a bit since Number 1 platoon hut was five hundred yards back the way I'd come. C Company occupied a number of huts set among the trees; the training battalion had been located round the barrack square and much more in the public view. The company office was in what had probably been an old woodcutter's house in what must have been a forest once upon a time; the hut was two storied and had a curious balcony all the way round the first floor, with a pulley and a chain hanging from the roof.

The hut I'd been assigned to was at the far end of the company line, practically in the forest still. Hut C3. I was first in there, though two bunks were already made up, one in the corner obviously for the corporal and one half way down, near the stove and the table. I'd had a bit of being near the stove and the table in the middle of a barrack room. It means that everybody uses your bed to sit on when there's a good card game going, so I chose the top bunk in the corner at the far end of the hut, opposite the corporal. I guessed he'd picked the quietest place. Locker above my bed, locker beside it. Three 'biscuits' on the bed. Three blankets. A window if anyone near me turned out to have bad feet. But I'd be far enough away from the card school to get to kip if they played late. Anyway, I hated cards. One of my biscuits was soiled; another was a bit off square and would make my bed look untidy when I set it out for inspection.

1 wandered round the barrack room, finding three biscuits that matched exactly and were practically brand new. I put my kit bag on the bed, and my large and small packs, with the ammo pouches beside them. First impressions count, and I hadn't met the corporal, didn't know what kind of a man he might be, except that if I dumped my stuff in a shambles opposite his bunk he'd chase me.

I sat on the bed. Now I had an identity. I was a private in the Royal West Kent Regiment. Now I could sew name tapes on my shoulder at the top of my arm, and a division flash below. I could buy a brass cap badge and polish it with spit and Duraglit, although first I'd find somebody to machine buff it for me, make it look as if it had seen some service. I'd meet a platoon of lads and have time to get to know them, because no one was being posted back where they came from the following week. I could settle down, dig in, and make a nest for myself, confident that this would be my home, these my companions, until we were all shipped out together. To fight in the war.

The war still seemed remote. North Africa, the Far East, were places men came back from, but you had no feeling of them ever having been there. They told you tales, of course, but you couldn't always believe them; there was a lot of old soldiers' bull about. Like the lad they'd sent to the training battalion, who came out of hospital, came into our platoon, told us all about being with the Long Range Desert Group, and killing hundreds of Germans from the deck of a jeep with a machine gun, and it turned out he was bonkers and had been posted to some nut house. Or the lad we got who said he'd been in the Far East and it turned out he'd been in the glasshouse, and they caught him doing a burglary and he went to civvie prison in Maidstone. If you believed half the stories he told. . . . Lieutenant Asquith, in the training battalion, had been in North Africa and now had a limp, but he didn't ever talk about Africa, except once when a lad called Irish Paddy was on a charge for never washing, and said, 'I've lived all my life, sor, without the sight of too much

36

water,' and the officer told us all what the sanitary conditions were like and how important it was to keep our bodies as clean as possible because of the risks of disease and infection. The corporal was the first man to come into the barrack room. He held out his hand, very friendly. 'My name's Corporal Runton,' he said, 'but everybody calls me corporal on parade, Runty off parade.' He referred to a list on a clip board. 'Which one are you?' he asked, and I said I was 4732849 Wilkins T., which stood for Thomas but everybody called me Tom. He said, 'We'd better not break the habit of a lifetime,' and put a tick against my name on his list. Once again I got the feeling of belonging. He looked at my bed. Presumably saw the three matching biscuits and the three clean blankets, the way I'd laid out my stall. 'You and me'll get on together, I can see that,' he said. The barrack room gradually filled that day as different people arrived from different places, and gradually Runty's list was filled.

One man had come down from Scotland the previous night; three had been posted from a training battalion at a place that sounded like Bally Kinley in Ireland. At twelve o'clock, Runty formed us up outside and marched us to the cookhouse. It hadn't opened yet, and a number of men were standing outside, in a ragged queue. Runty marched us to the head of the queue, and kept us in formation at ease. When the door was opened, he used his corporal's stripes to hold back the queue, and marched us inside, in file. When we got our dinners we all sat together, Runty opposite me. 'That's how to use your loaf,' he said. 'Remember that marching men can get through anywhere.' And then he said, 'I'll give you a tip. Dead unofficial, of course, but if ever you're late coming back to camp, and there's a group of you, just form yourselves into a squad, and one of you march behind going "Left right left," and the guard will let you straight through. It never fails. Unless I happen to be the corporal of the guard . . .'

He had the neat gaunt features of a man from the north, but when he told us this his cheeks filled out with laughter,

37

and as he said to me earlier, I knew we'd get on. Because he was filled with this quiet confidence, not one of your brow-beating or bull-shitting types, but a man who knew what he was about. He didn't talk about Africa that day, either, although I found out later he'd been there, and wore the oak leaf for mentioned in despatches, and four wound stripes.

The bunks around me filled during the day: White, who Runty immediately called 'Chalky', and Cutler, and Hargreaves, and we even had a 'Taffy' and a 'Nobby'. When Lance Corporal Smith arrived, Runty, who was sitting on the edge of my bunk at the time reading people's paybooks, said 'Oh, Jesus,' and called across the barrack room, 'Lance Corporal . . .' Smith came over and Runty stood up and said 'This is your lance corporal, everybody, called Smith, and I don't want anybody swearing in front of him or showing him dirty pictures because he always carries a prayer book next to his heart and he's liable to hit you with it.' Lance Corporal Smith smiled the first of the many thin-lipped self-satisfied smiles I was to see, and said, 'You can't provoke me, Corporal Runton.' He walked all the way down the barrack room on one side, and all the way up the other side, standing in front of each bunk, and he had to ask everybody's name, whereas each of us had volunteered his name to Runty. And a funny thing happened because one of the lads, who had a very pale face and long fingers and spoke as if he had a toffee in his mouth, had got into bed, only he'd brought a pair of sheets from home with him and mauve striped pyjamas. I'd been there when he'd checked in with Runty and his name was C. Clements, and Runty, not un-kindly mind you, said 'What's the C for?' but Clements went all pink and Runty didn't press the point. But Runty had the paybooks and later he whistled and showed me Clements's and his name was Cecil.

Well, when Smithy was walking round, first we had a 'Tom', and then a 'Fred', and then a 'Bill', and so on, all good solid names, and we were all stripped down to our singlets and drawers cellular by then, but Smithy came to

38

the bed where Clements was lying, and no doubt saw the sheets, and the mauve pyjamas, and said, 'What's *your* name then,' and Clements said, 'Clements, corporal,' and Smithy said, 'What's your first name?' and Clements looked round the other men in the barrack room, and blurted out 'Bert, they always call me Bert,' only he tried to say it in a deep voice and it came out rumbling and Runty caught my eye and I caught his and we both wanted to laugh. But we didn't. Life could have been hell for a 'Cecil'. The next day he sent his sheets and his pyjamas home, and we all called him Clem.

At each bed the lance corporal had something to say about the condition of brasses, or boots, or webbing, and I heard Runty quietly say to him, 'Anybody would think your dad owned the bloody NAAFI, the amount of dubbin and blanco and brasso you make 'em buy.'

Lance Corporal Smith, who by then we were all calling Smithy, marched us down for supper, and we had to go to the back of the queue and when we got inside they'd run out of steak and kidney pie and chips, which I love, and we had to make do with mincemeat, mashed and cabbage, which I hate. Before he dismissed us outside the mess hall, Smithy addressed us and said, 'First parade in the morning and I want to see you turn out clean and well polished, because a clean and well polished soldier is a good soldier,' and Taffy muttered, 'Because cleanliness is next to godliness,' but Smithy didn't hear him.

We spent all evening bulling up for tomorrow, and I missed the NAAFI and didn't get a drink that evening, but next morning I could have stood guard outside Buckingham Palace.

When we paraded again after breakfast, Smithy marched us to the parade ground in front of the woodcutter's hut. The corporal marched at the back of the squad and said nothing. Smithy had 'inspected' us, and had given more rockets than buckets, as the saying goes. So far we hadn't seen a sergeant or an officer, and I'd begun to think Runty

39

was our highest authority, and I wouldn't have minded that, but when we were right dressed on the parade ground, a sergeant major was waiting for us. 'I'm Arthur Corby,' he said, 'but you lot can call me sergeant major, because that's what I am, the sergeant major of C Company. I know that all sergeant majors are supposed to be bastards, but I can tell you that my mother and father were married two weeks before I was born.'

That old chestnut got a bit of a nervous laugh. Three platoons all standing at ease but not feeling very easy. We should have been feeling relaxed; there were no officers in sight and again, I had a feeling of belonging, as if we were all joined together against a common enemy who would appear later and be carrying a stick and have pips or crowns on his shoulder.

The sergeant major waited until the laugh had fizzled out and then he said, 'I'm not going to give you a lot of bull about being good soldiers. I'm going to treat you, first of all, as human beings. See how we get on together. But I'll be watching each and every one of you.' Runty was standing in front of our platoon, and I noticed he was fiddling with his fingers. Smithy had his hands together as if he were praying. 'Any of you who don't shape up,' the sergeant major was saying, 'I'll get rid of. Simple as that. I'll arrange for you to be transferred out of my company.'

Simple as that, eh? It might be worth remembering.

'I can't be bothered with bolshies, or barrack room lawyers, or skivers. I like people who do what they're told, when they're told.'

Then he pointed dramatically towards the sun, and his voice took on an urgency different from the bored way in which he had been speaking.

'Somewhere over there is Europe, and we're going there together. I will want to know when we leave here that you've all learned enough to keep yourselves alive, to protect me, and bring me safely home. Above all, I don't want to die because one of you didn't learn how to shoot straight.'

40

He looked around our ranks, and smiled. 'Now you can all piss off to your barrack rooms, make sure your kit is okay; get to know the camp, and that means the fastest way from any point to the NAAFI and the dining room. Parade tomorrow and we start work.'

We were the only company who had that day off. Free all day to lounge on our beds, take a long NAAFI break while the other poor sods were working their guts out, go twice round the dinner queue, kip afterwards. But the next morning we were fit and ready for work and out of that barrack room like greyhounds. We didn't have a sergeant with us in those days, but we had Smithy, and from the word go he was a pain in the arse to everybody, including Runty, and, I suspect, the sergeant major. Because Smithy always did everything by the book, and often as not the book had a gold edge to its leaves. Funny thing, Smithy's name. Runty from the moment we arrived was Runty to everybody, but corporal to his face and to other NCOs. The sergeant when he eventually arrived was always the sergeant to everybody, the sergeant major was always the sergeant major. But Smithy somehow never had an identity. Though Smithy was our section corporal and slept in the barrack room with us, there never was any question of inviting him out with us. If he was in the NAAFI or the dining room we'd never ignore him. But we'd never invite him. Rumour had it he spent three evenings a week socializing in the Methodist chapel half way to the town, but we were never interested enough to find out, whereas when it was rumoured Runty had a blonde cracker we lay in wait to verify her for ourselves and it was true.

I'm trying to give you the general background to the start of my life in Maidstone because I believe it's important to the way I felt running up that beach, and even before I left that landing craft. Up to then I'd had an easy life in the camp, with good people about me like the sergeant major, Runty and Chalky and even, I now realize, Smithy, and I'd come to a certain way of thinking and it all had to end.

41

That day on the beach, after that long summer and the short winter of 1943.

They used to hold dances in the camp every Saturday night, but at first I preferred the Star in Maidstone where there were more birds although it was a bit pricey if you were unlucky enough to pick one who wanted gin and orange. Mostly, before I'd make my move, I'd watch and see what kind of glass they had in their hands, though you could get caught out that way because many a girl who'd been buying lemonade for herself and perhaps a half of beer would switch to gin and orange, or port and lemon, when some fellow was doing the buying. Still, the way I could dance, strictly Nat Gonella and the Palais de Dance in Huddersfield and all the twirly bits, I could keep the good dancers on the floor when many a clodhopper was asking for another drink. I had a technique – neat, tight, short steps except in the tango, all done from the waist and hold your head up – and it really got to them. I'd have my hand delicately round their waists and one thing I can say for myself, when I was leading I could make any bird look like Ginger Rogers.

After I'd been in the camp for three months I got to know the unit tailor, right old grumpy bugger he was, but I fetched him a length of cloth from the mill when I came back from a seven day once and he made us up a couple of shirts. I gave him my best uniform to work on and he brought in the jacket and put a couple of tucks in the front just above the pocket and shaped the trousers to the way I hang and the width of my leg and I looked really tidy. He told me a trick you can do with that rough serge when you want to make a crease; you thin the cloth by scraping it gently with a razor blade and burning it off, so that it'll take a real knife edge, and you stiffen it with soap. When all the others are bagging around the place with bulging knees, looking like Laurel and Hardy, there you are dead neat. Also you stiffen the collar of the jacket and put a corset bone in it so the points lie flat, and tack the points with a couple of tiny stitches, and Ramon Navarro is nothing to the way you look. I was sharp as a knife, and it paid dividends. I never had to walk alone from the Star Ballroom, Maidstone. Only I didn't like to take them into the pleasure park on the way home because that spoiled my creases.

I started to go to the camp dance because there, if you knew the boys on guard, you could take a bird into a barrack room, and nip off your trousers, and that way you didn't lose the creases. One night, when Chalky was on and Smithy was off, we used the guard room because the girl I had picked up was with her sister, and the sister was a real dog, just Chalky's type since he never minded how their faces were and always said 'Never look at the mantelpiece when you're poking the fire.' It turned out to be quite a night because Chalky's bird was a real deliverer and all six of the guard had her. Except Chalky for some reason. Even I was tempted but I knew that if I let the one I had off the rope they'd all want her and I wasn't sharing. Not mine.

It was at one of the camp dances that the RSM got up the idea of a ballroom competition and I won one of the prizes. I could have won them all but I didn't bother entering for the waltz or the quickstep, which to my mind lack the subtlety of the slow fox and the tango. It was a good night, and I'd got a good partner. She worked in the NAAFI, not much to look at off the floor but once she got into my arms she was sheer poetry, though I say so myself. I'd danced with her several times during the past months and we had such a good relationship going that when they'd start the music of a tango, automatically our eyes would come together even across the gymnasium and I wouldn't need to invite her except by holding out my arms. Many's the time some fellow's been chatting her up and doing well, or so he thought, until that music started, and she'd look around or over his shoulder and I'd beckon and he'd have had it. So when the RSM called the tango in the competition, it was natural who I'd dance with. We walked away with the first prize. The second prize went to the RSM but he had a tight arse and danced flashy and once or twice he out-reached his partner. Which is fatal in a competition. Major Brassingham had 'kindly consented to honour us with his presence and services as a judge', and also Lieutenant Soames and the RSM's wife, which made everybody say it was all a fiddle. But nothing the major had to do with was a fiddle. Except, perhaps, getting me a few extra camp passes so I could teach Mary.

Next day Smithy almost pissed himself when word came I had to go see the battalion adjutant. 'Retribution comes to us all,' he said woefully, but Runty and Chalky only laughed. 'Some girl, bun in the oven, that's what it is,' Runty said.

'Only with you,' Chalky added, 'since you don't share, they'll know who the daddy is.'

When the orderly took me to the adjutant's house and not to his office, I was even more surprised. He took off his cap as he went up to the front door. 'Take off your cap,' he said to me, 'and stick it under your lapel.'

'Am I on a charge, then?'

'No, but he doesn't like saluting in his house.'

We rang the bell and waited like civilized people. Frankly, I felt afraid, standing there on the front door step. I'd been to the house before on fatigues delivering stuff, but only to the back. The major himself opened the door to us and asked me to come in.

'Wilkins, isn't it?'

'Yes, sir, Wilkins T., 4732849 . . .'

'Yes, quite, well, we shan't need all that, lad. Thank you very much, Rogers.'

The orderly turned round and left, and I stood thinking what to do. Should I go past the major into the hall, stand there, or follow him? He quickly put me at ease by gesturing for me to go past him, and we went into a room off the hall I later discovered was his study. The time was five o'clock. I heard the klaxon go on my way to the house. Strictly speaking I was off duty. Any other day I'd be back in the barracks, smoking a cigarette on my bed, planning the evening ahead, counting my money to see what I could afford in the way of entertainment.

'The sun's over the yard arm, I think,' he said when I'd sat in the chair he'd indicated. I hadn't a clue what he meant. In those days, that wasn't my sort of dialogue. But I understood the translation.

'Care for a drink, lad?'

'Yes, please, sir.'

'What's it to be?'

'Could I have a sherry?' That was the thing to ask for, I knew that much. But he laughed. 'You're not visiting the vicar,' he said, 'and I've never met anybody who really likes sherry . . .'

I'd had it once. Got drunk on it, in fact. I couldn't stand the stuff. On the sideboard I could see three matching cut-glass decanters, each with a silver label hanging from a chain round its neck, and the one in the middle was the colour of whisky.

'Could I have a glass of scotch, sir?' I asked, and he smiled.

'Water, soda, or naked as nature intended . . .?'

'On its own, sir.' I felt quite bold and had drunk whisky so rarely I didn't want to dilute the pleasure. He poured a drink for himself and for a moment I worried that I had done the wrong thing when I saw him squirt soda water into his, but he turned to me with an apologetic smile. 'Can't take it on its own,' he said, 'damned indigestion.' I relaxed because I guessed somehow I'd done the right thing. We talked together for about fifteen minutes. Mostly he asked me questions about my life in the camp, and I told him what I thought, honestly and fairly. But I didn't tell him about the wrong things. It wouldn't have been right for me to criticize *his* camp on such a short acquaintance. The nearest I came to a criticism was when I told him how much time and money I spent eating in the NAAFI, and quickly he asked, 'Cookhouse food not too good?' I shook my head. 'Not like home cooking, sir, but then, you wouldn't expect

45

it to be.' For the first time I saw a glint in his eye which later I realized meant he had recorded a fact he would not forget, and would put to use later on. Though the cookhouse food didn't materially improve, from that day on we got a little more on our plates each meal time.

After we'd been talking fifteen minutes or so he looked at his watch but apologized for doing so. The commanding officer and his wife were coming for dinner and the major had a few things to do. Did I mind if he came to the point? He had seen and admired the way I danced the previous evening. Did I think it would be possible to show his daughter a few steps? Of course, it would take up my off-duty time, but he hoped I wouldn't be offended if he were to offer me 'a little something' for my trouble – should we say, half a crown an hour? It wasn't an excessive amount, but I realized later it would not have been in keeping with his character if he had offered me a larger sum. It wasn't intended as a bribe, merely a just and appropriate wage for services rendered. And I accepted it as such. It meant two packets of cigarettes and a pint of beer for every hour I worked, or two of us to the pictures, or beans on toast six times.

It wasn't until the major had shown me out, still using the front door, that I gave any thought to my would-be pupil. We'd all seen her around the barracks, of course, hurrying here and there, not looking at anybody or stopping to talk. We'd all dubbed her 'stuck up', and nobody that I knew had made a try for her. I'd noticed she limped. Why hadn't the major mentioned it when he asked me to take on the job? Why hadn't he come right out with it? Look, my daughter limps but I want you to teach her to dance. And wasn't teaching a cripple to dance worth more than teaching a fit person? It would be that much harder, take that much longer. Wouldn't it be harder to teach someone who'd shown herself to be unfriendly? What if it did take longer. I was being paid by the hour, wasn't I, and he hadn't given me a deadline, and I'd smoked two of his fags while we were

46

discussing it, so what the hell? I *wanted* to do it. I truly wanted to do it. It would give my days a fixed point.

What I did between seven thirty in the morning and five o'clock in the evening was routine. I could recite the training programme, knew what nights I'd be on guard duty, what nights on fire picquet. Let's face it, what I was doing in the evening wasn't much better than a routine. Tuesday and Thursday out with my bird from the British Restaurant. Married to some navy type up in Scotland, she couldn't go out weekends because her mother-in-law wouldn't like it. So she'd invented classes Tuesdays and Thursdays; we'd either go to the pictures or into the bushes in the pleasure park when it was fine or she was exceptionally hungry. She was one of the ones who never got used to being without it, and sometimes she'd go at me as if I was the last man alive. 'Give it to me,' she'd say, 'give it to me,' and I'd say, 'I'll bet you wish it was a black pudding you could wrap up in paper and take home with you,' and she'd say, 'Don't put ideas into my head or I might not need you,' and I'd feel disgusted with what I was doing and ram it hard into her and fast so I could come off as quick as possible. Because I've never liked being used. Not by anybody. And she was using me as a stud bull. Mind you, she paid for her pleasures, always brought me a bit of something to nibble, like a sandwich with half an inch of ham in the middle, though you couldn't buy ham in the shops, and tea and sugar and milk powder so that we could have a brew up on the barrack stove, and sometimes cigs and a bar of chocolate or some boiled sweets. And I'd say, 'What have you brought for me?' and look in her handbag, and she'd say, 'What have you brought for me?' and feel in my trousers; and for a long time it was all a routine game, and I felt big because, needing a man, she'd chosen me.

My weekend routine never varied. Walk round the town Saturday afternoon if I wasn't on duty, dance either in the Star or the camp Saturday night. Sunday either church parade or stay in bed, pictures in the evening probably with

47

the bird I'd picked up the previous evening at the dance, or if she hadn't delivered or I hadn't fancied it again, with the boys. Chalky, Runty, Cutler and me often went out together in an informal way, not committed to each other, but relying on at least one of the other three to keep company with, rather than be alone. Alone was a taboo word. Smithy was 'alone'. Sergeant Hunter was 'alone'. And so, curiously enough, was Lieutenant Soames. I caught him coming out of the library once and he looked very embarrassed. One night he was at the pictures, alone. Some British picture I couldn't stand, nothing at all like the Betty Grable and Alice Faye pictures I like. Captain Best was never alone. I used to see him at the Star Ballroom and always with a party, always with smashing girls, always a bottle on the table, or supper in the corner where they had the private alcove and nobody ever knew what went on, but it was said to be a marvellous place for a grope during the waltzes when they dipped the light and brought on the mirrored ball that swung around with the spotlights on it. Once, I did hear, some artillery major was kicked out for having it off across the back end of the table in the alcove, but I don't believe all the rumours I hear.

Walking back to camp after my talk with the major, I realized I'd have to make a few changes. Tuesdays and Thursdays, the major had said. Those were the only evenings his daughter could count on being free. But those were the nights for my bird from the British Restaurant, Gladys, and I couldn't see her hanging about some street corner while I finished the oblique turn in the foxtrot. So it looked as if British Restaurant had had her day.

As my feet hit the water alongside Chalky, I suddenly knew the fear of complete exposure. For a brief moment I wanted to turn round and snuggle back into that landing craft. At that minute I felt the pain of a child leaving its mother's womb, delivered unprotected into a cold and hostile world. But the man behind pushed me forward and I was carried as one link of a chain that was snaking its way forward to the dry exploding sand of the beach ahead, and I pumped my knees up and down, stepping high to keep from splashing the water. The man in front of me was hit and he came back before he folded forward and I reached out my arm and callously pushed him aside and went past him. I forged my way through, bent forward, head down protected by the helmet, heart thumping, blood pressing along my forehead as if it would burst out and drench my face with the splashes of water and sweat. Just let me get to the beach, I thought, just to the beach. Not here. My father died, drowned in water, and they pulled him out, but not here, don't let it be here, where they'll never find me to pull me out. I'll float back into the sea. Don't let me be an unknown soldier, dead at sea. Don't let me go down here, before I even get to the beach.

I felt a grip on my arm like a steel band and thought I'd been hit, but it was the sergeant major's hand and his voice in my ear – 'Go right lad, go right' – and I looked up to see I'd been pulling off to the left, a link breaking the chain. I looked forward up the beach, to the top of the crest where the waiting gun was firing. The rounds came out in a continuous stream and I could see the source of them because of the tracer and thought, So it was there after all, right where they said it was. And I wondered why they do that to give away their location, but knew that the minute they fired even a non-tracer the location would be exposed to a real soldier, a real trained soldier like the sergeant major, not a part-time flunkie like me who's learned his lessons and had forgotten every one of them. Head up. A fragment of something hit my steel helmet; I felt the blow, heard the fragment whang away. Christ, I thought, is that all there is to it? I'd shit my pants, thinking about being hit. Now it had happened, and I'd come through it without damage. I felt a great relief. Or was it the knowledge that the sergeant major was near enough behind me to help me, like he had corrected my course? The curtains in my mind opened and I saw the reality of that beach and the exploding sand and the gun shooting from above and the barbed wire we had to cross and suddenly it all became a clear picture, a jigsaw puzzle I knew I had solved.

# 4

We used to go on schemes from the camp, and they'd put up a pretend enemy. Sometimes it'd be another platoon and they'd even dress them differently. I remember once they let Number 3 platoon wear pyjama trousers and wind towels round their heads, pretending to be dervishes I suppose. They had to retreat along a fixed route and we had to chase them, miles and miles over the rough country of South Wales. Every so often they'd set an ambush for us and we had to take it seriously because one of the corporals in that platoon had been issued with live rounds and tracer. You didn't fuck about because he was a right sadistic bastard and wouldn't have minded knocking a few of us off.

We'd had lessons in all the weapons, map-reading, stalking, fire and movement, but it hadn't made much sense. But there came one time behind the railway track of an old mine, that we were going along, when suddenly, whap, a tracer came out of nowhere. We all dropped down. Then the buggers hiding up top dropped thunderflashes on us, and because we'd trained we were quick enough to throw them back. I was glad we'd trained. My rifle jammed because the blanks were bloody awful. The powder had clogged the bolt slide so I whipped it out the way Runty had taught me and then everything was all right again. One by one, the lessons we'd learned came to life, because we needed them. But worst of all was when Cutler and me were going across a bit of a ravine and we'd thrown a rope across it and another for a hand rail, but the joker who'd climbed the other side, Chalky, hadn't tied the rope properly and it slipped with Cutler and me left hanging from it. It took all the lads of our section to get us out. That taught me two lessons: you must never depend on other people, but you've got to learn to rely on them. At the time it seemed a contradiction. Chalky had tied the rope and made a balls of it, but the rest of the section had got us out of the mess. From that moment, when I felt the relief of being dragged over the lip of that ravine in Wales, I knew a bit about being a soldier.

I didn't know anything about fighting; it took the sight of that beach and the exploding sand and the gun shooting from above and the barbed wire we had to cross, to make me see that all the lessons we'd had, and all the schemes, had been designed to bring us to this point with understanding. It was familiar ground we had to cross, and like a jigsaw it all fell into place. The barbed wire was back in Detling quarry, the gun shooting down on us was in the hands of that sadistic corporal, the exploding sand was at Morecambe. Would there be little sticks poking out of the sand with french letters on them? The fear drained from me like the piss down my legs, washed away by the reality of the water, which could have been the water of the Medway river.

Already there were men ahead of me dropping in the water; three landing craft were in front of us and the Engineers had started to run forward but many were stopped by the fist of that gun smashing them back and down with shots from the crest of the ridge. The first rank of Engineers carried Thompson machine guns with which they sprayed the beach ahead of themselves as they ran. Half of them keeled over and down before they got to the sand and I wondered what the hell they could be doing firing their guns low into the sand that way when the enemy was up on the top of the ridge. And then I realized they were using the heavy impact of the .45 rounds to clear the strip of beach of mines. Several exploded, struck by bullets, and of course logically that was the only way the beach could be cleared quickly, by running the machine guns over it like vacuum cleaners in reverse. One Engineer held a length of chain and another the other end as they ran apart and pulled the chain out between them, the links of the chain dragging across the sand. Two more behind them had the same method, and two more behind *them,* and slowly along the sand a clear path was emerging. When I looked along the beach I saw the same sort of technique being used, but over on the left it was not working because the chain was becoming entangled in dead bodies.

I flicked my head to the right and saw at that moment the explosion of a mine which carried one length of the chain up into the air. Despite the deluge of noise I heard the scream of the man on the end of the chain, the end nearest to me, as the chain whipped up into the air, with the man's arm still attached to it. The man himself had been thrown backwards into the whirling sand. Water splashed up my legs and I noticed it, not to do anything about it, just to be totally aware of it. The trouser leg must have pulled out of my gaiter again and I had an almost irresistible impulse to stop and bend down and poke the end back into the gaiter but I ran on. All my senses were alert and all my feelings alive, and that disturbed me, because I had expected that once I got moving out of that boat the adrenalin, or whatever it is that pumps inside you, would rob me of all feeling except the fierce drive to go forward. When you do a hundred yards dash, when you throw yourself into a high jump, even in my case when I placed my arm around a girl's waist to start a tango, you don't know the details of what you do. You start and you finish and the adrenalin takes care of everything that happens between. People ask you afterwards, 'How was it?' as if you could remember every detail, but you remember nothing if you're truly concentrating, just as I wanted to remember nothing of that run through the water and up that awesome beach, just as I hoped that the adrenalin would get me through.

I wasn't sure I could get through without it.

The sergeant major had seen the Engineers with the chains. 'Spread out,' he shouted, 'spread out, and stay behind the chains,' and we started to skitter away from each other. Chalky moved about four feet to my left, just in time, because as he went I heard the whang of some kind of shell ricochet as it screwed between us, and realized it would have hit either one of us at waist height. Those first six steps through the water took as long as the two years I'd served in Maidstone, and even now I can remember the thundering pattern of the sound and the vivid flashes of colour, almost all yellow and red and the kind of purple they call royal; the khaki uniforms stained red, and the men falling.

That was the start of D-Day for me.

# 5

The first dance lesson I gave Mary Brassingham was a night-mare. It was on the Tuesday after the major had 'appointed' me. I'd seen Gladys on the Monday and she was livid.

'How can I tell my mother-in-law they've changed the night of my classes from Tuesday and Thursday to Monday and Wednesday?' she asked. She was whining, and for the first time I noticed she had quite a pronounced growth of hair on her upper lip and tiny beads of perspiration in it, and I remembered the way she sometimes smelled like an animal when we made love, and felt a flicker of revulsion. Why shouldn't she smell like an animal? That was all it had been, a couple of alley cats, back-street dogs coming together. Damn, there was a war on and a man had a right to make himself happy any way he could. That was the way Chalky would have justified it; well, perhaps not Chalky or Smithy, but certainly Runty or Cutler.

'Suit yourself, but I can't manage Tuesday or Thursday any more.'

I'd lied to her, of course. Told her the major had given me an extra duty, hinted it was something special. I hadn't said anything about Mary Brassingham, nor that I was being paid. 'I'll tell you what, see what you can arrange, and send me a postcard.'

She looked at me; the sweat was really running, and now the animal stink was starting to come from her, or perhaps that was my imagination. 'Just like that, eh? See what you can do and send me a postcard? Not very romantic, are we . . . ?'

'We agreed, remember, no romance. No getting involved. You're a married woman.'

'That hasn't seemed to bother you too much.'

That was where she was wrong. It had bothered me. Oh, I knew the old saying – nobody misses a slice off a cut loaf – but sometimes I'd thought about the poor bugger whose missis I was knocking off, and it was worse when once I'd caught a glimpse of them together. Would you believe it? The cow was taking him to the Star Ballroom. Showing him off, I suppose. Only I had been there early and the band was playing lousy and I'd decided to go on to the camp dance because I knew how I could get in without paying.

Mary Brassingham herself opened the door, and took me into the drawing room. Somebody had pushed the chairs back to the wall and had rolled up the carpet. It made it awkward. There was nowhere to sit. We had to stand inside the door. A large wind-up gramophone on a mahogany table; beside it a stack of records.

'Is this all right?' she asked. Those were the first words she'd said. Dead awkward.

'Fine, it looks just fine.'

What the hell do you do? Girl you've never even seen close up before. In her father's house. Walk up to her, put your arm round her waist, say 'Now what we're going to do, is . . .' Different in a dance hall, isn't it. Different class of girl to start with. The Mary Brassinghams of this world don't go to dance halls of a Saturday night. So I walked across to the gramophone. Somebody had wound it up. I lifted the lid. Inside was one of those kits for sharpening fibre needles. The needle was new, newly sharpened. Looked at the records. They were new too. Roy Fox, Victor Sylvester, Geraldo. Strictly music to dance to. No Artie Shaw. No Benny Goodman. You can't have everything.

'Are they all right?' she asked, anxiously.

'They're fine, absolutely fine.' They were also brand new. I could imagine the conversation – only it would be a monologue.

'We require a few tunes for dancing, send up half a dozen of each, will you? And put them on the bill.' I bought my

56

first gramophone record second-hand for threepence.

I turned to her; she was wearing a wool dress in soft brown. She'd obviously had her hair done and the curls were tight. The fringe was a neat straight line across her forehead. But she hadn't done so well with the lipstick, or the rouge. She was looking at me, and I found it hard to analyse her expression, except that it wasn't haughty. She seemed a little frightened as if wondering what I was going to do. I picked a record, lowered the needle head and slid it into the first groove. The gramophone, as I had expected, had a beautiful tone. All that good wood. 'You can make it louder by opening the doors,' she said, but I shook my head. I walked to the wall and turned round a small sofa so it was facing into the room. Then I went back to the gramophone and looked through the tunes with my back to her.

'Sit on the sofa,' I said, 'and we'll have a bit of a chat.' I didn't want to have to watch her first walk, didn't want to force her to model it for me. When I'd given her enough time to sit down I turned around, walked across the room and sat down beside her, though as far from her as I could get. 'It's all a matter of rhythm,' I said. She nodded as if she understood. 'Dancing,' I said, 'is all a matter of rhythm.' Then I clapped my hands together, not loudly, to emphasize the beat of the music. I'd deliberately chosen a waltz, and clapped each first beat of the set of three louder than the other two. Dah, dit, dit, dah, dit, dit. She looked at my face, not at my hands. 'Now *you* try to do that . . .'

'Should I clap my hands, too?'

'Yes.'

She tried. I knew at once what a hell of a job I'd let myself in for. She had absolutely no sense of rhythm. She couldn't even clap a waltz. I picked out the beat for her and hummed it as the record played, tried to get her to hum it with me. But she just couldn't separate the different elements of it, couldn't space them out. The record ended and I wound up the machine and started it again. Dah dit dit, dah dit dit. But she couldn't find it, couldn't isolate the strands of the beat within the tapestry of the music. I got up and danced around, feeling like a charlie, moving my feet in time to the beat, dah dit dit. But she still couldn't find it. I tried explaining it to her, taking long steps and short steps. She didn't play any musical instruments, knew no songs, had no idea of what music tries to do. I grew desperate because music and rhythm have always been so much a part of me: the songs we sang at school, the choir I joined after school, the choir my dad sang in, my mother bashing away on the old joanna in the church hall whenever she got a chance and telling us how she'd been brought up in a house that had a piano in it. I'd come up with the lot: the Messiah, Elgar – all the big choral works were second nature to me. And then I discovered ballroom dancing and dance music, the pleasures of melody and rhythm plus a girl in my arms.

'Have you never heard any music?' I asked her, wondering what kind of life she could have led without it, and she said, 'Yes, I've heard lots of music, regimental bands, and I've been to concerts with my father.' She was on the defensive and I hadn't really meant to attack her, but I suppose I sounded incredulous and she equated a lack of musical knowledge with a lack of something more important, like the lack of the ability to walk gracefully like all the other girls. When I realized that, I felt the blood rush to my face. How could she have known anything about rhythm. Rhythm must develop from walking and balance and movement. How can you have any balance in your walking and your movement when your bloody foot is sticking out at an angle of thirty degrees. You go to a concert and all you hear is noise because there are several different rhythms going together, and you hear the army band playing and all you see are soldiers walking along doing one two one two one two, chopping the rhythm and the melody alike into meaningless pieces. Rhythm comes to us from the natural motion of our bodies balancing on our feet, skipping, running, standing, walking, but Mary Brassingham had only one good leg, and the other played some part in propelling her forward,

58

certainly, but contributed nothing to her sense of balance or rhythm.

I suppose I would have given up. I would have said to her, 'Look, there's no point in your learning to dance so badly, so unrhythmically that nobody will ever ask you twice,' but the door opened, and the major was watching me make a charlie of myself sliding over the floor and Mary looking with an air of eager anticipation and I did a turn and saw him and stopped dead. The pleasure he was getting from knowing his daughter was being taught was so apparent.

'How's everything going?'

He looked across at Mary. 'Just heard the music,' he said, 'and thought I'd pop my head round the door to tell you supper's in half an hour, if you'd care to invite Mr Wilkins to join us.'

Maybe the Mr Wilkins did it. Maybe the eagerness with which she said 'Oh, good.' Maybe the glow of pleasure I got at the thought of actually being invited for supper and becoming an insider. I couldn't resist thinking of what Runty would say, and Chalky, if I could tell him – 'Had supper with the major . . .' Of course, it'd be something vulgar but they'd be jealous and I'd know.

'Would you,' Mary said, with a heartwarming spontaneity, 'like to stay for supper? Or do you have an engagement . . .?'

An *engagement* . . . Not a date with a girl, not a half a crown's worth of the pictures. But an *engagement*. 'No,' I said, 'I have no engagement.'

'Good,' the major said. 'Then you'll stay and take a bite of supper with us?'

It was all so different for me. In my world, you don't 'take a bite of supper'. In my world you 'eat your supper and get on with it'. Supper is what you get just before you go to bed, a hunk of bread to eat with your cocoa, with maybe a piece of cheese and a pickled onion, and don't drop the crumbs on the floor.

'Yes, I'd like to . . .'

I was hooked, for without the dancing lessons there'd be

59

no 'taking a bite'.

The major closed the door after him. I walked to the sofa, stood in front of Mary. 'We'd better get started,' I said.

I've often wondered how it happens on a honeymoon. Do people really rush into each other's arms the minute the door closes behind the porter? I felt the same kind of embarrassment as I stood in front of the sofa with my hands outstretched. She put her hands in mine and I drew her from the sofa. But not into my arms, the way I would have done with Gladys, or my NAAFI partner. 'You'd better walk across the floor,' I said, 'and I'll see how you walk on that leg of yours.' No point in pissing about. I had to know how she walked, I had to watch her; she had to know I was watching. Her face went white under the powder and the rouge. She'd had to learn to screw up her courage to be able to cross a room full of folk, knowing some would watch and pity her. She must have walked across hospitals' and doctors' consulting rooms while medical men examined her posture and stance. Possibly they'd even made her walk naked so they could see her entire body, not just her affected leg. This was different; this test was without social or medical justification; this was brutally individual. I stepped away from her and turned, knowing how *I* would glide across that floor, dah dit dit, dah dit dit, with the NAAFI girl in my arms.

Mary took a step forward, and another, and my nerve ends jangled when I recognized she had no knowledge of the beat of that music, no ability to move her body in answer to its rhythm. She hobbled across the floor in something like three seven time. At the other side of the room she turned to look at me; she hadn't cheated; she'd walked the longest distance possible in that room. There was a tear in her eye. One in mine, too.

'I'll teach you the waltz,' I said, knowing that for both of us the nightmare had just begun.

# 6

I didn't get to the beach. Nor did Chalky or the sergeant major. Nor did Lance Corporal Smith or Lieutenant Soames. Suddenly the water in front of me opened and raised itself in a deluge that cascaded up and over me. I felt the water smash violently into my face and catch under the rim of my helmet and throw me backwards as if I had tried to walk into a wind of gale force. In the wave was sand and a shingle of small stones that solidified the water as if it were concrete; first my run forward was halted and then I felt myself being thrust backwards and down by the weight on my head and my shoulders and my pack and I was forced into the raging water. The others were lying beside me and Chalky's face was lacerated by it, red stabs of blood on his cheeks like the bleeding marks of smallpox and I knew from the pain on my face that it too was marked in that way and I felt it smarting. I wanted to shout out but I knew I didn't have sufficient air in my lungs as I lay there gasping and looked about me and saw the others floundering in the water. A bomb had exploded in front of us but mercifully its blast had been taken by the water and the sand and shingle or we would surely have been torn to shreds.

I tried to rise from the water but heard the sergeant major shout, 'Stay down Wilkins,' and obeyed him instinctively. Then I noticed the whipping of the shots above my head, a moving ceiling of shots as that gun on rapid fire sprayed the air above us, seeking a target beyond us, but not caring if we should come between. I plunged my face into the water, lifted it again, and for a brief moment saw the place where my face had been stained red by my blood. Salt water stung my cheeks and went into my eyes and I lifted a hand to wipe it away but my hand was covered in salt water, too, and that stung even more since I'd rubbed it into my eyes. I tried blinking rapidly, but all that did was to create haloes of light where the explosions were still happening on the shore, and prismatic effects on the water that was being gouged up around us by the falling shrapnel. The sergeant major was now crawling forward through the water as if through long grass and I crawled forward with him, arms and legs held down, arse screwed down low as it would go, and I felt bullets tug at my pack and one must have caught a buckle because it pulled the strap of my pack tight into my shoulder, tight enough to make me think my shoulder might be torn. But the next movement of that arm forward, my right arm, went well and without pain, so I knew the shoulder wasn't broken.

The pain was familiar to me, and the pain I felt inside my knee was familiar as I slipped on the stones in the sea, cobbled smooth by millions of years of rolling in the water, but now broken by the force of explosions. Arm forward to make the distance, then the weight forward to shift the balance and sea rolls up my arse, again and the sea rolls up my guts. Left hand, rifle hand, sod it, the stones bite at my knuckles, right leg, sequence, tight, low, smooth.

I'd done it so many times, grown good at it in the days when it was a game and the sergeant major's stick not pounding down on your buttocks the only prize you could expect. Once he made us crawl all the way across Detling quarry, through everything, stones, thistles, nettles, muddy water; hands and knees for what seemed a mile, but was actually no more than five hundred yards. Crawl, crawl, and him walking behind the three platoons, with the three sergeants and the three corporals. The lance corporals crawled with us, and Smithy enjoyed it. Every time an arse came up, the sergeant major's stick came down. Runty gave me the best tip on how to do it. 'Imagine you're in a woman but you've finished doing it and your leg goes to sleep and you want to change your position but you don't want the damn thing to drop out.' Cutler laughed and jerked his buttocks up and down and brayed. 'Like this, corporal, like this?' he said but Runty hit him hard with the flat of the old-fashioned bayonet he carried and Cutler stopped pissing about. All that crawling, all that training for two years, and they never made us crawl through water because they never knew we'd have to crawl to the beach. We'd trained, dammit, to run through the water. Like we'd trained to run out of the landing craft but they'd never trained us to leave the sergeant in there, tucked under one of the seats and left there as if he was a lump of shit, and they'd never trained us to crawl over broken cobblestones with edges on them like knives that rolled as you rolled and chopped into your kneecaps and into your elbows.

I held my head down and water splashed up over my face, rushing into my nostrils, and I closed my eyes for a moment, for one step only, but I could not keep my eyes closed even though the salt water hurt them because I couldn't conceive of myself crawling sightless through that water. I'd gone five or six paces forward and had come to the edge of the crater the bomb had blown; the water was running and sucking down into the crater and I knew if I tried to crawl through that I would drown and if I stood up to wade through it I would be shot and if I stayed where I was I would be blown to pieces by one of the bombs or shells or whatever was exploding in the water, and so I had to do something. But what? They hadn't trained us to crawl through a crater filled with rushing sea water scoured by sand and shingle, with a machine gun firing rapid straight over your head.

I looked around me, scared out of my wits, scared for the first time since I'd seen the sergeant shot, and saw that Chalky too had stopped on the crater's edge and the sergeant major was drawing level with me and Chalky in the water. Nobody was left standing on the whole stretch of water between us and the shoreline. Everyone was lying in the water. Many had their heads down and their faces in the water, and one was on his back and that was Cutler, and his arms were outstretched, and he was floating gently, bobbing with the force of each explosion and rolling as the sand and shingle rolled, and already dead. And I didn't even bother to wonder how. I was thinking of my father. Lying alone in the water. Floating alone in the water through the long quiet night, his face down, his arms outstretched. I saw the dark mill pond again where I had stood as a boy looking right into the water that had taken my father. Tears welled into my eyes and the salt of the sea water was washed away, though I could not know I was crouched in the sea, seeing again only the sombre water of the mill pond, remembering my father who was dead, but thinking about Cutler who was dead and all the other men in the water who were dead. Just as my father had died before he reached his goal, so Cutler had died before he reached the beach.

My father had been promised a good job at the mill and only two days after he died he would have started as an overlooker, with his feet on the first rung of the ladder. All the overlookers lived in houses with gardens up on the moors above the valley where we lived, and the company even helped the overlookers buy their houses on mortgages at a low rate of interest. When my mother heard my father was going to be made an overlooker I could see the pride in her. She made me put on my jacket, and took me up to Golcar where some of the overlookers lived with gardens, the house from front to back, not like in the terraces where we lived with another family backing on to us and a family each side, an individual cage in a double row of cages.

I laughed out loud; it must have come from me in a hysterical way because the sergeant major slid through the water beside me and gripped my arm below the elbow. All images of my father were washed away, because before we left Smithy, would you believe it, Smithy had been really ill with the shits and there'd been talk of leaving him behind and making Cutler up to lance corporal and Cutler had even bought the stripes. I knew how badly Cutler had wanted to sew that stripe on his arm and claim the end bunk in the barrack room which traditionally was not shared with anyone else as *our* bunks were, one up, one down. Ambition, even my father's, could be realized in simple terms, like a house on the moor or a bunk in the corner, but my ambition, my one and only ambition, was to stay alive and I knew no way of realizing that in simple terms. So I laughed.

'What's up, lad?' the sergeant major asked, and I laughed again. I was laughing and he wondered what was up. Death, that's what was up, in the sky above our heads, in the waves that pounded all about us, in the whee of the fragments of the shells and the bombs and the mines and the mortars.

I slid into the crater, striking forward, not caring how wide it could be. But it was only six feet and already the bottom had filled with sand and shingle firm enough to support my feet; from the lying position I was now in the standing position and still no more of me showed above the water. The others followed me across. I stood at the far end, looking out as if over the lip of a trench, and I poured the water out of my rifle. The beach only sixty feet away was littered with bodies. The Engineers were being hacked by the machine-gun fire, which went on despite the pounding the navy was giving it. And then one landed smack on the top of the second gun, the one at the shore end of the jetty, and, Jesus Christ; suddenly it wasn't there any more, only a smoking hole in the ground. But *our* gun, that bastard gun, was still firing.

I'd miscalculated the number of dead in the water because half of them were crawling forward. The Engineers had managed to drag those chains about fifty yards up the beach and despite the craters the mortars had made, I could see the cleared sand like smooth skin beneath pockmarks. Here and there the sand was burned black, no doubt by the explosion of a mine, and the barbed wire had been hooked and dragged into piles so that we would be able to pass it. As I watched I saw an Engineer crawl forward with a bangalore torpedo which he slid into an unbroken section of the wire; he struck the end of it and crawled back. The machine-gunner must

65

have spotted him; the sand spurts showed where the gunner was looking for the Engineer, but no shot hit him; when the bangalore went off, the wire was blown high and a gap had been cut, but what's more important the ends had been separated and the Engineer hooked into it and two pioneers by the pile of wire started to pull a cord to drag the bangalored wire so that the gap increased to twenty feet. I knew with tremendous relief then they were preparing the beach for tanks or at least armoured cars, and I thought 'Poor bloody pioneers, bunch of heroes to take that shit.'

Chalky beside me, the sergeant major between but behind us. Looked round. Lieutenant Soames behind him, trying to talk into his radio, though wearing a throat mike and the actual sound didn't matter since the throat mike worked on vibrations they said, but he looked at the meter on the radio to see if the signal was peaking as it should do, and wearing earphones. The lucky sod. Who the hell was he talking to? They ought to have told us that, I needed to know. Captain Best? Behind us oh, three boats back? It'd have to be, wouldn't it. That was the way the network went. They said Captain Best ought to have been a major since he had command of a whole company, but apparently he said the wrong thing at the wrong time to the colonel who commanded the battalion – at least, that was the rumour. Anyway, Soames to Best to colonel to, presumably, navy. Calling for more fire power to knock out the gun. Only one gun left after all, one bloody gun, and a whole company plus Engineers to deal with it in the little cove. They'd said the cove was useless as part of the major advance because behind that hummock a cliff and a ravine made the cove impassable for military vehicles. That was why it was not fully defended. Because it could not be used for a major advance without bringing in bridge-building kit. Farther down they had the artificial harbour but we had nothing like that. Away off to the south was the whole of the American Army, but I didn't know anything about that. But one tank on that beach would knock the shit out of that gun, which was certainly at that moment knocking the shit out of us. Lieutenant Soames took off his earphones. 'It's up to us,' he said to the sergeant major.

The sergeant major didn't reply, too busy counting moving heads. It'd have been easier to count the still heads and deduct from the total, because the still heads weren't ducking about and you could tally two of them at least to every one that moved.

'Corporal Runton,' Soames shouted.

From the right I heard a 'Here, sir,' unusually subdued for Runty.

'Captain Best's orders, you're made up to sergeant, as of this moment.'

'Fucking hell . . .'

But Lieutenant Soames wasn't listening. 'Lance Corporal Smith?'

'Yes, sir, here sir.'

'You're made up to corporal.'

'Full corporal, sir?' Smithy said, wanting it spelled out in front of witnesses.

'Yes, full corporal.'

'Thank you very much, sir.'

I could almost feel Chalky getting out the needle and thread. Don't be in too much of a hurry, Chalky, they may even have picked me.

'Private Cutler?'

No reply.

'Private Cutler?'

'He's dead, sir,' Chalky said, showing initiative, the short way to earn promotion or a bullet in the head.

'Right, White, I'm making you up to acting lance corporal.' The 'acting' wouldn't have bothered me, but it shook Chalky, now Acting, presumably also Temporary Unpaid Lance Corporal White. But remember, Chalky, all promotions in the field need to be 'ratified at the earliest possible opportunity, and confirmed in Company Orders, a copy of which shall be posted in a prominent position wheresoever the Unit shall congregate, such posting to be taken as full and complete notification of the contents of the Order'.

'Right lads,' the War Substantive sergeant major said, 'end of NAAFI break. Let's get on with it,' and we breathed deeply and scrambled out of the hole to start to run forward again, and Chalky took one right through the shoulder and screamed but, no doubt mindful of his new status, lurched forwards not backwards and I grabbed his arm and held him as we moved away, the blood running down his arm and into the sea spray on the top of my ammo pouches where I carried the spare bombs for the two-inch mortar, if ever we'd get a chance to use it. Chalky looked down at his shoulder and the blood was really pouring out of it and running down his chest and it wasn't a clean hole like a bullet would have made but the serge of his jacket was turned into the edges of the wound, large across as the end of an egg cup. As we started to lurch forward I fumbled with the button of my field dressing pocket but the sergeant major shouted in my ear, 'Use his, lad, you may need yours,' and I remembered all he'd ever said about not spreading myself too thinly and reached for Chalky's field dressing pocket, across his body on his right side. He said, 'I've got some more in my map pocket,' which was on my side, and I opened it and took one out, held it up to the wound. But of course the tying bandage was wrapped round it, and this wasn't one of the ones we'd prepared, but a gash one Chalky had lifted somewhere and I cursed and pulled it away and twisted it to let the tying bandage fall away which it did, neatly, and I was able to put the treated pad against the hole even though it was on the outside of his uniform and bring the tying bandage up over his shoulder.

'It hurts, Tom,' he said, 'hurts like bloody hell.' And all I could think of to say was 'I know, I know,' but I tried to say it as kindly as possible. It was the sea water that hurt as much as the wound itself. I fumbled the bottom of the tying bandage up under his arm to reach the other end, and the bandage dropped forward away from the serge, but I

68

pulled the top in again and tried to twist it round the strap of his pack, while he kept on saying, 'It hurts, Tom, it hurts,' as if there were something else I could be doing. But I couldn't think of anything. There wasn't room and there wasn't time for me to stick my finger inside to gouge out any metal that might be in there. Anyway, I didn't think I could bring myself to do that without being sick, and perhaps if I started to poke about he'd faint. It was best to carry on as I was. I wound the bandage round the strap of his pack and tied it there, and though I knew it wasn't tight, perhaps it might just stop the bleeding enough to let the wound congeal. It was all I could do, because we were moving forward, walking not running, through the water littered with dead bodies floating loose, and you couldn't have run without being tripped. They never trained us to go through water littered with the bodies of your oppos.

'He all right?' the sergeant major asked.

'I think so.'

'Get him to lift his arm,' he said.

It was easier to grab Chalky's elbow and lift it for him.

'No, let's see if he can do it himself.'

'Lift your arm, Chalky,' I said.

'Corporal to you,' he said.

'He's all right, sergeant major.'

As if to prove it Chalky waggled his arm, but looking at his face as we forged along I could see the effort it cost him. But he wasn't going to let them take away his stripe on a technicality.

Roberts was hit on my right. Beyond Chalky. Slept in the top bunk opposite me. Seldom washed his feet. Smoked and coughed after reveille. Bit of a loner. Good shot, could group better than me, and good with the Bren. Slower than me over the obstacle course. Wife was a singer or something in Sheffield. He wouldn't show her photograph around because she was wearing a bathing suit. Runty nicked it one time and we all had a shufti. Big breasts but not much else, in my opinion. Roberts was hit smack in the chest and went

back and down in one, legs lifting as he hit the water and
made a bloody big splash. But dead quick. Half his ammo
pouch blown away. Why hadn't it exploded? Dead, he
wouldn't care.

'It hurts, Tom,' Chalky said.

'Private to you, corporal.'

'Balls.'

# 7

'And BALLS to you, too,' Mary said.

I was shocked. It was so out of character. We'd more or less mastered the waltz. I borrowed a metronome and it stood on a thing you use for potted plants. This thing was hand-carved, a lady carrying a jug and the top of the jug was where you put the plant pot. We took out the plant pot, put a book on top, and the metronome on it, and as it ticked away we went round and round it, dah pause, dit dit, dah, pause dit dit, and every step she took jerked her like a prancing horse. I kept saying to her, 'Don't prance like that, keep your foot on the ground and slide it along.' I'd even brought some french chalk they used on the gym floor for the camp dance every Saturday, and I rubbed it in the soles of her shoes so that her feet could slide, but she would keep picking them off the ground. I lay on the floor and held her feet to show her how to slide them and was scared to look up in case she thought I was trying to see her knickers. Finally, when she was almost in tears, I lost my wick. 'Can't you slide your feet, like I keep telling you?' I shouted at her, and she said, 'My foot won't slide like yours will. You keep forgetting . . .' and then thinking she was after pity, I lost my wick completely and said, 'Oh, BALLS' and instead of her crumpling into tears as she would have done three or four lessons before, she stood her ground and said 'And BALLS to to you, too.'

Up to then I'd been treating her as a cripple, tailoring everything to that, which was a mistake. But when I realized she'd inherited her father's courage and had enough spirit of her own to say that to me, I started treating her as a girl. Which was better all round. I suppose without realizing it I hadn't been holding her properly in my arms. You can't dance with a girl you treat as a piece of china, like one of my mam's mantelpiece pots. You must grab hold of them, bring them up against you. I hadn't been doing that; I'd been holding her finger and thumb as if she was a cocker spaniel I was bringing through its paces at the Town Hall dog show, not communicating my sense of movement to her. From that moment everything improved. We finished the waltz in the next two sessions and started on the quickstep.

After the dancing lesson we always had supper, the major, Mary and me, except when the major had some regimental duty to carry out. At first the major's batman used to look after us, but after the second supper a lady from Maidstone started to serve at table. The major arranged that so as it wouldn't embarrass me to be sitting down to a meal which another private in the same regiment would have to serve. He also did it not to embarrass his batman.

Batmen are born not made, like pub waiters, and it wouldn't matter to him who he served, though the major wasn't to know that. So many little things the major did to make life easier for me, and prick that I was I recognized so few of them at the time. Like asking me did I want to use the bathroom? not, did I want to wash my dirty hands? They were all courtesies he didn't owe me but showed to me willingly because he was that kind of man.

We were having roast lamb for supper one evening. Roast lamb for mid-week supper! Where I came from we'd been lucky to see it for Sunday dinner. He always called it 'mutton'. 'Would you like to take that mutton over to the sideboard and carve it, Tom?' he said to me. I was surprised. He'd carved the roast meats himself, prior to that. I'd watched him with great interest; once I'd said I'd never learn how to do it, and he did it so well, and he chuckled. But a couple of meals later, over to the sideboard! I'd seen how he did it and I think I made a fair imitation. Why take it to the sideboard? Because he wanted me to try my

72

experiments without feeling they were watching me. If I'd brought the meat back in lumps he'd have eaten it like a stoic and would have contrived somehow, in a roundabout way, to tell me where I'd gone wrong.

'How's the dancing going?' he asked. It was the night Mary had said balls to me, but I didn't tell him that. Usually I'd been the one to reply to that question, never very truthfully. This night I didn't speak but looked at Mary. For the first time I'd learned she had firm breasts, and a well shaped back. I'd held her that close. She blushed faintly, and said, 'It's going very well, don't you think, Tom?' That was the first time she'd used my name. The major knew it, looked very briefly at me and no doubt discovered I too was blushing or anyway coloured, and said, 'Try some of this mint sauce. I always think mutton's quite tasteless without mint sauce.'

When we'd finished dinner, instead of Mary going to powder her nose she stayed in the room with us and the major gave her a cigarette and a glass of port, and I had a couple of cigarettes out of a silver box while he smoked a cigar and told us both about growing fruit in a greenhouse and how you must be careful to take away some of the fruits before they are ripe because a tree naturally tries to outstrip its own strength by growing too many fruits, and even offered to show me a pair of scissors he had to go upstairs and rummage for, while we just sat there and looked at each other.

'I never knew you smoked,' I said.

'I don't often. Only when I'm relaxed.'

'You're not tired, after working all day, and dancing . . .?'

'Good Lord no. I could dance for hours.'

'You really like it . . .?'

'I love it.'

'I never knew.'

'I didn't know either. Until tonight. That silly metronome.

Can we have the music again tomorrow? Seems so, well, foolish being close like that, with only a metronome ticking. What would people think, if they saw me . . .'

'We'll have the music next time.'

# 8

I took the mine-detector from Chalky as we struggled together through the water. It seemed pointless to leave it with him. I took the bag that hung down the front of him and hung it round my neck. He'd shown me how to use it when we first got on the landing craft in the middle of the Channel. We'd all been singing then and interested in things. Switch it on, put on the headphones, and listen. In the boat we'd got a loud clicking noise in the earphones, because of the metal, but over soil you just get an occasional click. If you hear too many you thin them out with the knob on the right-hand side. You sweep the plate on the end of the handle backwards and forwards just over the level of the soil and when it passes over the metal of a mine, it starts to click like hell. Trouble is, no matter what metal it passes over, it still clicks. By now there was a hell of a lot of metal of one sort and another strewn over that beach. They said the mine-detector was invented by a Polish radio expert, but I couldn't understand what radio had to do with detecting mines. No more than ten strides to go through the water before we reach the sand.

Before we set off some American gave us a talk; all I could remember from his charts and his mass of figures was that, from the moment we landed on the beach, we had two hours to live.

'I don't think I'm going to make it, Tom,' Chalky said, and the sergeant major reached forward, clapped his hand over Chalky's mouth and Chalky swallowed.

'Make you feel better,' the sergeant major said. The sergeant major was a walking chemist's shop.

My rifle was sopping wet and covered in grains of sand

and if the bolt ever worked I'd be a lucky man. And if the rounds ever fired, because they must all now be sopping wet too. The mortar bombs and the grenades, would they work? I was past caring, six paces to go.

'Sorry I don't have any tea, corporal, to wash the tablets down,' the sergeant major said. Chalky managed a smile. They'd done right to promote him. Lieutenant Soames came forward. 'At the edge of the beach, get down and go for the gun.' A command from a superior officer.

Have a go for a gun at over three hundred yards? What a load of bollocks. I nearly said so.

'What do we use for cover?' That came from Thomson. Silly bugger, always asking daft questions. Used to drive Smithy mad, asking him why, and Smithy only knew a why that was printed in the manual.

'Use your loaf,' the sergeant major said.

'It's big enough . . .' That came from Hargreaves, coming in closer, knitting us all tighter together now we had a direct order and something positive to do.

'What do you use for cover, with dead bodies littering the beach?' Runty said, angry as hell. 'You choose the fattest corpse you can find, and if there's two close at hand you pull them together and get behind both of them and while you're down there, you check their pockets to get out any rounds they've got, and any field bandages.'

Three paces to go and all hell let loose. I looked straight into the slit, saw the muzzle blasts of three separate guns, all poking out of that one long slit. No wonder they'd made a bloody porridge of us. Three guns all firing from one place, no wonder the firing had never stopped. One gun empties its magazine slowly. While they reload, the other takes over. One gunner spots for the other, swinging his gun to have it ready to pick off individual targets, like the pioneers with the bangalore, like us when we bunched like all the other poor bleeders now lying face down in the water, but now we're at the shoreline and they open up together and it needs not one shot through the slit but three. Impossible. Us with only a two-inch mortar, and what's a two-inch mortar against concrete the navy can't smash. Because it's a solid mass of concrete with a sprinkling of soil some gardening joker has planted grass seed on during the two years we've been pissing about in Detling quarry. Two hours. The Yank must have been joking. We didn't have two minutes.

'Three guns in that bunker, sergeant major,' I said.

'Well done, lad, but there's four. I think one of 'em must have jammed.'

That's a grain of good news, a mite of cold comfort in a stinking noisy hot world. Explosion nearby deafened me, searing flame ahead as a shell landed and burst its case. By now we were past ducking, even for near explosions. By now we were picking out places to drop down, and adopt the so-called 'firing position,' loosening rifle fingers that had grown knuckle-white from holding on too tight. What the hell was I going to do with the mine-detector in my right hand like a bishop's wand?

Hargreaves dropped, Thomson dropped, they hit Chalky again. This time on his left leg, my side, only three inches away from my leg. I still had my arm under his elbow when they got him; he spun to his left; his rifle came over and banged me, and he was face to face with me; my right arm slipped round his back and we were in the perfect position for a quickstep, except that I could feel the hardness of his ammo pouches, not his tits. He buckled at the knee and started to go down, but the sergeant major was behind him one side and Runty the other and they turned him back. His arm got entangled in the cord of the mine-detector and he pulled me round with him but they didn't see and they started to rush him up the beach and I had to go with him, half sideways half backwards, and when they got him past the water line there was a body six feet out of the water and they threw him down and I had no alternative but to go down with him since his legs were now entangled in mine and I fell down and backwards and landed with my face cradled between his wet face and the face of the dead man lying there.

'Fucking hell.' I tried to scrabble away, but I couldn't because I was attached to Chalky at so many places. The mine-detector strap had locked round his arm and my ammo pouches were locked in his and even the buckle of my gaiter had locked inside the gap in his gaiter and I couldn't pull myself away from him and that bloody corpse.

'Fucking hell!'

The corpse jerked as a machine-gun bullet spammed into it, and I ducked. Now they'd got the target and the range and were putting those bullets into him one after one and every one was jerking him on the sand and would have moved him along the sand like a ping pong ball if the weight of Chalky and me hadn't stopped him. But then I had the strap free and my ammo pouch free and I was able to move my leg free by pulling the gaiter up and saw Smithy lumbering towards me carrying that bloody telephone exchange and clutching his stomach; and when he let his hands go, his stomach dropped out and fell on Chalky's face like lights from the butcher and Smithy spun round and the telephone exchange came crashing down into my face.

# 9

When I arrived at the Military Hospital in Maidstone they lifted me out of the ambulance that brought me and placed me on a trolley. The atmosphere was close, hot and humid, and my body felt wet. A man passed his hand over my face. His hand was hard, and smelled of oil and ether. I was wheeled inside and the temperature immediately dropped. In the corridor, echoing long, the man gave the trolley to a woman he called 'Miss'. She, too, ran her hand down the side of my face but her fingers, long, soft, and dry, smelled of ether and feminine soap. As the man walked away his rubber soles scuffed the floor of the corridor as if he'd forgotten how to pick up his feet. The trolley started to move much more smoothly, and though I listened hard I couldn't hear the woman's feet, only the rustle of her clothes. She wheeled me forward then turned after a while and stopped. I heard the clank of a lift and the whoosh of the opening gate. The woman held a whispered conversation with a man, then pushed me into the lift, the trolley clacking over the space between the cage and the corridor. The door closed and the lift descended. It stopped, and the woman said, 'Damn.'

The man said, 'You can say that again.'

They rattled the buttons, but the lift didn't move. The man lifted the telephone out of its cradle, and clacked the cradle up and down saying, 'Hello, Hello.' He stopped clacking the cradle.

'Dead,' he said.

'Press the alarm button,' the woman said.

'This is the second time this week.'

'Press it.'

The man punched it, in and out. 'They'll pull my leg something rotten,' he said. 'This is the second time this week.'

'Keep on pressing.' In her voice I could hear the panic of developing claustrophobia. I'd heard it when Chalky got stuck in a drainpipe down which we were crawling as part of an assault course, though why they should ever assume we'd tackle the Germans through drainpipes and over fishing nets . . .

'Please get me out,' Chalky had said, as if afraid we'd go away and leave him there. 'Please.' He'd wriggled and somehow raised his knee, and couldn't get it back down again no matter how hard we shoved and pulled, me behind and Runty, facing backwards, in front, shoving and pulling. We had to break the drainpipe, which mercifully was concrete not cast iron, with a sledge hammer.

'Oh God,' the man said, 'now the alarm button doesn't work. That bloody electrician. I'll have his balls.'

'You don't gain anything by being crude.' The woman's voice was quiet and determined now. 'Perhaps you could climb through that hatch in the ceiling?'

Yes, I thought, and perhaps pigs could fly.

'I could try.'

'Stand on the arms of the trolley.'

Oh yes, and when it tips up, I fall off . . .

'Not this trolley,' I said.

Her hand stroked the side of my face. 'Not this one,' she said. 'Don't you worry.'

'I'm not worried, so long as he doesn't try to climb up here.'

'He won't. Now do as I tell you, and don't worry.'

Touch of iron in her voice, a familiarity with being obeyed by people like me. No question now of claustrophobia. I was not familiar with nurses' ranks and wondered if perhaps she were a sister.

The man climbed up onto the other trolley.

He wheezed and grunted and she had to give him a hand.

80

And he kept on grumbling. 'I'm too old for a job like this,' he said a couple of times. She had to give him a hand, had to push him. I could hear the sound of her exertion.

I'd expected the person on the other trolley to protest, as I had protested, but no sound came. Just an overpowering smell of washing liquor. I reached out my hand, felt a small pack hanging from the other trolley. The pack was open and I let my fingers dangle inside. Shaving kit. Knife, fork and spoon. Toothbrush. Towels, hand, one. Paybook, by the feel of it; I'd know that brown sticky cover anywhere. You'd think they'd make your paybook waterproof, wouldn't you, but the least drop of water on it . . . Also all the entries made in ink that runs.

'It's no good,' the man said in the air above us, 'I can't open it.'

Packet in the paybook feels like letters. You get curious.

'Try that handle. Perhaps that will do it.' Grunt, grunt, smell of sweat. You'd be better in the army, old lad, doing press-ups.

Hand along the trolley. Rough blanket, not smooth and soft wool like mine but shoddy like an every day every night army blanket that rubs your legs and keeps you warm; could even have been canvas.

'It's no use.'

'You'd better come down.' Perhaps the man's inefficiency had driven the claustrophobia out of her voice?

More grunt grunt, like a pig snuffling for food, and a stench of sweat and a smell of fear. Hand farther along the blanket. Identify the discs hanging on the rail that rub my wrists, the hard plastic clacking as they swing on the string, which feels damp. Mary gave me a silver chain for my going away present and Runty pulled my leg but they were a good idea, he said. 'Metal doesn't burn through as easy as string.' 4732849 Wilkins, T., Church of England.

'Oh, come down and let me try,' she said, impatient.

The man was offended. 'If I can't . . . a slip of a lass like you . . .' He's a long way from home. That's a North-country voice.

'Then what *are* we going to do?' Exasperation. She'd not yet accepted there are times you do nothing.

Hand along the blanket some more. The trolley moved and shuddered as the man leaned against it, and rammed it against the wall of the lift. The blanket was pulled under my hand beneath the weight of the man leaning against the trolley. Silence, except breathing, him hard and laborious, she quick and angry. Then the sounds of rummaging, the snap of a cardboard packet.

'You're surely not going to smoke,' she said.

'Calms my nerves.'

'I would have thought you'd know better.'

Hand at the blanket hem; the binding's pulled and there's a loose thread that curls over the binding like a wire worm. Hand moves along the thread, feels the stubble of a chin.

'It wouldn't be right to smoke.'

It was hot in the lift, but the chin was ice-cold beneath the stubble.

'No, I suppose it wouldn't be right!'

The lift started to move again. 'Thank God for that,' the man said, 'I thought we were going to be left here for the rest of our lives.'

# 10

I poked the rifle forward up the beach across the dead man's chest. The backsight was already set at three hundred yards but I checked it anyway and flipped it up. I was lucky, I had one of the old Lee Enfields with a slide. The others had a flipper, a choice between one hundred and three hundred yards. The slide backsight was beautiful to shoot, hell to drill with. But thanks to the sergeant major we hadn't done too much drill, and thanks to Runty, what we had done had not been too rigorous. I could have changed the slide backsight for one of the new ones, but I didn't. Arm jammed between the dead man's ammo packs, left wrist turned, holding the barrel, pulling it back to my shoulder. Right hand on the stock, take an aim. Must be four hundred and fifty yards to that bunker, stupid even to think of firing at it, but Lieutenant Soames had said have a go. The sergeant major was doing a quick patch job on Chalky, Lieutenant Soames talking into the radio. Four of us altogether. Mist in my eyes, a mist of salt water and sweat. I wiped my face with the sleeve of my tunic which did no good at all but made me feel better. Sand on shingle on the sleeve of my tunic got in my mouth. Spit it out, it might be a piano. Silly phrase, what did it mean? Like most army phrases. Two men meet – 'It's all right for you,' one of them says. What he's really saying is 'I've got nothing to say to you but I'm not brave enough to pass you by and leave it with a friendly smile.'

Eyes crinkled, looking through the backsight. There was the slit. I held it in the foresight. Lined the backsight to the foresight and the slit. The stammering flashes seemed aimed right down the rifle into my face. Range four fifty, so I aimed high. How much? How the hell could I work that out.

A backsight lifts the front of the gun approximately five-eighths of an inch to go from one hundred yards to three hundred so presumably two hundred yards equals five-eighths of an inch of backsight so lift the front end of the gun three-quarters of five-eighths of an inch because you only need a lift of a hundred and fifty yards. Allow for the fact I was aiming up the hill anyway, so that's a sixteenth of an inch less. There was a mark on the hummock above the slit. What the hell? Aim for that. I did. Squeezed the trigger. Nothing happened. Silly sod. Safety catch on. Push it forward, aim again for the mark, wrist pressure, pull the gun back, resight, everything's fine this time, squeeze the trigger. Fuck it. Nothing happens again. Of course it can't, you silly sod, the gun isn't even cocked and you can see that because the back of the firing pin, right there in front of your nose, is forward. Right hand forward, grasp the bolt handle, lift it, turn it, pull it back and never mind that you're ejecting a live round because it's quicker to do it this way than to pull the bolt slide back from the end, and slam the bolt forward and turn it, snap it down, and aim and fire, and feel the familiar smack in your shoulder as the butt kicks back. But watch the hummock, watch the target because that's the only way you'll know what the hell is happening, but in this morning light, now quite bright, with everything that is going on about you it's impossible to know if there's a puff, a small puff from the hummock and if there is a puff it's absolutely impossible to know if it was caused by the round from your rifle, hence the need for tracer, so whip the bolt back, eject the spent case, take a tracer out of your top pocket, check the rim for the mark, slip it into the breech, hold down the next round in the magazine and slide the bolt forward over it, snap the bolt down, take aim, and fire. I saw the round make one solid line between me and that slit, one solid line, and knew I'd put one round right in the slit, and the gun that had been splattering right down my line of fire had stopped.

'Bloody good, lad,' the sergeant major said. He'd been

watching behind me. I was glad I hadn't known.

One round, right into the slit. I felt a thrill of exhilaration.

That's what the training is all about. Just to get me there and teach me to handle a rifle right so I could put one round through that slit, knock one machine-gunner off the back of his gun. Did a wisp of smoke curling from the slit confirm my hit, just one thin wraith of smoke? The tracer had been red, incendiary. I felt no remorse. So all those thoughts about what it would be like, all that crap from Smithy about the life hereafter, and Chalky saying I could never bring myself to do it, and Runty saying kill or be killed and the sergeant major saying don't let them take advantage of you – all that speculation and even wondering if you should have a quiet word with the padre because the feelings you had were cowardly and you wondered if you would run away in the face of the enemy; but when it happened, you took your aim carefully, squeezed the trigger as you had been taught so many times and even aimed off for height and distance, and when the wisp of smoke came curling out of the slit and you hoped you'd hit a human being, you felt nothing but the satisfaction of having learned a lesson well and putting it into practice well and that's all there was to it.

'Good lad,' the sergeant major said.

But there'd been four guns in there and one had been jammed and I'd knocked one out and that left two and those two were well trained and swung round and plastered the beach where we were lying, over, beneath, round and at us and luckily the angle of decline was such that the rounds smacked into the man who I was lying behind. I never knew his name though I'd seen him hundreds of times in the NAAFI. We all hugged down and down and I left my rifle where it was and twisted a foot or more to the side of it which was good because a round hit the foresight of my rifle and smashed it and pushed the rifle crazily backwards and the rifle hit the sergeant major across his cheek and that long backsight raked his cheek to the bone as the rifle spun away over his shoulder. Lieutenant Soames had been hit, and I wondered what kind of protection I had because so far I was the only one wasn't bleeding except from the shingle on my face.

'We must move forward,' Lieutenant Soames said, 'towards the road.' How the hell could we? We were pinned down and more shit was being thrown at us than I'd ever believed possible. I didn't give a damn what Lieutenant Soames wanted. I knew *I* had to move and forward was as good a way as any. If I didn't, one of those bullets smacking through the tattered flash I was shielding behind was going to come through to me.

Three bodies in a pile – ten feet ahead, a big fat pile of corpses.

Gun's firing, gun stops. They were reloading.

I jumped to my feet and ran, the mine-detector flapping in the sand at my side, the webbing strap caught round my shoulder. I'd have dropped it if I'd had the time. One, two, three, now I'm really shitting. How long to change a magazine on a German gun? What type of gun anyway? We'd had an afternoon being shown the types of guns they use, but I couldn't remember the foreign names, except perhaps a Spandau. Was this a Spandau? Smithy had known all about them, of course, because they'd sent a manual translated into English and Smithy had taken it to bed with him the night before so that he could learn all about rates of fire and so on.

They opened fire again when I'd gone six paces, but the loading had swung the gun and it gave me another four paces before they got back to my line. By which time I had thrown myself behind the mound of bodies, startled to find the sergeant major, Lieutenant Soames, Sergeant Runty, and even Chalky beside me, 'Good man,' the sergeant major said, but he was talking to Runty who must have grabbed a rifle on his way and now handed it to me.

'Let's see you put another through the hole,' Runty said. 'Just imagine it's got hair round it and you won't miss.' In how many millions of places I'd heard that. Here, it was

86

comforting.

Chalky was crying with pain, but thank God they'd made him run. He looked like a patchwork quilt with the field dressings stuck on him and his uniform torn away exposing his shirt and his drawers cellular. Somebody had removed his pack and presumably left it behind, and his back was wringing wet; the blood had seeped into the sea water and sweat and had made a pattern beneath where his pack had been. He was clutching at his leg, but that wound appeared a lot neater than the one above, probably a through and through.

Tracer into the new rifle, quickest way to zero it because it has one of the new backsights and I don't trust them one little bit. Hold the rifle dead steady despite the mortar blasts that throw sand in my eye and create a pressure that lifts the end of the barrel off the body I'm using as an arm rest; this time check everything before I aim and take first pressure. Already Runty's fired two rounds but they're not tracer and I don't know where they've gone, only they must have missed since the guns are still spitting at us through the slit; so aim carefully along the line of fire and notice how bright the morning has become because now I can distinguish the whole shape of the bunker. Traverse right along the slit holding a steady line because I never like to find my targets and hold still on them but move to them, hold the slit below the sight aiming deliberately high and squeeze the trigger and whap, but watch, and before I can tell myself to keep looking the tracer has arrived, only it's green not red though it had the markings for red and it had smacked against the concrete at least four feet above the slit. Shit, the rifle's had a clout, the sights are aiming high, and there's no time to frig about waiting for an armourer, but load again and now aim for the slit itself and squeeze again and this time the tracer's red and lands just below the slit and now they're on to us, on to our position and there's no question of being able to shoot, just put your head down and keep it down.

It wasn't supposed to be like this, was it? This wasn't the way the scene had been rehearsed. You'd learned all the other skills – running, weaving, ducking, falling, aiming, lifting, running again. Fire and movement it was all supposed to be, one lot to the left firing, the other to the right running, then on the sound of the whistle, places change. Of course we'd been warned that perhaps we might not even hear the whistle and therefore we might be 'called upon' to use 'a little initiative', but we'd never rehearsed a scene in which all forward movement would be quite impossible, a movement that depended on what seemed like the only four men left alive. Damn it, there must be other men in the company left alive; you can't throw away a whole company of men, over a hundred men, all lost in the water; but if there are any others left alive, why aren't they also firing at the slit, why can't I see their tracer fire licking the lips of that slit, as mine were?

Detling quarry. What a bloody waste. And then the beach at Ramsgate, and the small arms school at Hythe because I happened to turn out to be good with a rifle, but not good enough for them to turn me into a sniper so they sent me home to Maidstone, not realizing I have never wanted to be a sniper in any case, only wanting to learn how to use the rifle as well as possible to defend myself. Because one of the things I remembered was how Major Brassingham had said, 'You can do anything with a rifle except sit on it,' and that stuck with me. Aggression breeds aggression, and I could never again become the aggressive party. Wasn't that the lesson of my childhood, that whereas the others in our valley quickly grew to be bullies, to be aggressive to get what they wanted out of life and usually ended up spending their lives on the floor of the mill, spinning wool, I never could do that, always looked for the easier way, perhaps the less direct way, but in the end the more successful way? Because I hadn't spent any time at all on the floor of the mill, spinning, I'd been up in the office taking it easy, learning how to lick the system. We had an old boy in the mill, a communist all his life and where did it get him? They let him keep his job because if he'd been thrown out of work he'd have become a martyr, and what he didn't see was that by keeping his job he was bowing down to the system. Whereas I wanted to learn how to bend with the system, to bend with it and take it gently by surprise, and conquer it that way.

'If somebody could move off to the side, sergeant major,' I whispered, 'and sort of draw their fire. I'm certain I could put one into that slit, given the chance.'

We needed a hero. I was quite determined it wouldn't be me.

# 11

The next evening we had a dancing lesson, Mary surprised me again. She was wearing a ball-gown.

Her father had let me in. 'Mary's already in the drawing room,' he said.

I always wore my best uniform for the lessons, and my shoes. Always polished them. The trousers had never seen a pair of gaiters and hung well, thanks to my tailor friend. The major looked approvingly at me, then walked across the hall and opened the door into the drawing room for me to pass. 'Here's Tom,' he said, as if he were a toastmaster announcing my arrival at some important function. She was standing by the table on which we kept the gramophone. She must have heard the front-door bell, because she'd started the music. It was a new Victor Sylvester. I'd heard it on Forces Favourites the previous Sunday and had mentioned it to her. The ball-gown was in blue satin, with a water pattern on it. You get to know about cloth, working in a mill. This must have set her back a fortune as well as taking her clothing coupons. Her hair was held in a couple of hair clips that twinkled, and I realized they were probably diamonds. When I got near to her she smelled marvellous, and standing there with that ball-gown down to her shoes, hiding her feet, she looked tall and graceful, unlike any girl I'd ever seen before. Of course, they wore ball-gowns in the Palais de Danse in Huddersfield, but this didn't look like a made-over bridesmaid's dress. And it didn't have a million sequins on it. I hate sequins.

'That's a quickstep,' I said, 'and we haven't mastered that, yet.'

Her face showed disappointment, but she said nothing.

She took the record off the machine, found an old waltz from the pile of waltzes and put it on. 'Is that better?' she asked, and I went forward and took her in my arms and we started to dance.

She'd been practising. I wondered who with. Her movements were much smoother than they had been. I took her into the forward turn. Perfect. Then forward again. Then backward turn. Dammit, she'd got it off pat. Smooth as butter sliding over the floor. She was holding her head back, looking into my face, challenging me. So, I turned the waltz old-fashioned, spinning her round and round, eight forwards, eight backwards, and you have to be either an athlete or Viennese born to do that, and of course she couldn't and half way through the reverse bit, she swung that awkward leg just that bit too far across and my next step went inside it and kicked the inside of her foot and if I hadn't held on to her, I'd have brought her down.

'The first thing you've got to learn in dancing,' I said, 'is that the person you're dancing with may not be as good as you are, and may make a mess of it, and the only crime is to fall down on the dance floor, because you look such a charlie picking yourself and your partner up.'

'Really?' she said. 'Then we'll have to be very careful not to let that happen, won't we?'

That evening, we ate cheese and onion pie in almost complete silence. The major had left me a note on a card. 'Sorry I shan't be in for supper tonight,' the note said. The card had a deckle edge, like a wedding invitation. The lady from Maidstone, Mrs Mullion, brought in a board and on it was one piece of cheese. 'I had a bit left over from making the pie,' she said, and I thought to myself that anybody else would have wrapped it in paper and taken it home, since cheese was on the ration. The major wasn't somebody you'd ever rob. His daughter wasn't somebody you'd ever succeed in diminishing.

'That's a beautiful dress,' I said to her.

'I didn't think you'd noticed.'

91

'It was the first thing I saw.'

'You could have said so.'

'I didn't know how.'

'Oh, come off it, you must have paid many girls a compliment in your time.'

I thought too highly of her, she thought too lowly, if there is such a phrase, of me. And neither of us realized the unnecessary gulf we placed between ourselves.

'Yes, I suppose I have, but with you it's different.'

'Because of my leg? That's why I wore the long dress, to hide it. It's not easy, dancing in a long dress. It took me all last evening to get used to it.' She blushed again, no doubt ashamed of having told me she'd spent last evening in that way.

'Nothing to do with your leg.'

'What, then?'

'It's something I can't explain.'

'You could try, if you wanted to.'

How could I? In my world, a compliment was meant as a come-on. If you fancied a girl you flattered her, said anything to make her feel you cared, to get her arm round your neck in the back seat of the pictures. A compliment was one of my weapons, the ones I was used to handling. Other fellows went bald-headed at it. 'Eh, love, I fancy you, I right fancy you.' But I'd never been able to go that way about things. A little compliment. 'Hair looks nice this evening, been using the Amami, have you?' and then on and on through the evening, watching the girl open like a flower for you. Till, at the right time, you could get real personal. 'You've got a fascinating body . . .' and meanwhile your hands are exploring and she doesn't mind because you've given her a touch of the Desert Song and you could be Nelson Eddy for all she knows and her Jeanette Macdonald. But I couldn't start that caper with somebody like Mary Brassingham.

'I'm a bit shy about dishing out the compliments, but that doesn't change the fact I like that frock . . .'

She burst out laughing; I suppose she'd never heard anybody call a ball-gown a frock, and she got up and went to the sideboard and asked me if I'd like a glass of port with my cheese, and the moment we nearly reached had flown from us like a pigeon going home.

When she sat down again with her own glass of port and mine on a silver tray beside us, she said, 'You must learn to speak your mind a bit more,' and though I didn't know what it was, I sensed that for the moment I'd lost something.

Let's face it, with Mary and the major, in that house and that style of life, I was out of my depth. I knew it, and wrongly supposed they knew it too, and held it against me. So, instead of going back to camp, I went looking for Gladys. You could say it was to restore my confidence, or you could say I was getting randy. To find Gladys, I had first to find a pal of hers called Sylvia who was always in the pubs, and could call at Gladys's house without arousing the suspicions of her mother-in-law. It took me a hell of a time to find Sylvia. I found a couple of mates from C Company and they shouted when they saw me and offered me a drink but I didn't stay in the pub once I saw Sylvia wasn't there. Eventually I found her in the Dog and Partridge, and she was with a lad from the Air Force and was pissed off when I asked her to go to Gladys's place, and so was he, but I talked her round, told her it was life and death, and she laughed and said 'I'll bet. I heard Gladys chucked you,' which was the story I knew Gladys had put round, and after she went I bought the Air Force lad a pint and looked round and compared the pub and the conversation with what I'd got used to at the major's. When Sylvia came back she was mad because Gladys had been out anyway and the Air Force lad had that owlish look on his face that meant it wouldn't be long before he wanted to spew, which made Sylvia even madder, so I left them and went back to camp, feeling that I was making a fool of myself, and ashamed for it. I knew damn well that even if I had been able to get hold of Gladys, it wouldn't have done me any good.

93

As luck would have it, on my way back to camp up the road from the barracks I saw Gladys in a taxi with two officers. She looked happy, laughing at what was probably a dirty joke. She saw me too as I saluted. One of the officers lifted his stick towards the peak of his cap in a negligent gesture, the other ignored me and kept on laughing through horse teeth, and Gladys waved to me.

Chalky was on the gate, and grumbled at me when I went into the guard room, through the counter into the duty quarters at the back. Smithy was on the counter and made a great show of crossing my name off the list. Runty was in the back playing cards with Hargreaves and Cutler.

'Leave the tea alone,' Runty said. 'That's for the soldiers around here, not the poxy dancing masters working their loaf to skive off duty.'

'Bollocks, I wasn't on the list.'

'You were on *my* list when I sent it to the company office yesterday but somebody crossed you off.'

'Well, I didn't cross it off.'

'What difference does that make? We still had to mount a guard one man short.' He was really narked. The others were narked, too. One man short on guard meant that much less sleep for the rest.

'I'll go put my boots and gaiters on,' I offered, but when Runty said 'Piss off' he really meant it. He must have meant it; they were playing brag and I'm useless at that game; they could have cleaned me out.

'Really, it'll only take me five minutes to get ready for guard duty . . . my kit's all ready.'

He got up from the table, and came across towards me. 'Look, you prick,' he said, 'we were one short when we mounted the bleeding guard. How the hell are we going to explain to the orderly officer that now we're back up to strength?' He was standing in front of me and he stabbed my chest with a finger like a bayonet. 'So far as the army is concerned, the real army that has duty lists and rosters and all that crap, you don't exist, Private Wilkins T., until

94

tomorrow morning at reveille. And if, in a purely military sense you understand, you don't exist, how the bleeding hell can you stand guard?'

I could tell he was angry beneath his heavy bantering tone. All his talk about orderly officers and explanations was just so much cover. If the lads had wanted me on guard, he could have sent me to the officers' mess to explain to the orderly officer, who was doubtless swigging a last gin before setting out on his rounds. The orderly officer wouldn't care if fifty soldiers volunteered for guard who weren't on the list. But the simple fact was that Runty and the others didn't want me on guard with them.

'One day you'll learn, my lad, you can't bend the army machine to suit your own convenience. Not if it means your pals have to carry the can. Soon you're going to wind up and find you have no pals, because nobody likes a skiver.'

It was true, of course. All for one and one for all, in the platoon, and nobody does anything that makes life more difficult for the rest of the platoon. I'd been thoughtless, allowing my guard duty and fire picquet patterns to be fiddled. In our company, guard duties were assigned by section, and the only way you could legitimately get off was if you were away from the section, sick, on a course of instruction, or on leave. In the eyes of the other lads in the platoon, teaching the major's daughter to dance didn't count as any of these things.

'Honest, I didn't ask for my name to be taken off the list.'

'I don't give a damn who did the asking. It was taken off after I put it there, wasn't it, and that's good enough for me.'

I was desperate. 'But *you* fiddle things, sometimes, you fiddle the duties around . . .'

He gave me a pitying and contemptuous smile. 'Look, lad,' he said, 'when I fiddle a thing, I do it for all of us, not just for myself, and there's the difference. Now piss off.'

I couldn't win. The next day I went to the major's house to see him privately. He led me into his study, asked me to sit down. Then he listened to what I had to say, quietly, gravely, heard my fumbling explanation of why I didn't want the guard roster changed so that I could teach Mary to dance, how it meant that the rest of the section had to work harder and sleep less. That was Friday.

On Monday they changed the system of selecting men for guard duty and for picquet. 'In future,' the posted company order said, 'all men will be selected for guard duty from a central pool of men . . .' It would be the responsibility of the company commanders to submit lists daily of men's availability. It was a real cock-up. Because it meant that nobody ever went on duty with his pals any more. That made me very popular in the NAAFI.

# 12

Fire and movement. One lot fires while the other lot moves. 'See that group over there,' the sergeant major said to Runty, pointing low. About five or six lads had fallen into a solid wedge. 'We're going over there. You and Wilkins stay here. When we get there, we'll give you covering fire, try to draw the gun on to us. As soon as the gun shifts, I want you and Wilkins to smack a couple of rounds right in that slit. Understood?'

We understood.

'And if you can cover us while we're getting there, we'd greatly appreciate it,' Lieutenant Soames said.

I could wedge my rifle down beside the head of the dead man. That gave me another three or four inches of cover. I didn't bother with the tracer. Now the mortar barrage was constant and I wondered where the hell they could be coming from, somewhere on the other side of the ridge, with the machine-gunners spotting for them. None of the mortar explosions was more than fifty feet from us, but the bombs buried themselves in that soft sand and the force went upwards over our heads. The navy still sent an occasional shell at the ridge, but Lieutenant Soames must have radioed back to somewhere that they were doing no good, and they'd switched to a more important target. Of which, no doubt, they had plenty. Now the sun was well up and shining straight at us over the crest, and in a way I was glad the guns had been mounted below the crest or we'd never have seen that slit. Bolt back, bolt forward, eject the spent tracer round, push another round up the breech. 'You okay?' Runty asked.

'Yes, sergeant.'

'You can forget that crap.'

He'd wriggled himself low down about three feet to my right firing round the end of the dead man's legs. Lieutenant Soames, the sergeant major, and Chalky started to move. I could hear Chalky groan like an old woman with rheumatism, but between them they managed to keep him going, and they must have kept him close down on the sand, because the machine guns didn't follow them.

'Don't waste your ammo,' Runty said, 'wait until they move their aim before you fire at them.'

'Yes, sergeant.'

'And stop taking the piss.'

'Yes, my old ducks . . .'

'That's better. I didn't want the bloody stripe, you know.'

'I know, but they lumbered you with it.'

'Only until we get back, then I'll tell them where they can stuff it.'

Runty was an odd man out. He joined the army in 1937 as soon as he was old enough to escape from going down the mines in Rotherham. He was at Dunkirk, and though he wouldn't talk about it we knew he'd had a bad time. He'd also been in North Africa, caught amoebic dysentery, whatever that may be, and was sent home.

At first he was in the training cadre at Maidstone, accepted a stripe for it so that, in his own words, 'I could teach some of you buggers how to behave a bit better than the new recruits they sent out to Africa.' We learned from another corporal who'd known him in Africa that Runty had had a hard time with a young lad who'd pulled the pin on a grenade and dropped it at Runty's feet by accident, or because he was shit scared or something. And then when Runty tried to get the grenade and throw it, the recruit had done the heroic bit and had fallen on the grenade, and Runty had had to pull him off, screaming hysterically, and slap his cheeks and pick up the grenade and throw it, all in seven seconds, while a tank tried to get into position to roast them with a flammenwerfer. Runty had made us spend hours and hours, practising picking grenades up off the ground and throwing them. And then he'd tried to get permission to do it one day with live grenades but Captain Best wouldn't allow it. So one night, on one of the Detling quarry schemes, he made us do it with lighted thunderflashes, and I think that was worse than with live grenades because the fuse length on a thunderflash was unpredictable. Three lads burned their hands but Runty said that was better than being caught with a German stick grenade.

They tried many times to persuade Runty to let them make him up to sergeant but he would never accept. 'Too many pricks in the sergeants' mess,' he'd say. I could see his point. 'The sergeants' mess,' he'd said to me one night on guard duty, 'is a club for people who've never learned how to behave in a club.'

The NAAFI had a separate section, the corporals' mess, but he wouldn't even use that except when they had cigarettes and we didn't. Then he'd go in and get a couple of packets over and above his entitlement and sell them to us. At cost price, of course. He even kept a spare battledress jacket that had no stripes on it, and I knew for sure he always took it on leave with him, and sometimes even wore it when we went out on the town together, him and Cutler and Chalky and me. Because they soon forgave me about the guard duty, especially when I explained how I had tried to get the major to stop fiddling the rosters.

'This is an almighty cock-up, isn't it Runty?' I asked.

'This is the way it happens, Tom.'

'One nest of guns. Taking a lot of good lads.'

'Make sure you and me are not among them. When the time comes to shoot, make sure you shoot bloody right.'

'But surely they ought to have put the armoured cars first up here? An armoured car could have . . .'

'Don't talk about armoured cars, Tom. Bloody useless tin cans. Anyway, this is too small a bit for that sort of caper. Do you realize that on the main beaches they have these buggers spread along the ridge every twenty yards or so. And they have a whole company of mortars backing them up. Whereas what's ahead of us? One gun and, at the most, two mortars.'

'Two mortars, doing all this lot.'

'Look, Tom, the Germans may be no bleeding good behind a gun because they haven't got the right temperament for it, but give them a mortar and a spotter, up two feet, ach ja, down two feet, ach ja, and they'll hit any bloody thing they want, in time.'

As if to confirm what he was saying, a mortar bomb landed about fifteen feet in front of us, dug in the sand and exploded on the hard stuff below. It showered us in a mixture of sand, uniform, and mangled bits of pioneer who'd been lying within a couple of feet of the blast. I wiped my hand across my face, but Runty had been watching the gun, a professional soldier ever, and he shouted, 'There they go, Tom,' and I realized the gun was no longer firing at us. So I aimed and fired at the slit, aim and fire, aim and fire. Five neat rounds. But they didn't stop the gun, merely made it traverse back in our direction. So I stopped firing. There was a scrabbling sound behind me, and as I half turned my head I saw that another pioneer had crawled up the beach behind us, and he must have been one of the bodies in the pile of bodies we'd sheltered behind and fired across earlier, but he was only just alive and how he could move I'll never know. He'd lost his right foot below the knee.

'Give us a sup,' he said and I could place him anywhere within twenty miles of where I was born, and that made it very personal, and I started to take my flask off my waist belt, but Runty saw what I was doing and said 'Don't do that, Tom,' and grabbed a flask off the belt of one of the corpses we were lying against and slithered back and pulled out the cork and stuck the neck of the water bottle in the man's mouth. The pioneer tried to lift his head to get more water down his throat and one of the machine-gun bullets went into the top of his head and made a neat hole in his brain and killed him. Runty crawled back to where he had been, silent. He looked across at me, and I sneaked a look back at him. I knew we both wanted to be sick but neither of us would be the first. Without saying anything, Runty lowered his head to the sand, took off his steel helmet, lengthened the strap all the way, then put his hat on again with the strap under his chin. I didn't say 'I told you so.'

'When I was a young lad,' he said, 'it was all the mines in our village.'

'It was all the mill with us.'

'Now, it's all the war. Life doesn't change much, does it?'

'Not for people like us.'

'The mines, the mill, or the army,' Runty said.

'The mines are a reserved occupation.'

'So is the mill, I bet. Somebody has to make the cloth for all these lovely uniforms. My dad died of silicosis. On his lungs. Like his dad before him. My mother's dad was killed in a mine accident, along with my two uncles and my two brothers.'

'My dad fell in the mill pond. My dad's dad worked on a farm.'

'Lucky bugger. That's another reserve occupation.'

I looked across at the sergeant major, with Chalky and Lieutenant Soames. They were stopped. Soames was talking into the radio, lying flat on his back with the radio on his chest. Chalky was lying flat on his face with his head to one side, looking back at us. The sergeant major was lying flat on his stomach, but he was scanning the lie of the land, that sloping billiard-table beach on which they had to hide. Soames appeared to be arguing with somebody on the radio and kept gesticulating with his arm. But only in the horizontal plane. I looked all around me, confident Runty would be watching the gun. Counting the live ones. I could see about twenty, and they didn't appear to be any better placed than we were. One gun was picking targets, the other was systematically raking the beach, end to end. Absolute bloody suicide to try and get up and run. We were pinned down again.

I looked back. The landing craft had all withdrawn from

101

the beach. I couldn't see Captain Best, or any of the other officers from the other platoons, or any of the other sergeants or NCOs. So where the hell is Captain Best? My guess was in the water, face down. One gun, one small beach, one company. Sounds logical, doesn't it. But it wasn't working, it couldn't work until somebody could smack one through that slit. About twenty yards away I saw a two-inch mortar lying on the sand. I had four two-inch mortar bombs in my ammo pouches. If I had that two-inch mortar . . . Now that's something I'm really good with, a two-inch mortar. When I was a lad we used to take bits of cane and a piece of string, and we used to put a knot on one end of the string and loop it round the end of the cane so's it would fall off easy. Then we'd bring the string down the cane, holding it tight to keep the knot down, and we'd throw the cane. I could throw a piece of cane farther, by the time I was ten, than you could fire a bow and arrow. And I got to be dead accurate with it. I could chuck a piece of cane up into the air, and the cane would drop a hundred yards away into a dustbin. Don't ask me how, it's a knack. The mortar was second nature to me. Hold the mortar on the base plate, drop the bomb down it. Point the mortar, which after all is only a straight piece of tube, up into the sky, apparently aiming at nothing, and pull the string. The string fires the cap that fires the bomb. And I quickly got so I could drop a mortar bomb just anywhere I wanted within a six foot circle. We practised with smoke bombs, and put our names on them in chalk, and had a sweepstake, and I won every time until the lads got so disgusted they wouldn't play any more. Not for money. That was another bit of Detling quarry.

If I had that mortar, I bet I could lob one right in that slit.

But I didn't have the mortar, and I'd be damned if I was going to crawl all that way to get it. A VC job, that was. Who needs a posthumous VC?

'It's taking them a bloody long time,' I said.

'Then why don't you go across and tell them to hurry up?'

I had a bar of chocolate in my map pocket. With vitamins added. Hard and tasting like the chocolate they put on the buns we used to get sometimes on a Saturday from the bakers, six for a penny, six buns with a piece of crisp chocolate on top the size of a halfpenny, and all the terrible decision of whether you should lift the coin of chocolate off and save it while you ate the bun, eat it first, or eat it with the bun, which was usually hard and difficult to swallow because the buns were baked on Friday when they were a halfpenny each and only came down to six for a penny last thing on a Saturday. I wriggled the chocolate out of the map pocket. It had been in a tin, but I'd thrown the tin overboard on the landing craft because it was bright metal and Runty had tipped me off about reflections. Daft, isn't it? They make you paint your brasses, then give you iron rations in a tin that gleams gold like a mirror. I broke off a piece of the chocolate. 'Want a bit?' I said to Runty.

'Giving food away in face of the enemy is classed as a self-inflicted injury,' he said, 'and liable to court-martial.' But still he took a piece and popped it into his mouth.

'Ah, bacon and egg flavour,' he said.

If you closed your eyes and forgot about the bangs, or thought back to the mill where there was so much noise you couldn't hear yourself speak and learned to lip read, yes, you could taste the bacon and egg flavour. Every morning, during that long summer, bacon and eggs or kippers in the dining room, and I'd always taken bacon and eggs and don't ask me why because they were a symbol of the good life, bacon *and* eggs in the plural, and I got to know the cookhouse corporal by booking him in early one night when I was on guard and he was late, and I'd sit at my table and watch and he'd tip me the wink and all our lads would go round a second time and have second helpings. I think that's why they forgave me for the guard business, because I could always work the oracle for them on a thing like that. And shared it.

Like ration cards for going on leave, and if you went on

a forty-eight you were only entitled to a forty-eight-hour ration card which was bloody useless as a trade with a girl, so I got to know one of the lads in the orderly room, because I fiddled him and his girl into a dance one night past the chucker out, and ever after that any of our section going on a forty-eight always got a fourteen-day ration card to go with the pass. But he couldn't do much with the travel warrants. Whenever we were legally entitled to a warrant, he'd arrange for us to have a Glasgow-any-route-return and we'd go to London and flog them there for a couple of quid. Dead easy. Look for any lad hanging about King's Cross Station wearing a kilt or a pair of what we called pyjama trousers.

'Watch it, Runty,' I said. The gun had moved again.

'Hang on, it's gone the other way.'

If only I'd had that mortar. And was a hundred yards farther up the beach, of course.

'My dad once won the North of England,' Runty said, 'with a bird he bred himself from an egg.'

'What the hell are we doing in the Royal West Kents?'

'That's what they call the fortunes of war . . .'

I was thinking of something else. 'Runty, have a skeg up the beach, see if you can see a two-inch mortar.' He got the idea right away and we both looked. 'Come on, Tom,' he said, and was up and off and running before I could get to my feet. I left the mine-detector where it was and set off after him, running zigzag the way we'd been taught. We'd got twenty paces before they could get the gun round to us and then we dived, long and low. There was a slight hump in the sand. Enough to hide us. We hadn't seen it because of the angle of the light, but the light had changed during the few minutes we'd been behind the barricade of corpses and Runty had spotted it. When a gun's traversing right, as that one had been, it's slow work to stop it and traverse it left again. Well, comparatively speaking. Slow enough to give us twenty yards.

'Now wait for the shit,' Runty said, gasping.

'You ought to give up smoking.'

'I'm trying to.'

'They may make you.'

I wished immediately I hadn't mentioned smoking, because I wanted one badly. But they were in my inside pocket. Now the shit came, the mortar shells, both machine guns concentrating on tearing away the crest of that tiny hump behind which we had scuttled. But the range was long, and the angle didn't help them. Personally, I hate firing downhill. But they were having a bloody good try. The mortars were all shooting long and the spray of sand came from behind us, splashing us like a water shower, and it got in my hair and down the back of my neck and several times my tin hat was lifted forwards over my eyes and each time I yanked it back. If it had been strapped at the back it could have lifted the back off my scalp. I turned round and looked back and from where I was lying I could see that the sergeant major's group – although Lieutenant Soames was the officer I didn't think of it as his group – had almost reached the mound of corpses from which they had intended to give us covering fire. I wondered why the hell they hadn't got up and run when we had, but realized that Lieutenant Soames had been lying flat on his back and anyway they had Chalky with them.

'If we only had one Bren,' Runty said.

'Sod the Bren. Give me a two-inch mortar.'

'Sod the Bren?' Runty said, 'I'm glad Smithy can't hear you say that. He'd have a purple fit.'

'Our Father, which art in Heaven, give us this day our daily Bren.'

A small group over on the left started rapid fire from four rifles. No Bren. What the hell were they up to? I saw a couple of them scuttle sideways, trying to get to the shelter of the jetty. 'Wrong bloody way,' I shouted, but they couldn't possibly have heard me. The gunner at the top had seen them. The shooting stopped above my head. 'This is it,' I said to Runty, 'watch him try for double nine.'

Runty was up again and running and we made fifty yards to another pile of corpses, this time four, and even had time to drag two of them closer in. When I looked to the right I saw the sergeant major and Lieutenant Soames had got Chalky up and running; well, you could hardly call it running, more shambling, forward, and they had only thirty yards to go to a narrow dip where they arrived while we were dragging the corpses across the sand. One of the guns came back and it was target practise time again, see how many you can put into that khaki lump. The first gunner had switched to single fire and was aiming, and he picked off the two men running for the jetty one after the other with two shots. It was beautiful shooting. When for some reason the two who had been giving covering fire also got up and ran, he picked them off, too, and I knew that if anybody ever looked at their corpses he'd find a bullet in their backs. Which wasn't the best way to go. I didn't have time to bother about them. Once again I could hear the rounds smacking into the bodies we were lying behind, and I asked myself how long it could possibly be before they started to come through. So I got out the trenching tool that was strapped down my leg and started to scrape away at the sand to make a trench for myself.

Runty said, 'It's not worth while, we'll be moving soon,' and I asked him why and he said, 'Because a lot of other people will have the same idea as those four only they'll be running backwards not forwards and while the bastards behind that gun are having fun picking 'em off one by one, you and me, Tom my old lad, will be running forward under the range.'

'Lesson number one, eh?'

'You've got it.'

We learned lesson number one the first time we went out on a scheme with Runty in charge of the platoon. The sergeant was on leave. The scheme was supposedly to teach us compass and map reading, and we set off over the Downs, point to point to point. Every so often we'd stop, and bivouac, just for the exercise, and somebody would get out the fags and pass 'em round and we'd brew up and have a smoke.

106

Very relaxed. When night came, we set up a camp in a fold of the hill and put out guards. The company was spread all over the Downs and Runty pointed out other camps to us, stupidly set in exposed places. The next morning we struck camp and set off again. It was a pleasant holiday ramble. Until we ran out of cigarettes. I'd taken thirty with me, but Cutler had forgotten to bring his, and Chalky had only brought ten, and what with lashing 'em out, all of us who thought we'd brought enough were soon without. We had to last the rest of the day and a night without a smoke between us. That's when Runty got us all together. The crafty bastard had been keeping count.

'Cutler,' he said, producing a list from inside his jacket, 'how many cigs a day do you smoke?' and Cutler said seven.

One by one he asked us all how many cigs a day, and we all gave him the answer. But then he read out the figures he'd written down. Cutler, who normally smoked seven cigs a day, had smoked fifteen in the time we were out, only one day. Even Hargreaves, who said he only smoked one cigarette a week and that after his dinner on a Sunday, had smoked three.

'I don't want to get philosophical with you lot,' Runty had said, 'but if somebody's offering, somebody's taking, even if they don't bloody want 'em. So in the future, when you go out on a jaunt like this with no possibility of buying any more, don't flash your fags about, because you'll wind up having none left.'

It seemed a load of bollocks about a packet of fags, but then he got to the real point. 'One day,' he said, 'you're going to be out there and your life is going to depend on you having the things you need. Not cigs, for God's sake, but food, and water, and what's more important, ammunition. And if you've been offering those things to your pals all the time, what are you going to stick in your rifle when a dirty great hairy-arsed German comes leaping over the top at you with a machine gun full of bullets and a belly full of knackwurst. Because right at that moment, if you try to get a round back from anybody, they'll say "Piss off." The first lesson in the bloody army,' he said, 'is to take care of number one. And number one is you, each and every one of you.'

He still had a packet of twenty Capstan full strength left, and every time he lit one my finger nails grew shorter. But I never forgot the lesson. Until the time came to offer Chalky my bandage. Now why the hell had I done that? Like the sergeant major had said, Chalky had his own bandages. The sergeant major carried the supply of spares.

Two more lads started to run, without even giving themselves covering fire, and we ran forward. The machine-gunner picked off the other two, no doubt too lazy to change the range setting on his gun, or swing it round through thirty degrees of arc. This time we only made fifteen yards and I felt the second gun, the one that had been traversing, plucking at my sleeve, and when I looked down my sleeve was tattered, but there was no blood. The sergeant major's party had run forward about ten feet and at first I couldn't see them but realized they'd been lucky enough to find another ripple on the beach, and from where I was lying I could see that the ripple extended up almost as far as the road; if I could get into it, I could crawl practically all the way up that beach without being seen by the men firing the gun. But to get to the ripple was a sixty yards dash, all at the same range. Half way along the ripple was a heap of men, and down the side of his pack one of them I could see had a two-inch mortar barrel and it was a safe bet the base plate would be strapped on his front, between his ammo pouches, and a man running next to him and probably killed in the same burst of fire or mortar would be carrying a case containing six mortar bombs. Six plus the four in my ammo pouches, ten mortar bombs. If I couldn't hit that slit with one out of ten, I wasn't bloody well trying. I opened my ammo pouches, checking I had the bombs there. Two left, two right. Even if I can't find the pack of six, I've got my own four.

'See that gully, Runty, right of arc. It goes all the way to the road.'

'So it does.' No surprise in his voice. No eager anticipation.

'See half way along it. That lad has a mortar.'

'So he has.'

'We could run up that gully, piece of cake.'

Runty turned to look at me, his face angry. 'I don't know why I bother with you,' he said, 'I just don't know why I bother. Why do you think we're running up this bit of beach so easy, eh? Because the Engineers' chains have been over it and the chances of our meeting a mine are nil. But look at the lad with the mortar. He'll never play football again.'

I looked again, and wanted to be sick. Stupid bastard that I was. Of course the Germans knew about the gully, knew we'd be attracted towards it. So where had they planted the mines? Where the feet of anybody using that gully, like the mortar team for example, would play football with them.

'Ought we to tell the sergeant major?'

'Sometimes, Tom,' he said, 'you get right on my tits. The sergeant major bloody well knows. He wouldn't crawl up that gully if you paid him in cig coupons.'

'All right, clever dick. So I'll go across to the gully, and I'll get that two-inch mortar and then get out of the gully again.'

'Now you're bloody well talking.'

I can't explain why, but somehow I had the feeling the man in that bunker belonged to me. He was strictly *my* target. Not as a personal vendetta, because, of course, he was completely anonymous. But those guns had been shooting at *me* and I wanted them. And if you want something badly enough, you go and get it. And at that moment I badly wanted that two-inch mortar.

So I held my rifle low in my right hand, almost touching the sand, and sprang to my knees and started running. Across the swept sand, zigzagging, dodging the mortar holes, running as fast as I could in the crouched position, but Runty had made us run miles in this position telling us we'd be lucky if ever we got a straight spine to run on, and when the

109

mortar bomb landed about twenty feet to my side and blew me sideways, peppering me with sand spray like bullets, I kept on running. I could see the spurts of sand where the machine-gun bullets were hitting and said thank God they're aiming too low because if they'd been aiming at my body the sand spurts would have been a hell of a lot higher and any shots when they came would have been in my body, not in my legs. But I dodged through what seemed at the time like a spray of machine-gun bullets and not one of them touched me and the blood was pounding in my ears and I realized too late I'd been holding my breath all the way and threw myself down in a long curling slide that must have rammed half a pound of sand up my rifle barrel and certainly scraped all the skin of the left side of my forehead; but I was down, flat down, behind the body of that mortar man, and my fingers were outstretched, and when I got my breath back and the salt out of my eyes I would have a two-inch mortar and ten bombs to play with.

# 13

I was a good hundred yards runner, could easily beat anybody in the platoon. Thursday afternoon was always battalion sports and the CO was very keen. Nobody was ever excused Thursday afternoons except on medical report or definitely on duty, and they said Lieutenant Colonel Springfield used to look at the reports himself. You were marched by platoon up to the sports field, and there you were checked off by the RSM. At the end of the afternoon, you were checked off the field again by the RSM. He used to piss off to his quarters, they said, between two o'clock and five, while we were on the field. It was just one glorified bloody PT session.

Take the hundred yards, for instance. They had loads of hundred yards distances laid out, and each platoon took one of the places and raced by section. The three section winners then had to race against the three winners from the other platoons in the company. The company winners had to race against the battalion best. Well, I quickly saw who had the easy time; the ones who won the races. If you won you could loaf around for a half an hour while they got the next race assembled. I've seen men spend all afternoon running the hundred yards a total of four, five times. Whereas if you lost, then the PT instructors got you and they had hundreds of games up their sleeves, like the Eton Wall game, whatever that was, using a medicine ball that weighed a hundredweight, and you had to push and pull your way to a wall with it while another platoon had to stop you, and no holds barred. Or they had inter-platoon boxing, out there on the grass. One of your lads in the makeshift ring with one of the lads from another platoon, then after one minute of scrapping, another two came in and that made four in the ring until you had the whole platoon in the ring, all scratching and clawing and punching away. Just to look at that field on a Thursday afternoon would convince you the PT staff were sadists, and some of the lads complained bitterly to the padre when he took us for ABCA, but he never did anything.

So I always made damn sure I won at least the first race. And then if I lost later on, I could stand around watching the soccer. I've never been good at soccer, coming from rugby country, and I found it a cissified game, but they used to play it at the far end near the NAAFI truck, and I was usually first in the queue for the 3.45 NAAFI break, and could get a drink and a wad for our entire platoon. One day I had a good idea and suggested to Runty we make ourselves some bows and arrows, and when we were good enough we should ask the RSM why our favourite sport of archery was being neglected. 'An archery match,' I said to Runty, having been to the library to check my facts, 'can last as long as three hours.' Runty laughed, and said the RSM would have his bollocks. I did mention it once to Lieutenant Soames and he said he'd see what he could do, but to the best of my knowledge he never did anything about it.

One Thursday night, after sports, when I went to give Mary her dancing class, the major answered the door and asked me in. Apparently Mary had to work late at the hospital and wouldn't be back until supper time. Would I like to come into his study and take a drink with him?

Yes indeed I would and thank you very much.

That afternoon I'd won three of the races, but it was getting near NAAFI time so I lost the next one and went up to watch the football. The pukka battalion team was playing an away match, so a scratch team had been made up, containing Runty who wasn't half bad with a ball.

The major poured us a couple of whiskys and sat in his leather armchair on one side of the fire. I sat at the other side. Very comfortable. By this time I felt I knew the major a bit, I understood him. He was good to be with. Never difficult to talk to, always interested in anything I had to say, though I always kept strictly away from camp gossip. Mostly, I asked him questions about things that puzzled me, all sorts of things. I once asked him a question about a clock he had in a glass case, and he told me it was a carriage clock and went on to tell me a lot I hadn't known about the different types of clocks there are. The one he had, for instance, was worth more than five hundred pounds because it was a unique example made by some man I'd never heard of and whose name escapes me at this moment. Mind you, I could see he wasn't interested in the money side. Anyway, there we sat, completely relaxed. At least, I was completely relaxed, but *he* seemed a bit put out. Couldn't settle. Offered me a cigarette, took one himself. I lit mine and offered to light his but he put it in the ashtray saying, 'I don't want to smoke that. Can't think why I took it.'

Finally he looked across at me and said, 'Do you mind if I say something personal, Tom?'

I thought he had some problem on his mind he wanted to discuss with me, something on which he wanted an ordinary man's opinion.

'Not at all, sir, anything you like.'

But he had to cut and light a cigar before he could start, and I watched him with mounting apprehension because I realized the something personal was going to be about me, and I rapidly reviewed all he might have learned about me, all the things I'd done I wouldn't want him to know about, like flogging that railway voucher and hitching to London that time to fetch Mary's shoes and using his name in the record shop so they'd let me into the booth at the back to hear records I couldn't afford to buy on a Saturday afternoon, or maybe he'd heard about Gladys and felt his daughter might be contaminated.

'I often go up to the sports field on a Thursday afternoon, Tom,' he said. 'You're a good runner, aren't you?'

'I try my best, sir.'

'But that's just the point I wanted to make, Tom,' he

113

said, gravely. 'Watching you, it occurs to me that sometimes you *don't* try your best. Take that fourth race today. You could have won that hands down if you'd tried. Last week, as soon as you'd won your individual platoon race, you seemed to lose interest. You could have won that company race, too. I've been having a word with Lieutenant Soames . . .'

Oh, my God, I thought, what the hell is this. Just because I come to his house and give his daughter dancing lessons, he sets out to Gestapo me. I suppose my annoyance must have shown.

'Don't lose your shirt, Tom. You'd be surprised how much interest we take at battalion level in all our young men, not just you.'

But I couldn't be mollified that easily.

'I only do my best, sir.'

Then he laughed, and some of the tension went. Now he felt more easy in what he was saying because, I suppose, I'd shown him how little understanding I had. You can't offend a stupid person.

'That's the point I'm trying to make, Tom. Lieutenant Soames said something to me that confirmed what I've noticed on that sports field; that you do your best only when the mood moves you. I was interested to try to discover what does move you. Look at it from my point of view. I know our training could be a lot better if only we could discover what motivates you chaps. It can't all be brighter curtains in the mess hall, longer NAAFI breaks and more weekend passes, can it? Take yourself, purely as an example you understand.' He got up and stood with his back to the fire and there he looked a commanding and authoritative figure, an officer and a gentleman, while I sat feeling scruffy, small, and insignificant, wishing at that moment I'd had a proper shower after the sports day instead of a quick wash round my balls and a quick dip under the armpits. 'Take yourself as an example,' he said. 'You seem always to go so far, but no farther, almost as if there were a hidden line of achievement you refuse to cross. Lieutenant Soames believes, for example, that you could have passed that snipers' course if you wished, and watching you run I believe you could win the battalion hundred yards, even go on to regimental level if not farther. So let me ask you this question, Tom, and believe me when I say I do so in a purely friendly way. Is something holding you back? Is there something in your mind, and the mind of other chaps like you in the battalion, that says, so far and no farther? I've been watching you very closely, and it seems to me you're racing like a horse that has its reins too tight. And for my part, I'd like to give you your head, if only I knew how.'

All I could think to say was, 'I don't fancy the responsibility, sir.'

I could see the look of disappointment on his face, and though I knew he was genuinely seeking for information, to try to help me and others like me, I couldn't bring myself to help him. Because the only things I could say would seem incredibly petty. Fancy telling him I'd blown the race so I could be first in the NAAFI queue. Fancy telling him I'd blown the snipers' course because I didn't want to be a paid killer separated from my mates.

'Let me put it to you another way,' the major said. He went and sat in his chair again, conscious perhaps that standing before the fire made him a dominant and perhaps frightening figure. 'The way the army is today, anyone with a grain of common sense, and an ability to be a little bit better than the rest, can rise up through the ranks, even be selected for officer training. In my day, to be an officer you had, unfortunately, to belong to the privileged class of so-called gentlemen, though many of my fellow officers were perhaps bigger scallywags than you'd believe possible. But nowadays, thank God, we've changed our mind about that, and some of the best officers in this regiment started out as ordinary working men. A chap like you, Tom, could make OCTU with no difficulty at all. You're a natural born leader – no, don't sneer when I say that – you're a natural

115

born leader. Take the things you've told me about your young days and your employment. Why do you think you didn't become a bully like the rest of your chums, and why do you think you went into the office instead of on the what did you call it, the mill floor?'

But I couldn't answer his questions.

'Why do you think you are always the first in that NAAFI queue, and supply all your platoon with tea and cakes . . . if that isn't leadership, then I don't know what is. My God, Tom, if you put as much energy into your running as you put into working out how to beat the system, you'd be the champion sprinter in the British Army.'

# 14

Running across that beach towards the two-inch mortar, I'll bet I beat every record in the British Army. But now there was no NAAFI queue to worry about. No tea and wads for the boys. Most of them were dead. But I had the mortar. It seemed to be in good shape, but there's not much can go wrong with a mortar except perhaps the barrel can get bent. That's all it is, after all, a piece of two-inch pipe with a pin in the bottom that is first pulled back when you start to move the cord, then thrown forward again by the force of a spring. When it goes forward, it strikes the firing pin at the base of the mortar bomb, and the bomb is fired out of the barrel. At the bottom of the mortar a knob fits into a hollow in the base plate, simple as can be.

I laid the mortar down on the sand and gingerly turned Poston over. I'd recognized him as Poston as soon as I came near enough; he was the only man with ginger hair in our platoon. He wasn't in my section. Now, he wasn't in anybody's section. The segment of the mine had got him in the throat and there wasn't much left. The base plate was okay, tucked between the straps of his ammo pouch.

Funny how your mind remembers little things. Poston and me were fighting it out in one of those silly intersection team games where you have to go round the assault course carrying all manner of unlikely things. This time it was a dustbin. The last part of the course was across a pond, and you had to float the dustbin to the middle of the pond, get undressed down to your PT shorts and put your uniform in the dustbin. Then you swam across the pond and carried your dustbin over a wall, got dressed again, and ran a short distance. The trouble was that a dustbin doesn't float too easily but tries to tip up and your clothes could get soaked. I worked it out, and put two bloody great stones in the bottom of mine because it was worth while carrying the extra weight for the sake of keeping the dustbin upright. Poston had a hell of a job with his and it tipped over and filled with water and he almost drowned himself getting it upright again. When he got to the winning line where I was waiting and laughing he said, 'You cheated, you bastard,' and belted me one in the guts and another in the mouth and ruined my weekend. Later, when I told Runty, he said, 'You didn't cheat, you used your loaf, and Poston's only mad at you because he didn't use his loaf.'

I slipped the base plate out from under his straps. Shots pinging over me, and the continuous explosion of mortar shells, but by now I'd stopped hearing them except as a thud in my head and stopped seeing them except as a brilliant flash of light and a shower of sand. Base plate flat down, scooping out the sand to make a firm base at an angle. If you try to fire a mortar too shallow it can kick off the base plate and break the arm of the man holding it. Runty once showed us how they'd used them in street fighting in some wog town in Africa, resting the butt end of the mortar against a building with the mortar almost parallel with the ground, and one time he'd done it to knock out an armoured car and the mortar had gone backwards right through the wall which was only made of mud and cowshit.

Poston was half lying over his oppo. Jenkins I think his name was, though we all knew him as Taffy. Taffy had gone down all spreadeagled, and I had to get his legs together before I could flip him over, since I was working lying down and couldn't raise my body to lift him.

Now the sergeant major was firing, slow rounds, just keeping their heads down I supposed, and Runty was firing too, covering fire so I could work. But nevertheless, shots were still zipping around me, looking for me in that tangled mass. And I had a sudden and frightening thought of what would happen if one of those bullets caught the pack of fused mortar bombs Taffy had been carrying, six of them going off together and me crouched over them.

No case. Taffy hadn't got the case of mortars underneath him. Oh shit, he must have dropped it somewhere, or maybe it was under the pile of them, or much more likely the mine they'd trodden on, silly buggers bunched like that, had blown up the mortar bombs. But six, exploding together, they'd have been bound to make a crater and there was only the normal shallow crater of the mine exploding, no more than a foot deep because the mines were placed to throw all their force upwards, not downwards. I looked about me in case the bombs had been scattered, but I couldn't see any of them, and Jesus Christ, I didn't want the job of lifting them all and moving them to see if they were lying on a case of bombs but it had to be done. How do you move a dead man? You twist his feet and his body flops over. But how can you do that when his bloody legs have been blown off to the knee. So I did the best I could wriggling among them and feeling under and round them.

Poston and Taffy, and Wilson, and Roberts who played the saxophone night and bloody day whenever he was off duty but wouldn't join the dance band because he said he couldn't read music. No bombs. Shit. I'd have to do the best I could with the four bombs I had. I glanced down at my ammo pouches and I'd forgotten to do up the last pouch again, oh damn and blast and bugger it because the ammo pouch was empty and the two bombs I'd stuffed in there must have fallen out as I was running over the sand, but the other one was still fastened and I opened it, half expecting to find nothing there, but I still had the two. Two bombs. Two? Impossible!

I looked back at Runty. No, he had no bombs. Chalky? No, he had none, too busy with that bloody useless mine-detector. The sergeant major and Lieutenant Soames wouldn't be carrying mortar bombs. Look around the beach, as much of it as I could see from where I was and though the light was good now, I couldn't see any mortar bombs lying loose. A German bomb exploded about fifty feet away and a cloud of bitter-smelling smoke drifted across to me after the explosion and I started coughing. Damn, damn, damn. With even four bombs I'd have had a hope, but not with two. The sergeant major and Lieutenant Soames, and Chalky, crawling slowly now along the beach towards me. Runty had been right, they were keeping clear of the gully and from my low down position it looked as if their arses were sticking up like skyscrapers. Bullets kicking up the sand around them. You take a million chances and maybe the statisticians were right, maybe the area of the beach divided by the area of one man does give you a million chances because although those bullets are flicking the sand all around them, not one of them had hit. Runty's hull down, firing like mad, not now really bothering to aim but keeping them busy in that slit, and now quite a number of people are firing from different places and it seems as if all the runners have been stopped by seeing six people butchered that way. One bomb into the mortar. Mortar onto the base plate. Don't bother to lock it there. Look up, force myself to lift my head so I can see the slit in the bunker. What an impossible target. Too bloody right it's impossible. How long have they been making it impossible? Two years or more, while I've been frigging about in Detling quarry and in the camp, going to Saturday night dances, carting dustbins across ponds, teaching Mary Brassingham how to dance. I pulled the cord. The bomb exploded. My wrist felt as if somebody had hit me with a steel rule, and the mortar slipped backwards hissing on the sand beneath the crump of the explosive. Lovely weapon, a two-inch mortar. The bomb sailed up into the air and I watched it fly, or thought I did, and then swung my gaze to the face of the concrete bunker and saw the bomb land a fraction short, a fraction short, dammit, but when it exploded it blew a mountain of shit of earth and stones up and some of it spread like a blanket across the mouth of the slit and must have gone inside and that can't have been too pleasant for anyone squatting in there, looking out through the sights of a machine gun.

The guns stopped. All up, all up and running, but it can't last long, it wasn't a hit, it was only a momentary halt while they curse and wipe the shit of soil and stones out of their eyes and come back at us blazing mad. Suddenly I remembered I hadn't buttoned up my right pouch and reached up my hand just in time to stop the bomb, but running with my rifle in one hand and the mortar in the other, lifting the hand carrying my rifle to stop that mortar bomb from dropping out, the sight of my rifle caught me in the eye and I stumbled and fell flat on my face in the sand. Oh Jesus Christ, where's the nearest corpse, where's the nearest place I can get to fast? and there was a small bend in that gully but if I jump into it what the hell will I find there? So I half lifted myself and sprang forward but stayed outside the gully, on the shoulder, and flopped down on the sand again and not six inches in front of my face was the half-inch metal spike of a mine, sticking innocently out of the sand where my throat would have been if I'd gone a half pace farther forward. Mines on the shoulder of the gully. The crafty sods. They knew anyone coming up the gully would leave it at this point before negotiating the bend, so they could see up to the top of the shoulder above.

Would the sergeant major be wise enough to see this one? I looked round, turning only my head. He was still coming up the side of the gully towards me though he'd gained considerably from his short run, and I turned quickly and Runty was almost up to the road way, and even I had only about thirty or so yards to do. But then they started again and this time – though it could have been only my imagination – they seemed to be firing and placing their shots with an anger I hadn't detected before. But I dismissed the thought as fancy and started to dig my fingers into the sand about four inches from that point of metal sticking up and found the canister below. I traced its outline in the sand. It was about nine inches long and five or six inches wide and I brushed the sand away from the canister avoiding the point. All the time my instinct was saying leave the bloody thing, leave it, there must be a thousand on the beach, but I couldn't leave it, not with the sergeant major and Chalky and Lieutenant Soames heading this way. I worked my fingers below it looking for wires because we'd had a course in mines that Runty took and he really put us through our paces and I knew that sometimes they peg these mines down into the sand so that if you lift them you trip another fuse; but this one had not been pegged so I lifted it out of the sand, holding it level, and then I screwed out the plunger and it came out easy and I threw the mine into the gully where it would be seen. Once you take out the plunger they're safe. Trust Runty for that, and I knew I could trust him. Because this was one lesson he hadn't left to Smithy.

He brought the mines into the barrack room, put them on the table. 'I'm going to leave that little lot with you,' he said, 'and I want you to play about with them. Don't be worried, they won't go off, but I want you to become so familiar with them that you won't be afraid of them when it comes to lifting one, only the ones you'll lift, if you should ever get so lucky, will be live.' We handled them, got to know the feel of them and the weight of them and then he took them out into Detling quarry and hid them and said 'Find them.' Which we did. Faulkner found a Schu mine and lifted it out of the grass and Runty had pegged a smoke bomb under it so that when Faulkner brought it up, grinning all over his face, the smoke bomb went off and Faulkner couldn't sleep for two nights for the coughing and eventually had to be put in sick bay while they washed him out. But none of us would ever forget, thanks to Runty, and none of us would ever be afraid. Mark you, the bloody sweat was pouring down my forehead into my eyes and I had an almost uncontrollable urge to crap. But I didn't.

Gun zipping over my head again, mortars probing the beach, no doubt looking for the bastard who fired that bomb so close to their spotters, which was me. And I was bloody hungry, I suddenly realized, and also realized I'd stuffed that bloody chocolate in my left ammo pouch when I gave a bit to Runty and now that ammo pouch was empty as a virgin's tit. Oh, bugger. I opened a couple of buttons of my blouse and reached inside. Shortbread biscuits, strictly against regs of course. They were broken to powder in the bottom of my pocket. I scooped out a few crumbs and broken bits, but they tasted like the lining of a battledress pocket should taste, and I washed them down with a swig of the whisky and tea.

It all seemed so bloody pointless, me on a beach with a two-inch mortar and one bomb, two years of training, against a gang of gunners, reinforced in a bunker, with limitless ammo and no doubt a fry up for breakfast at this very moment and passing round the steaming mugs of coffee in between tapping off a few bursts to make us keep our heads down. Okay, so what if we did get to the bloody road, would we be any better off? I could smack one into the slit from the road, that wouldn't be too difficult, but who's to say that would stop them. They could have twenty men in reserve in that bunker and as fast as I'd knock one down, another would pop up. So what was the point? In the end, one of the bullets or one of the mortar bombs would be sure to get me.

There was a tremendous blast behind me and I looked round and the sergeant major, Lieutenant Soames, and Chalky seemed to be in the middle of a blazing fire of reds and yellows with a brilliant white centre and I realized a mortar bomb had hit right in the middle of them. My face dropped to the sand and I wept. Because somehow with them gone it was all so pointless, all such a waste of time and energy and effort and people, just mortar bombs fired over the hill at random by people who'd never even see us, and we'd never even see; all Chalky's arguments about whether he could kill a German face to face, if it really came to it, and Smith's bloody Holy Joe attitude and now Chalky had stopped three shots and had gone on, but the one last thing, a mortar bomb chucked over the crest of the hill by some anonymous bugger, had got him, and that's what choked me. I didn't give a shit about Smithy, lying on the edge of the water with his guts chopped out, because in a way I felt he deserved it. If the life hereafter was all he cracked it up to be, harps and clouds and the pearly gates of heaven, then he bloody well deserved to go there as soon as possible and I had no pity for him. But Chalky had hovered somewhere between heaven and hell, belief and non-belief, good and evil, and most of all he'd been a human being I'd known for two years and learned with through the whole of that long summer.

# 15

What a summer it had been, long continuous good weather and the sort of life that made you glad to be healthy, alive and involved in something that let you spend your days with a bunch of good lads, marching around the scented fields of Kent, the blossom and the hops and the fruit. Nights out under canvas, when you'd finished a bit of training, and a fire going sometimes if you weren't on a scheme, and your rations from the cookhouse grizzling in the bottom of your mess tin.

I always used to be the one to collect the rations, the dry rations as they called them, because I could always get a bit extra, and if it was meat there was always plenty if I was the one to get it. We'd catch a rabbit, perhaps, and once we shot a sheep – by accident of course – but it had to be eaten. We had the big dixies they used for tea that came up on the lorry and we'd boil a marvellous stew for ever on a fire while we were over the hills practising stalking until the smell of that stew drove us all home again. Always the lads to talk to, to be with, to give you a lift over a wall or into a tree. Always someone who knew whatever skill you were training and could lead the way, or knew how to tie a knot, or had brought a few extra socks when your feet got wet. I could never understand Runty trying to destroy that element of our lives, the being together, sharing everything in a wonderful team spirit. Because everybody else drummed that into us, night and day. Team spirit. Learn to work as one unit. Now, of course, I realized that Runty knew that on the beach it'd be every man for himself.

But what a summer it had been, and how I shall always remember the smell of the apples in the orchards, and the plums, and eating as many as you wanted, and even going hop-picking that one time when they let us off duty. Walking along those roads, route marching really, but it was only a walk in step with others, and you lost the feel of your pack, you knew you were alive and even though you might have a bit of a blister on your foot it didn't matter because for the first time in your life you were a man and you had your own abilities and you were alive. And I hadn't even had my twenty-first.

'I wonder where you'll be for your twenty-first birthday,' my mam had said. 'We shall have to give you a party.'

I was home on leave at the time. I tried not to go home too often, but I hadn't been home for six months because the previous leave I'd been invited to Scarborough with Chalky and we'd had a marvellous time together with two birds from the ATS stationed there. But this time I went home because I thought my mam might be missing me. I had no brothers or sisters, but my mam had her own friends and still worked in the mill which was all given over to making cloth for uniforms. She was very active in the darts team and had her regular route: Mondays the Crown and Anchor, Wednesdays the George, Fridays the King's Arms, and then at the weekend there'd always be a match. When I got home she looked at me, anxious for a moment, but then clasped her arms round me and laid her cheek on mine. 'That's my lad,' she said. She was very proud of me and insisted on taking me to the club with her, where she went when she wasn't playing darts, and introduced me all round. I had my pay packet in my pocket, and was in a mood to stand a drink to anybody, but even though most of them were pensioners from the mill they wouldn't let me buy so much as a half.

One old lad, must have been about seventy-five – I remembered he'd been the night watchman at Blakey's Mill when I was a young lad but I hadn't seen him since – he bought me three halves and wouldn't leave my side. He kept touching my uniform and calling me the war hero, and I got a bit annoyed at it but my mam said, 'Don't mind him, he's had three grandsons killed in the navy at Dunkirk,' so I kept him nearby. He kept on saying, 'I could tell you a thing or two,' and at last when we were sitting by the cribbage table, though nobody was playing, I said, 'All right, tell me a thing or two,' only by then he'd had a few drinks and seemed to find it difficult to focus. Eventually he got it out. 'It's easier for your lot than it was for mine.'

'How do you make that out?'

'You don't have the trenches.'

He fell silent, thinking no doubt about the battles of his war, and when I said, 'Was it bad?' he shook his head from side to side, but then said, 'It was 'orrible.'

My mam heard this and she sat down, and her look embraced both of us, a woman's compassion for men who go to war. 'It's horrible for both of you,' she said, 'though it may be in a different way, but when a man is taken away from his family and set upon a foreign field . . .'

'*Set upon a foreign field?*' I said, 'where did you hear that? Anyway, I haven't been farther than Maidstone yet.'

'But you will be, lad, one of these days, mark my words.'

That cast a bit of a gloom over things but the waiter was passing – well, he wasn't a waiter only old Frank helping out – and so I ordered another round and by the end of the evening I could feel the room going round me whenever I stood up. So I went into the gents and stuck my finger down my throat and when I came out feeling better the old lad was standing there and he said, 'I still say it's easier for your lot,' and wrapped his white silk scarf round his throat and started for home. My mam was waiting for me and a woman called Florrie who was captain of the Ladies' Darts Team, and they said, 'Let's see if the fish and chip shop's got aught tonight,' so we walked along the street that way but when we got there, the fish and chip shop was closed. The man in there, still swabbing the frying machinery, and Florrie knocked on the window and said, 'We've got a war hero out here and he's hungry.'

But the fish and chip shop man waved his arms and I could see he didn't care if I was the mayor of Oldham. So I tucked my arms into the two ladies' arms and we went along the cobbled road singing, 'I know that she's my lady love, she is my dove, my turtle dove,' and carried it on until we came to the bottom of Florrie's street. She clasped me in her arms and kissed me on the cheek and I could smell she'd had a beer or two, but then so had I, and she said, 'God keep you and preserve you and bring you safely back to us,' and she went up the street, crying. Mam and me didn't talk for a while until we walked along past the mill. We both remembered.

'He'd have been too old for the war,' she said. 'He'd have been at least a foreman, now.' But she said it as if she didn't care too much any more, as if that was all in the past. I could feel a new strength in her, something I'd never thought of before, as if she'd become an individual, not his wife, not even my mam, but a person capable of looking after herself. I really liked that, and I tucked my arm in hers and said nothing.

When we got home, she made me a supper of sausages and a couple of eggs and a rasher of bacon and I didn't feel guilty because I'd brought home the ration cards for four people for a month that I'd fiddled, and chocolate from the NAAFI and lots of cigs, but when she'd fed me and not until, she said, 'Let's have a look at you, let's have a right look at you,' and I could see the pride and the happiness in her eyes.

'On your own now,' she said, 'tha's a man.' I was a bit embarrassed, because she'd always treated me as a lad before this, and then she said what she did about the twenty-first party.

But the nicest thing she did was to press a key into my hand and say, 'Don't lose it, that's the key to the front door.'

I realized she'd never forgotten Golcar, never forgotten that fate had robbed her of that privilege, because we only ever had one door on the house and it was called the door.

128

I turned round and hugged her and said, 'Us'll have the biggest bloody twenty-first party this street's ever known . . .' and she said, 'Don't swear to your mam, there's a good lad.'

Oh, mam, what a twenty-first it would have been, I was thinking with my head in the sand, and the image of Chalky on the backs of my eyes, and I closed them against the sight of that beach, as I closed my ears against the incessant pounding and the explosions and the whang and whee of those bullets passing over my head and the stench of the cordite and the smell of the sea on my uniform, dank and heavy and nauseating.

I lifted my head, reluctantly turned around. Lieutenant Soames and the sergeant major were crawling up the lip of that gully, but I could see no trace of Chalky at all, and the sergeant major's face was blackened by the explosion and Lieutenant Soames had lost his steel helmet and the top part of his uniform was covered in blood and sand and the radio was missing. So I pressed the base plate firm into the sand, trying to control my anger, and I got the barrel and placed the last bomb inside it, and placed the base of the mortar against the base plate and held it there firm, and then I looked up and above the gully and there were tears in my eyes, but I brushed them away again and resighted the mortar and I was boiling with anger and if I hadn't been holding on to the mortar my hand would have trembled with it, and I grasped the string and pulled. It came away in my hand.

The knot had become untied.

My anger drained away at that moment, and I threaded the string back through the hole, and doubled it back, not bothering to tie it into a knot because I only had this one bomb to fire, and resighted the mortar. I could tell that if I'd fired the mortar during my moment of anger the bomb would have gone anywhere but at the bunker, though of course a mortar is something you fire as much by instinct as by sighting, like a cricketer sights but chucks the ball by instinct. I pulled the string and the mortar bomb exploded out of the barrel and flew. I didn't even bother to duck because the gun had switched to the left of me near the jetty. The bomb flew and crashed against the concrete of the bunker and so far as I could see it was a near miss on the lip, but the guns suddenly were quiet again. So I started running, back to where the sergeant major was lying and Lieutenant Soames, and I heard Runty shouting 'Come back, you bloody idiot, come back,' but I slid down beside the sergeant major.

'You all right, sergeant major?'

'Yes, I'm all right, lad.'

I could see he wasn't. 'Done something to my shoulder,' he said, and when I touched it he shouted in pain and I guessed his shoulder was broken. There was no blood. Lieutenant Soames had blood seeping out through his uniform, and a dazed, glazed look in his eyes. He lay gasping and wheezing, and then his body slumped onto the sand, flatter than a live body could have been, and I felt a gasp come out of him and noticed his face was flat down in the sand and he couldn't possibly be breathing, so I tried to turn him over, but the sergeant major said, 'Leave him lad,' so I did. The sergeant major had seen more people die than I had. He said, 'Can you just give me a bit of a lift, and maybe we can make the road.' I helped him get up and we started to shamble up the side of that gully, past the place where I'd disarmed the mine, and now I was glad I'd done it, and the guns were absolutely silent, and I said, 'I think that last mortar may have got them,' and he said, 'You could be right,' but we kept on running.

Runty was already at the road, and had his rifle in his hand and was half standing and waving. Other figures got up in the sand and started to run up the beach and I was really surprised to see how many were still alive; there must have been at least twenty, and we all ran up towards the road, and I was twenty paces from it, no more, with the sergeant major trotting beside me, when the gun started again. As we fell down the sergeant major gave a short

130

scream, with the pain of his shoulder, and passed out. I turned him over quickly so he wouldn't suffocate in the sand.

He was still breathing, I was absolutely sure of that, but I didn't know what I could do because we hadn't been taught in first aid what you do when a man has passed out because of a pain in his shoulder, and while he was unconscious I got a grip on his shoulder wondering if it was a dislocation and I could push it back in somehow, but I could feel it grate when I touched it and knew there must be some bones broken in there although they hadn't come out through the skin. So I thought, there's nothing I can do. But then I remembered the board I had in my small pack, strictly illegal of course but I kept it in there because it made my pack more square and looked better on parade and so I twisted round and got my small pack and opened it and took the board out. Then I opened the sergeant major's jacket at the back where it buttoned on to the trousers, and shoved the board up it, right up to his shoulder, and when I rebuttoned his tunic to his trousers, the board acted as a temporary splint. At least, it might stop the shoulder jogging about too much. I stripped off all his webbing on that side, fumbling to get the straps through the brass buckles, and dropped off his pack and his ammo pouches. Then I took the long strap off his pack and brought it from behind, under his armpit, over his shoulder and back into the buckle on his belt. It brought his shoulder more in line again. The frigging about, the pain of it I mean, must have brought him round again, and he looked at me through watery eyes. We were lying side by side as I worked and as his eyes focused, he said, 'You didn't shave this morning, lad,' and I smiled back at him and said, 'Neither did you, sergeant major.'

'What's happening?'

'A few of them have got to the road.'

'Good.'

The lieutenant is dead.'

'Bugger. He was a good officer.'

'The gun's firing again.'

131

'I can hear it. How far do we have to go to get to the road?'

'Twenty paces or so.'

'I'll never make it.'

They say the blind lead the blind, don't they. 'You'll make it, sergeant major.' Cue for violins, hearts and flowers.

'You're a good lad, Wilkins, but a rotten soldier. You ought to have been an officer. That way, you'd have been just right.'

The bullets zipped over our heads, probing for us. Sand spurted in our eyes but by now I was so used to it I merely shook my head.

'What have you been doing to my shoulder. I felt you messing about in there, even though I was passed out.'

'I've put a splint on it.'

'Once a boy scout, always, eh?'

'I never joined. You had to have two shillings for the cap and the neckerchief and the two green things to stick in your stockings, and we never had two shillings to throw away.'

'Hard luck.'

'I've seen some of them scoutmasters.'

'Nobody'd fancy you. You're not the sort.'

A mortar bomb, close enough so that we could feel the blast move over us and our ears sang and my vision clouded, and when it cleared I saw the sergeant major wincing with pain.

'This bloody beach,' he said. 'The plan was for the navy to blast that gun to kingdom come. We were supposed to walk up the beach, clearing mines. They put the lieutenant in direct touch on the radio with the gunnery officer. That prick couldn't hit the side of a building at fifty feet.'

'If I'd had a few more bombs for the two-inch mortar . . .'

'When you're fighting, lad, never start a sentence with "if", or "when".'

'I'll tell you this, sergeant major, if and when I get up on that road, with a rifle in my hands, I'll give 'em hell in that bunker '

'If and when, and where and what and how, eh? But what about the "why", lad?'

'There is no why, you told us that many times. You've always said to us that the soldier who asks himself why is already dead.'

'I'm going to give you some orders,' he said to us very early on in the camp, the whole company assembled. 'I'm going to give you some orders, and your platoon NCOs are going to give you some orders, and you're going to obey them. That's what we call *discipline* in the army. The senior person present gives orders, the junior person obeys 'em. In this company no NCO is senior to me, so I give the orders, and you lot obey.' Of course, we stood in fear and trembling, recruits new to the battalion, and we all thought what a big-headed bastard he was and all prepared to hate him. But later, when he talked to us quietly, platoon by platoon, in the peace of the ABCA hut, when he'd told us all we could sit at ease and light up our fags if we wanted, he'd explain every order, that we had to learn to depend on those who gave us orders, and obey them, and above all, never ask ourselves 'why'.

Cutler, who seemed to thrive on sticking his neck out, took advantage of the sergeant major's mildness and asked, 'What happens if we don't agree with an order, sergeant major? What happens if we think an order is wrong?'

The sergeant major chuckled. 'You're a cheeky lad,' he said, 'but you're only expressing what's in half the people's minds, but they haven't the guts, or the cheek to ask. This is what happens. You carry out the order. Then, when you get back to your barracks, you ask the person who gave the order, nicely mind you, why he gave it to you, and if he doesn't jump down your throat you listen to his explanation, and if you're not satisfied, you ask to see the next senior NCO because that's your privilege in the army, and if *he* doesn't give you satisfaction, you go on asking, right up the

133

ladder, until one day you find yourself wearing your number ones standing outside a bloody great door in the war office, waiting to see a Field Marshal. If he doesn't give you satisfaction, you come back and start on the padre, and see if he can pass you up his line. Does that answer your question, Cutler?'

And, of course, we were all impressed but a little fearful because he knew Cutler's name. I don't think any one of us ever asked 'why' after that.

'What are you grinning at, lad?' the sergeant major asked, his face wincing with the pain in his shoulder again.

'I was just remembering the first time you talked to us about "why". And thought of Cutler, starting again at the padre and – what was it you said – working his way up from there . . .'

The gun had shifted again. I looked up over the gully. Five yards ahead, a group of bodies. The gully ran off to the left, a hundred paces to go before the road. We'd be better taking the short cut, the direct route.

'Can you manage five steps, sergeant major?'

'I'll try.'

I got him up. He fell one pace, walked two, fell one, and walked the other. The gun was coming back. We got down behind one body, one of the last to be cut down.

The lad we were behind wasn't yet dead. He'd lost a lot of blood but his eyes were open. He was delirious, babbling through the blood foam that soaped his lips, unaware of anything in this world except his memories.

Runty had got the lads on the edge of the road organized into some sort of squad and they were firing at the bunker, but not doing any harm. I could see from where I lay that the bunker slit had a lower lip to it, and the men were firing upwards and no doubt the slit was reinforced along that lip so that the bullets wouldn't ricochet inside. I would put one above the lip, easy as pie. But not from where I was lying. I had to get that other fifteen paces before I could do that.

The guns inside the bunker must be mounted high, so they had a good downwards vision, and the walls of the slit were not parallel; the slit narrowed through the concrete. I could put one or two in there all right.

'Leave me here, lad,' the sergeant major said, 'and get up there, to Runty. You're the best shot he has and he can use you. Tell him to knock that gun out, then come back for me.'

So I obeyed what was after all a direct order and as soon as the gun shifted I got to my feet and set off running, leaving the two-inch mortar behind but still clutching the rifle, and I'd only gone two steps when there was a roar from behind me and a blow in the small of my back, a giant punch that sent me rolling over bent double, down to the sand, rolling over, and I felt a sharp pain in my leg and the singing sound in my ears of the explosion from behind me and I slid forward with my foot somewhere up near my ear. You do see spots only they're not actual spots, just prints on the back of your eye where there's light and no light and bile in my mouth and my nose rubbing on the sand and I remember thinking not face down or I'll choke in the sand and trying to turn my head and the sand scouring the skin off my cheek like emery board and then passing out.

# 16

When she wheeled me out of the lift the nurse – or was she a sister? – took me along a short corridor and turned right into a room that sounded much smaller than the corridor had been, less echoing, and she went back to the door and called for someone named George and I heard the soles of his feet squealing on the linoleum and smelled the odour of cigarettes and this time beer, and then a sideways movement as they took me from the trolley and placed me on a bed. The nurse made up the bed around me; the sheets and the blankets smelled slightly of lanoline grease the way I remembered from the mill, so they were new and made of good stuff. The man's footsteps grew fainter as he went out of the room, and he banged the trolley against the door and the nurse said, 'Careful.' Her voice was sharp and hard and I thought I wouldn't like her for a section corporal, but she placed her hand down the side of my face and stroked and I wondered why, except perhaps that she wanted to make contact with me to show the difference between her and a clot who'd banged into the door and drunk beer, which she too must have smelled.

She opened the neck of my pyjamas and placed her long cool hand on my chest on the left side, and kept it there for a time – and I heard her click a stop-watch off. When I had my tonsils out the nurse didn't use a stop-watch, only her wrist-watch which had a second hand on it, and I'd never seen a watch with a second hand on it, in fact I'd never seen a wrist-watch that close up before. She took it off and put it round my wrist, just for play, and I loved it. It felt so grown up. The nurse with the stop-watch reached inside the blankets and the sheets and got out my hand and did the same to my wrist, clicking the stop-watch again, and I wished I had the money to buy her a wrist-watch which would be more humane than that stop-watch. She asked me if I wanted my bowels moved, as if they were portable, and I said, 'No,' and 'Did I want to pass water?' and I said, 'No,' and she said, 'Tea will soon be here,' so I knew it must be afternoon after all, and not evening or night as I had been thinking, so silent was the hospital.

She bustled about the room, arranging things, her stiff uniform crackling as she walked. She clicked her teeth in a dissatisfied way a time or two, and hung a metal board at the bottom of my bed.

I wanted to ask her some questions, but didn't like to. She wasn't the sort, from the sound of her, who'd give answers to lads like me.

She was silent for a moment and I wondered if she'd left the room, but I heard her open the window and knew she hadn't. She was silent again. Then I heard a different kind of rustle from her uniform, less crisp, more intimate, and that was followed by the crackle of paper, and she was silent again. But I could hear her breathing. And then, I realized she was crying.

I let her cry for a while, and then I held out my hand and said, 'Nurse,' and I heard her gasp in fright as if she'd forgotten anyone was there, and I heard the crackle of the papers again, and the sound of her uniform as she came to the bedside.

'What do you want?' she asked, her voice unfriendly, but she took my hand all the same and held it and I held her hand and said nothing more and hoped she'd understand that I wanted nothing, only to give her the comfort of not being alone with her memories. Eventually, she patted my hand. 'Tea will be here soon,' she said, and went out of the room. When the door closed I knew I was alone again.

I asked Mary once, 'Doesn't it bother you being alone with me like this, night after night?' I don't know why, but I suppose I felt a bit cheeky. It was like having a girl friend

137

and not having a girl friend. By now I was holding her close the way I would any dancing partner, and thought she must be aware of it. Perhaps I was feeling my oats or something that night, wanting to end this role I was playing of dancing master. Anyway, I asked her if it bothered her. We were having one of our 'let's just dance' sessions at the end of the lesson, when I'd put on a record and we'd go through without comment, to try to give her the feeling of an entire dance, and she pulled her head back from where it had been resting near me, and she said, 'Should it bother me?'

I said, 'No, I don't suppose it should.'

'To tell the truth, I was enjoying the music and the dancing. I can see why dancing is so popular.'

'For most people it's an excuse.'

'For what?'

'For holding a girl in your arms. Or a fellow.'

I felt her stiffen in my arms, as if I'd accused her of doing something cheap or common. She relaxed again.

'I suppose it *is* an excuse for a lot of people who can't find intimate human contact any other way. The British are not a race of touchers, are they? Nothing like the Continentals.'

'Thank God. All that pawing.'

But when she looked into my eyes, I knew she'd been enjoying the 'pawing', the intimate physical contact, just as much as I had. She leaned forward against me, even placed her cheek next to mine. 'You're a strange person,' she said, 'not at all what you seem on the surface.'

The ward door opened again and somebody else came in, another nurse because I could hear the rustle of her clothes but they were much less starchy than the other one's had been and she came to the side of my bed and I could smell a sweet perfume on her so I moved my hand from where the other one had left it on the bed and it touched the new nurse and she gave a little laugh.

'You're awake, then?'

Her voice matched her perfume, young and lovely.

138

'My name's Elizabeth,' she said, 'but everybody calls me Beth, though I don't like Beth, really.' I said nothing, wanting only to listen. 'Still,' she said, 'I suppose that's better than Betty. I'll be bringing you some tea soon. How do you like it, milk and sugar?'

'Two spoonsful.'

'Sweet tooth, have we?'

I didn't like the bright cheerful way she said that. Somehow the 'we' seemed to lump me with all the others and I needed at that moment to be an individual. I'd had enough of being treated as I was, because I was with the others. On that beach, they hadn't been shooting at *me*, they'd been shooting at *us*. So I said, 'Yes, *we* have.'

She laughed and came nearer and put her hand on my face. Everybody wanted to touch my face.

'Sorry,' she said. I knew she'd understood. 'Do you like chocolate biscuits? Wholewheat?'

'I love 'em.'

'My mam sent me a packet, but don't tell, will you?'

'No, I won't. It can be *our* secret.'

Again, that lovely laugh. 'Do you want to listen to the radio?'

'I wouldn't mind.'

She got the earphones and placed them on the pillow next to my head. She guided my hand to the side of the bed. 'There's a switch if you want to change the programme, or turn it off.' She went out of the room, closing the door behind her.

Somebody was talking on the earphone and I couldn't quite make out what he was saying with the earphone on the pillow, so I tried to push my head a bit nearer, but then I heard the studio laughter and I didn't feel like that, so I reached out and found the switch and turned to music. A Palm Court Orchestra, violins and all that, and a piano. Very soothing. But they started to play, 'I'll see you again, whenever spring breaks through again,' and I switched off, remembering the show.

I'd never been inside a theatre in my life, but one evening the major said, after supper, 'What are you doing tomorrow, Tom?' and I said, 'I have no engagement', thinking he wanted me to give Mary an extra dancing lesson, and he said, 'I've got three tickets for a show in town and wonder if you'd like to come with Mary and me.'

Of course, I thought it was a Forces Concert in Maidstone and wondered what the lads would think, me sitting up front with an officer and his daughter. But I said, 'Yes,' anyway.

You can imagine my surprise when I arrived at his house the following evening at half past five and a staff car was waiting, and the major sat in front next to the driver, while I sat on the back seat with Mary, feeling like Lord Muck as we drove out through the gates and turned left instead of right. I said nothing but by listening, which has always been one of my techniques, I learned that the show was in London and a musical. We didn't talk much on the way up. I didn't know what to say in the presence of the army driver, a lance corporal from our battalion who'd given me a few odd glances when I got in the car. The major was busy reading some papers he'd brought in a briefcase and the car drove into Whitehall just as he finished. When the car stopped the lance corporal dashed out and opened the front door and I didn't know what to do so I opened the door my side and got out and stood to attention on the pavement. The major had a bit of a chat with the lance corporal, asking him if it would be convenient to pick us up at the Savoy Hotel at midnight and the driver said yes. The major drew me away from the car a few steps, and he said, 'Look, Tom, I've got an hour's work to do here, that's why we were able to use the car, but I don't like to ask him to run you round the West End, so would you mind awfully taking Mary somewhere for a drink and I'll meet you at the theatre. Mary knows where it is.'

'Of course, sir,' I said, glad I'd thought to put a pound in my pocket before setting out. Though I'd meant it for an ice cream for Mary during the interval, if they served them in the garrison theatre. I saluted him, and he saluted

140

back, and gripped my hand, and I didn't know what to do so I shook his, and when he took his hand away there was a crinkle of paper in mine. I didn't look down. 'See you later, Mary,' he said, and she got out of the car and kissed him, and he went into the building, the sentries saluting him as he went towards the guard box. The car drove round the corner, and Mary and I were left together on the pavement. It wasn't dark yet and Whitehall was seething with people.

'Where do you want to go?' I asked her. 'Your father said to take you to a pub.'

'Let's cut through and walk along the Embankment. We can stop for a drink somewhere near the theatre.'

We crossed Whitehall and ducked through a street, down some steps, crossed the Embankment to the riverside and stood against the wall looking down at the water. 'I love London at this time of day, don't you?' she said, and of course what else could I say but, 'Yes.' We walked slowly away from the Houses of Parliament and Big Ben, which I recognized. I looked furtively down into my hand and almost had a fit. It was the first five pound note I'd ever seen, let alone held, but I'd heard of them. Big and white and crisp, a ticket to a new world. When we arrived at the bridge which carries the railway and turned left to go up to Trafalgar Square, which I also recognized, I saw this little pub tucked to our right at the end of a narrow street, and I said, 'Let's pop in there and have a drink.' Now I was even talking like the major.

She looked at me, amused no doubt, but said she'd love to. I ordered whisky and soda and she had gin and tonic and she said she was hungry and could she also have a piece of pie, and I grandly said, 'Please order whatever you want,' quite forgetting for the moment that she came from the class of people who always do precisely that. I produced the fiver and put it on the counter and we both had a slice of pie with pickles and chutney, a serviette and a knife and fork, and I held the world in the palm of my hand.

'This was a good idea,' she said. 'Daddy's ordered us

141

a cold supper at the Savoy, but I was ravenous.'

And then I remembered I hadn't asked for a late pass. I wouldn't have needed one at the garrison theatre.

The play was a musical with lots of tunes I'd heard many times, so I could understand it quite well, and enjoy it, though I thought the story was a bit romantic.

One of the tunes was 'I'll see you again, whenever spring breaks through again. Time may lie heavy between, but what has been, is past forgetting' or something like that, and when they started to sing it, Mary astounded me by reaching across and holding my hand. She was sitting between me and the major, and I'd managed to get myself comfortable although the man in front of me wearing an American Air Force uniform kept bobbing about. The couple singing the duet were alone on the stage for the song, and the stage went darker, and spotlights shone on them, and suddenly I felt Mary's hand creep into mine. To tell the truth, I was feeling a bit choked myself, because it seemed people were always saying hello and goodbye and if you bothered to think about the future you wondered just who you would see again; so I held Mary's hand and it had a different feel from when I was holding it for dancing, more personal, and I could have cried. Because sooner or later the invasion was going to happen and they'd already been talking about it for months and I would be going to take part in it. I'd have to, since we'd avoided being posted to the Far East where the Second Battalion had gone, poor sods. And it was useless to say I wanted to go because I knew I didn't. My present life was too good for that, had too many new and exciting things in it for me. I looked sideways at Mary. She had her hand in mine, but seemed to be avoiding my eye, looking resolutely at the stage. But I could see how bright her eyes were and I felt uncomfortable as I always did when people become emotional around me, like Florrie that night I was home on leave and my mam, though she was better at hiding what she felt. Anyway, my arm got cramp where Mary was holding it and I needed to move it because the pins and

142

needles were painful, so I gave Mary's hand a bit of a squeeze and placed it back in her lap and left it there.

We went for supper in the Savoy Hotel. I'd never imagined such busy, bustling, and luxurious places existed though I'd heard they had hotels like that in Leeds. She talked very brightly about the show and said how amusing it had been in a way if you liked that sort of thing, and the major looked at her and looked at me, and said there's nothing wrong with a bit of honest sentiment and anyway it made a change, and for some reason I couldn't put my finger on I got the idea he felt the same way as I did, wishing she wouldn't talk like that. But I said nothing in case I might offend her or the major, just answered when spoken to and minded my table manners and revelled in the absolute unbelievable luxury of it all and wished mam could see me so she'd have something to crow about to the darts team.

On the way back to Maidstone I couldn't keep my eyes open and fell asleep on the back seat.

# 17

I thought I was blind. I couldn't see anything and I couldn't move my eyelids. I wasn't afraid. 'My God, I'm blind,' I said aloud, and the sound of my voice made me know that another world existed beyond my eyelids. I lifted both hands to my face and found my eyes encrusted with sand, full of substance sticky to my fingertips. It had to be blood. I smeared it away and could flick my eyelids and I could see after all and I wasn't blind. I couldn't see clearly. The explosions of the mortar shells had become like the images you see in the bottom of those triangular tubes with mirrors and bits of coloured glass in them they used to sell in the grocery shop down below our house. Once a box of them had been chewed by rats and Mrs Lubbock couldn't sell them of course with the paper all chewed so she gave one to me. When I looked down the triangular tube it seemed a miracle everything could settle itself so quickly into such a pattern, and when I shook my head the orange and red and purple blasts of the bombs on the beach formed into the same sort of pattern and I was glad to know I could see again.

I felt myself crying and the tears washed away the triple vision and I saw my leg was twisted in a funny sort of way and felt the pain in my hip. It was such an excruciating pain I wanted to scream but couldn't. I lay back and clenched my firsts and looked up at the sky. Ironically my first thought was 'Do they give you a wound stripe to wear on your uniform for a broken leg or does it have to be a wound made by a bullet or a bomb?' The sky was bright and thick white clouds looked as if they had been washed so white the explosions would never stain them. For the first time I saw the aeroplanes and some were flying along a straight path and bombs dropped from them, and some were diving, with flashes of fire where they were firing at each other. Dancing tight round the sky in a waltz, one of the planes, suddenly reduced to a puff ball of fragments and smoke, began to fall. A formation of heavier machines laid a stream of eggs which, instead of remaining black and screaming and deadly, grew white like the new mushrooms my Uncle Albert used to grow, with men dangling from the canopies. I thought to myself, 'Thank God the paras are here.' It was like those films we used to go and see for two-pence at the Carlton where the goodies were fighting the baddies and losing and suddenly the cavalry would arrive. Only the paras had no bugle, no flag, and arrived not hot at the charge but with a cold, slow and deadly intent. I wondered how men could live falling unprotected through such a sea of explosions, fire and flame. I was lying on my back watching them slowly descend when I heard Runty's voice close to my ear.

'Gone to fucking sleep, have we?' he asked and I turned my head and said, 'What's a nice boy like you doing in a place like this?'

I heard Runty scrabble down beside me and felt his fingers under my gaiter, surprised I could feel anything at all; he grabbed my foot and ankle and the pain in my hip brought a scream out of me and sweat to my forehead. Runty said, 'You'll be all right now.'

'You mean I'm not wounded?' I said with a great sense of disappointment, thinking about the stripe.

'Wounded, you daft sod, I've seen worse happen falling out of a NAAFI girl's bed.'

So I got up on my knees and we scuttled like crabs all the way up the road and they never fired the gun once at us.

Five of us got to the road, Runty and me and three men from 2 platoon including one fellow, Corky, who nobody liked because he had been a corporal and they broke him for striking another rank. Five of us lying full length below a pile of granite chippings and the gun. Four rifles between us. Runty checked the grenades; we had twelve. No mortar, no mortar bombs. No mines, no Bren guns, sweet fuck all. What a way to fight a war!

'We could always throw a few lumps of this bloody granite at them,' I said, and Runty laughed.

'We've got to get that gun,' he said, and for the first time I asked myself what was so bloody important about that gun, about those guns which had done their job of keeping C Company off that beach. From where I was squatting I could see the road down to the beach curved by a building that once had been a café, and now was derelict. I knew the road would be mined all the way up but to the left was an escarpment of rock with a shelf on it which ran upward and round the side of the cliff.

'They can't put mines in rock,' I said to Runty, and Corky, who couldn't forget he had been a corporal once, said, 'What the hell are you talking about,' and I said, 'You shut your gob.'

Runty had seen what I meant but he shook his head. 'The gun's the other way, Tom.'

'Who cares?'

'I care,' Runty said.

'Weren't you the one said to look after number one?'

'Do you think I want that lot left behind me?' Runty's eyes had been flicking over the gun emplacement while we talked. It stood ahead of us, impregnable, menacing. I looked back and saw where they were raking the beach and knew anything that moved was a goner. The sand was littered with bodies of the men I had known and I felt an almost uncontrollable urge to stand up and yell and curse, but Runty said, 'See that knoll about fifty yards to the left, in line with that telegraph pole?' I saw it at once. He said, 'I'm going to make for that. When I get there I'll give you covering fire. You, you bastard, better smack one right into that gun's kisser or I'll put you on a charge.'

I laughed, but he was already up and running and the

laughter continued even when the two other men from 2 platoon went running after him but the laughter died like cold froth on my lips when the machine gun sighted on the three of them and despite the rounds that Corky and I instinctively began to shoot, rapid fire with no time to re-aim, the bullets from the gun ripped into Runty and the other two and he jerked his arms like a mad marionette and pitched forward still on his face in the scree at the other side of the road, and the two men with him.

As for Corky and me, well, when we saw Runty pitch to the ground we got up and ran to that escarpment of rock. Corky cupped his hands and I put my foot in and he hoisted me onto the rock ledge. I reached down a hand and Corky jumped up and I pulled him up beside me.

I was right. There were no mines on the ledge. The surface of it crumbled from time to time and often we had to move sideways with only our fingertips and toenails holding, but we went up and up like mountain goats and soon were round the side of the ridge where the gun was ringed by a solid concrete wall about a hundred metres in circumference with slits in it. Corky took one look at it and said, 'Fuck that little lot.' I agreed with him and said, 'Let's go and find the paras.'

Call it cowardice in the face of the enemy. Call it running away. Call it fear. Call it what you like; I knew damn well the two of us could not take that gun. The instinct to survive is the strongest instinct we have. Runty had wanted to guarantee his own survival by knocking out that gun, by the one fixed idea of neutralizing what he could see as our greatest danger, but he was wrong.

Even in danger you must preserve the flexibility to stand up and fight when it can do you some good, and to run like bloody hell when the time comes. Corky and me were like-minded. We ran and left that lousy horrible stinking bleeding gun to somebody else. Dammit, a whole air force up there had bombs, and a whole navy out there had shells, hadn't they? Me and Corky, well, we had two .303 rifles and

147

two pocketsful of ammo and a few grenades. To me, at that moment, finding the paras seemed my only hope of salvation. So I ran and the tears rolled down my cheeks for all the men left on the beach, but I brushed them angrily away.

When I was eight years old I came home one evening and found the gas had already been lighted. The table in the centre of our living room was already covered by a heavy dark green cloth which was my mam's pride and joy. The cloth hung over the edge because I suppose it was made originally for a much larger table. When I got into the room I thought something was wrong. My mam and dad were looking at me in a funny sort of way. My dad said, 'Where have you been?' and I said 'Out' and that reply normally would have made him very angry but at eight you can be very stubborn. Mam put her hand on his arm and said in that beautiful soft voice of hers, 'Look under the table, Tom.' I lifted the green table cover and under the table was a bicycle. First I felt very strange and started to think what a silly place to put a bicycle, but then the thought grew in me that you'd only put a bicycle under the table to hide it. So I pulled it out. It was lovely. I looked at it: new twist grips on the handlebars, and a new bell and the rest of it cleaned and polished and I could even smell the ammonia tang of the Brasso my mam had used on it. It was the first bicycle I'd ever had.

Well, of course I had to take it out and try it and as he watched me go down the street touching the pedal only with my toes my dad said, 'It's a bit big for you, lad, but you'll grow into it.' I rode the bicycle down the street and round the corner and then went down Grape Street which I never liked to do alone on foot because of Sam Davis and his gang, but I thought on a bike I'd be safe. Sam rushed out of the waste ground near the bottom of Grape Street where they pulled down a mill and grabbed the handlebars of the bike. The gang came all round me and shook the bike, jeering, 'Look at Tom, he's got a bloody bike.' Then Sam kicked the spokes and one of the gang hit me on the nose because I was using my hands to hold on to the handlebars, so I fell off and ran home to get my dad. When he came back a quarter of an hour later he was carrying the bike because the spokes on both wheels had been kicked in and the new bell had been smashed with a brick and he said, angry, 'Why didn't you stop and fight?' That was the first time I ever saw my mam lose her wick because she struck out at him and said, 'He did the right thing. What does a bicycle matter?' I was crying but I heard my dad say, 'That bicycle cost me five bob. I wanted him to have the use of it. He's got to learn to stand up and fight for what he's got.'

My mother went to the mantelpiece and took the tin that contained her money and with great violence she threw the tin so it hit my father on the chest and the lid burst open and all the coins she had saved from the housekeeping, all the money that was hers, showered out over him and she shouted, 'Take your five bob and what do I care.' She put her arms around me and I cried. I knew my dad was right. I ought to have stayed and fought for the bicycle and I ought to have been the one to carry it home with the spokes broken and the bell smashed. My father never mended that bicycle and it lay in the coal cellar and gradually was covered with coal dust and is probably there to this day.

But that gun wasn't mine, was it? It wasn't mine to stand up and fight for and I knew that even my father would have approved this time of me running away to look for the paras.

I ran away from Mary Brassingham, too, and didn't know what my father would have thought about that. We were in the drawing room. I'd just shown her that fancy cross over-step in the quickstep where you put your right foot in front of your left then take a short pace back and go left and bring your right foot inside behind your left foot. It's called the butterfly and if you can get the timing exactly right you can go all the way down the side of the ballroom, and it looks very spectacular and you finish it off with a tight inside turn and even a three-spin twirl. Somehow or other she got the step the first time and I was very pleased because, let's

149

face it, it's an intricate step and I know a lot of people who've been going to the Palais for years and they've never got it; but right from the start we went butterflying down that drawing room like a pair of professionals and I finished it off with a three-spin twirl that left us both breathless.

'That wasn't half bad,' I said.

'Coming from you I take that as a compliment.'

I have never seen her looking more lovely. My face moved forward and hers towards me and I knew at that moment I could have kissed her if I'd wanted, but something held me back. I let go of her hand and took my right hand from the small of her back and walked over and lifted the needle off the gramophone record. When I turned she was standing just behind me and must have followed me across the room. She was looking at me again, cheeks flushed, eyes bright and shining, and she put both her hands on my arm, gave me a squeeze and said, 'We go well together, don't we?'

'When you remember to slide your foot across the floor and not pick it up.'

'I didn't just mean the dancing.'

Her face had a look of quality I'd seen on no one I'd ever kissed. Her body smelled of a clean delicate perfume. On her hand where it rested on my arm was a ring that must have cost as much as my dad would earn in a year, diamonds and emeralds that I knew were real and didn't shine with the sort of mauve glitter that was on the brooch I bought for my mam from Woolworth's the previous Christmas. How could I reply?

'You're getting to be a good dancer,' I said, 'and I've always believed that a good dancer can get on well with anybody.'

She winced, and that evening I did not stay for supper.

I suppose you could say I thought of Mary Brassingham in those days in a way I thought of that gun. It wasn't mine. It wasn't mine and I ran away from it.

When Corky and me circled round that emplacement we set

150

off along a track at the edge of a field. To the right about a hundred yards away I could see the road and the ravine between the beach and the road which made the beach militarily useless. I knew from the briefing that if we followed that road for twelve kilometres we'd come to where the paras had landed, so we set off jogging along the path keeping the road always in sight. A lot of movement along the road, German Army transports going in each direction, and once on a bend we saw a lorry run into a tank. Infantry running along the road until the planes came and strafed them with machine-gun fire. The infantry left the road but came only half way to where we were running and did not see us. I was glad of all the chaos for it meant we could move faster, taking less care than if we'd been alone and conspicuous in a deserted landscape. Running most of the time in a steady jog trot we covered the first eight kilometres without incident then sat in a hedge bottom beside an orchard and smoked a cigarette. Corky had a tin of M and V stew in his pack that we ate cold. We didn't talk. I for one had nothing to say. I had fixed my mind on getting to the paras. I had no idea what I was going to do when I got there. I was a soldier without a platoon, without officers or NCOs, a nonentity. From where we were sitting in the ditch we could see a farmhouse. One part of it had been bombed but a good half still remained standing.

'We could lie low in there,' Corky said, 'probably find some grub. Even wine. We could lie low in the cellar and wait till it's all over. When the troops come and the fighting's finished, we can make our way back to the beach, a couple of heroes, and get ourselves a soft job loading and unloading lorries. That'll see us nicely out of the war,' he said. 'I had a job like that in Southampton, when I was a corporal. Loading stuff for North Africa. Nicked and flogged no end of cigs, and chocolate rations.'

'You would, wouldn't you?'

'You've got to look after number one,' Corky said.

Corky didn't bear comparison with Runty and hearing

those words coming from him was an obscenity. 'Shut your cakehole,' I said, but nevertheless followed him when he got out of the ditch and headed for the farmhouse. Once again, something Runty had said to us many times on training turned out to be true because many times he told us you shouldn't try to do anything when you're angry. Anger puts you off balance and clouds your eyes and your judgement.

I was staring at Corky's back and hating him so fiercely and passionately that I didn't see the three Germans until one of them clobbered me on the back of the neck and I fell down on the ground next to where the second one was lying and the third one had stuck the end of his gun so hard into Corky's kidneys that Corky gasped and could not scream. As I went down to the ground I saw that the German lying there looked like a heap of butcher's meat and the German who'd clobbered me said, surprisingly in English, 'Your guns did that' and I was pleased to think we had at least done some damage. But I said, 'You can't blame that on me, cock.' The German hit me again and I realized he was using the butt of his gun which was covered with polished brass. The blow couldn't have been intended viciously because it hardly hurt. I turned and sat on my hunkers and thought about the possibility of kicking his legs from under him.

Runty and me were in a pub once in Morecambe and there was this bloody great pilot from the Canadian Air Force. We were with a couple of girls and the Canadian thought he could buy them off us. He was offering double whisky all round from the hidden bottle the landlord had produced at the sight of the Canada tabs and that had made Runty mad enough for a start; but this girl Runty was chatting up, an ordinary looking brunette from Carlisle and I don't know why Runty bothered, she turned down the whisky and the Canadian made a nuisance of himself insisting she drink it. When he tried to pour it down her throat, Runty, in a nice sort of way, told him to piss off and the Canadian chopped the side of Runty's neck. Runty went down like a sack of barley. Before I had time to do anything about it

Runty hooked one foot behind the Canadian's ankle and used his other foot to kick him on the kneecap and the Canadian went down. We scarpered out of the pub, but I heard later the Canadian had a broken kneecap. While I was looking at that German and wondering if I could break his kneecap and remembering how Runty had showed me how to do it he took a couple of paces backwards and said, 'You have no chance,' and I said, 'Where did you learn to speak English?' and he said, 'In the Merchant Navy.'

'Then why aren't you a bloody sailor?'

'Because I get seasick.'

'Shut up, you silly sod,' Corky said. He was sitting up rubbing his kidneys. The German who'd clobbered him had also stepped back level with his mate, and he said something like '*Was gibt's?*' and the English-speaking one said something like '*Augenblick bitte,*' his eyes watching us all the time, flicking from Corky to me.

'I suppose we're prisoners.'

'I do not know what we will do with you.'

'You're not going to shoot us,' Corky said, his voice revealing his fear. The German smiled at him. 'You have been listening to propaganda,' he said. 'Now get up and we will go to that farmhouse, and do not provoke me.'

We got up without provoking him. His mate bent down and emptied the pockets of the third German, picked up his knapsack made of a sort of fur, but left the dead man where he lay. It seemed all wrong. We had time to bury him, but I was not going to be the one to put the idea of a burial into their minds.

So these were the Germans, the first I had ever seen close up. These were the 'Krauts', the 'Nazis' as Winston Churchill had called them. These were the enemy, and as I looked at them I remembered something the major had said to me one evening sitting in his leather armchair.

'I could never be an officer in the line again,' he said. 'It's all so different now. I know my mind tells me I've got to hate them, but somehow I can't find it in my heart to hate any group of people.' He coughed and looked embarrassed.

'I shouldn't be telling you this, young lad,' he said, 'because you're the one who's got to take the bayonet practise but, you know, I quite believe that if you asked *me* to stick a bayonet in anyone I wouldn't be able to do it.'

Looking at those two Germans I felt no hatred.

I looked at Corky, his face twisted with fear and his mouth working and thought Corky is going to shit himself, but I didn't feel anything like that. I was curious. The Germans must have thought me crazy because I said, 'What are your names?'

The German smiled. 'What are *your* names,' he said and I told him I was Tom and the other Corky and it seemed the most natural thing in the world and he said, 'My name is Rainer and his name is Peter,' and I said, 'That's funny, I thought Peter was an English name,' and he said, 'No we also have Peter. He comes from Wuppertal. So do I.' We set off and Peter walked behind Corky with his gun pointing at the small of his back and I shouldered my rifle on the sling. Rainer and me walked side by side as if we'd known each other all our lives.

Most of the activity on the road had subsided and I guessed that either the Germans had stopped the invasion or had settled down to a long hard battle. I could hear the crump of mortars and shells were bursting all over the ground between us and the beach almost as if they were being fired at random. The aeroplanes were still flying and ahead of us parachutists were still dropping through the Ack-Ack fire. Here we were in a small oasis away from the war. I no longer even felt the need to hide in the hedgebottom every time a plane came screaming low over us. One of them had been hit and smoke trails behind it suddenly burst into flame and the plane crashed into the ground at least a mile and a half from us. It was British, but I felt no anger, no remorse. I was numb with all the feeling that had passed through me that day. I no longer cared, no longer felt any emotion. As we walked along I saw Corky's head moving from side to

154

side and he kept glancing over his shoulder. Rainer said to me, 'Your friend is the nervous type.' I told him the story of how Corky had once been a corporal.

'Many men are given responsibility in war they do not merit,' Rainer said, and I found myself saying 'We'd use the word "deserve" there,' and he said, very politely, 'Thank you very much,' and I wondered at myself for giving him English lessons at that moment.

'What are you going to do with us when we get to the farmhouse?' Corky asked, calling back over his shoulder. Peter thrust his gun menacingly forward and turned round to look at Rainer who, I suddenly noticed, was wearing a better uniform. I remembered the lesson Smithy had taken in the ABCA hut when he'd explained the German ranks to us, and showed us markings on their uniforms, and I knew Rainer was a Leutnant – which is like our captain – and Peter was only the equivalent of a private. Corky turned round and looked and doubtless saw that Peter's attention had turned off him briefly. He must have been holding the grenade in his hand, must have worked it out of his battle-dress blouse as he was walking along. In a blur of movement I saw him yank the pin out of the grenade. The percussion lever flew off and he tucked the grenade into Peter's trouser pocket at the same time as he pushed him sprawling into Rainer. Peter was entangled in Rainer's legs. Both fell to the ground. Corky shouted, 'Run, Tom, run.' Instinctively I started forward. Corky was bringing up his rifle to fire into them and at the same time turning to run and his first shot went wide. A burst of fire from Rainer's gun went into the ground. I don't know why but I grabbed Peter's shoulder and dragged him off Rainer and grabbed Rainer's hand and jerked him to his feet and said, 'Run for it.' He looked down at Peter now lying half on his side, half on his back. The grenade was in the trouser pocket under him and I knew he had no hope of getting it.

I ran with Rainer pounding beside me and on the count of five I threw myself to the ground. Rainer threw himself down just in front of me. The grenade went off behind us and some of the fragments spun crazily over my head. The blast rocked my brain and I remember thinking not again, not again. The bullets from Corky's rifle were hitting the ground beside me. I got up and said, 'It's me, you silly bugger,' and saw him sitting against a stone wall firing his rifle at Rainer still lying on the ground, and not really caring that I was almost in the line of fire. I dashed forward in an arc and he had time to fire another round before I got to him and there was no time to lift my arms to hit him so I pushed and he went over and down with me on top, cursing and shouting, 'What the bloody hell's the matter with you Tom? Get the Kraut.' I said, 'We won't get the Kraut because he could have got us back there and he didn't.' Now I had my rifle pressed against his neck and was using it to push his head down on the ground. He said, 'Give up Tom, you're bloody killing me,' and I said, 'I know I am, you bastard.' He managed to say, 'All right, we'll leave the Kraut.' I let go the pressure. The sling swivel had been against his jaw bone, now white with pain. He reached up his hand and rubbed it and looked angrily at me. 'You're out of your bloody mind,' he said. At that moment I felt out of my mind with hatred for him and all he seemed to represent, all the brutal, senseless, unnecessary slaughter of ordinary human beings who had names and identities just as we had.

Rainer was crouched over the dead body of Peter, with his head in his hands and no doubt waiting for the shot that would finish him too. I went across and pulled at his forearm and said, 'It's all right, Rainer, it's all right, we're not going to kill you.'

'I no longer care,' he said.

'Come on,' I said. 'We've got to get away from here.'

He took one last look at Peter and shuddered as he got off the ground and brushed himself with hands which were surprisingly clean; mine were filthy dirty and I had the same impression of him I'd had of the major, that here was someone of social standing, a gentleman. Mary had talked to me several times about it and once when we were dancing and I'd surprised myself by tripping over her feet and she knew it was my mistake and not hers, she said, 'I think the trouble is that you're not holding me, almost as if you're afraid to hold me properly.' This wasn't the old thing of not holding her properly because she was a cripple – I'd long ago got over that – but I realized I was holding on to her in a deferential sort of way, like I would hold the wife of the mayor if ever I should have to dance with her and wishing I was wearing white gloves and wondering if maybe the sweat of my hand would be staining the back of her dress, and if my breath smelled. I tried holding Mary in a more intimate way, reminding myself that I was the teacher and she was the pupil, in the matter of dancing I was the leader and she the follower, but it never worked. Looking at this man Rainer and knowing he was an officer I got entirely the same feeling again.

Corky got up, still rubbing his jaw, and came up to where we were standing.

'You could have killed me. For a bloody Kraut.'

'Bollocks.'

'Tom is not the killing sort,' Rainer said.

'I wasn't bloody talking to you.'

'He's an officer,' I said.

'I don't care if he's bloody Adolf Hitler.'

I was angry. I knew Corky was letting us down in front of Rainer. I did not want Rainer to have reason to despise us.

'We're going to make for the paratroops,' I said, 'all three of us.' I looked at Corky. 'All three of us, Corky. You understand?'

He grinned at me. 'Anything you say, old lad. I stopped making decisions when they took my stripe off, but if you want my advice, you'll take his rifle off him and throw it away. Or better still, I'll take it. Nice bit of loot that is. The lads coming back from North Africa got twenty quid for an Iron Cross, so a jerry rifle should be worth thirty.'

Without saying a word Rainer took the clip from his Schmeisser, and threw the clip away over the hedge. Then he hefted the gun and tossed it at Corky who caught it deftly and said, 'Thanks, mate, now you're getting a bit of sense. For a Kraut.'

I had seen the look of utter contempt in Rainer's face when he threw the gun and wouldn't have wanted him to look at me in such a fashion.

We set off walking, Corky in front, Rainer and me behind, side by side, and this time I kept my eyes open and not on Corky's back as before. This time nobody was going to jump me. I held the rifle by my side pointing forward with my index finger in the trigger guard. The magazine was full except for the one up the spout and my thumb was on the safety catch. About two miles ahead of us I could hear the sounds of a battle and see the flashes of exploding bombs and mortars. I knew we were going into a danger zone but no longer had any desire to hide in any farmhouse. We went over the crest of a small hill keeping off the skyline and saw the planes flying low over the battle zone, firing at targets on the ground. The chatter of their guns was so loud I got the impression it was a miracle the planes could continue to fly forward against the backward thrust. When you think what the kickback of a normal rifle is. Once, in Detling quarry, Runty let us all fire a Bren from the hip, holding it like a rifle, and we wondered why he made the rest of us squat behind sandbags. When it came to my turn to fire the recoil spun me like a top and if I hadn't been on single rounds I would have sprayed the butts like a hosepipe.

'Why did you join the army?' I asked Rainer, 'or do you have conscription?'

'Why does anyone join an army? At the time it seemed the only thing to do. It even seemed noble. We are all cattle, you know, and it only needs one fellow to start a stampede.'

'Don't they have conscientious objectors in Germany?'

'Yes, but they are called enemies of the state and shot as traitors.'

158

'You could have shot us back there.'

'Looking at your comrade Corky and remembering my soldier Peter, I think I ought to have.' Rainer said this without emotion.

'One day,' he said, 'we will learn that the life of every individual is sacred.'

'What are you then, a bleeding parson?' Corky said. He'd dropped back and been listening.

'You got anything to eat in that pack of yours?' he asked. We stopped and Rainer brought out the end of a loaf of bread. It was like no bread I'd ever seen, dark brown and very heavy. He handed it to Corky who looked at it and sniffed. Rainer got out a piece of cheese screwed up in paper. When he opened the paper you could have smelled the cheese for a mile.

Corky's nose wrinkled. 'What the bloody hell is that?' he said and Rainer answered him, 'It's a cheese called limburger.' Corky said, 'It smells like shit to me,' and Rainer said, 'You can't always go by the smell.' He got a penknife from his pack with a long fold-in blade. Corky said, 'Careful, I'm watching you,' but Rainer smiled at him and used the penknife to cut off a piece of bread and smear a portion of cheese on it which he gave to me. I ate it. The bread tasted like malt and the cheese was strong and satisfying. I said, 'You're right, you can't judge by the smell.' Corky wouldn't even try it. When Rainer prepared a slice and handed it to him, Corky threw it away in disgust.

'You learn never to throw food away,' Rainer said.

'Call that food? It isn't even fit for animals.'

'I thought that's what we Germans were,' Rainer said.

'Don't get bleeding smart, because if it wasn't for Tom here, you'd get yours, animal or not.'

I belched loud and Corky laughed. 'That'll teach you to eat shit,' he said. Rainer cut me another slice, and when I ate it I didn't even smell the cheese, but it tasted nourishing. Rainer ate a couple of slices and we washed it down with a mouthful each of my tea and whisky, which I didn't offer to

159

Corky. We started out again, heading towards the paras. This time Corky tried to walk behind us, but I motioned him forward with my rifle and said, 'Don't get behind me, Corky, because you make me nervous.' He walked in front.

The sun was high above our heads and the day had settled into one of those peaceful June days I shall always remember from that long summer and Maidstone.

# 18

One Saturday afternoon I got bored and walked until a PU truck gave me a lift for a mile to the edge of the town. I went for about a mile along the country road that led towards Sittingbourne. On the old Pilgrims' Way I knew a pub that did cups of tea outside and I could be alone. It was a beautiful and peaceful afternoon.

They served me a pot of tea and a plate of plain buns and I ate three with my back to the road. I heard a vehicle draw up on the car park outside the terrace, but didn't think anything about it until I felt a light tap on my shoulder. I turned and Mary stood there grinning. She'd been riding in the ambulance back to the hospital, had seen me sitting there and told the driver to stop. The driver called out, 'All right Miss?' She nodded and he engaged the gear and drove off. I said, 'Aren't you on duty?' and she said, 'I've just taken a patient to Sittingbourne. I'm finished now for the day,' and I said, 'Do you fancy a cup of tea?'

After the tea we walked down the Pilgrims' Way. I never even noticed if she was limping or not. There were a lot of brambles and we picked some blackberries and ate them, although they weren't yet ripe. Maidstone and the camp seemed a long way away. The air was sweet and fresh and the white trumpets of the convolvulus were everywhere. She told me the names of some of the plants we saw, red campion and meadow sweet and one we both laughed at called the greater stichwort which had a few white flowers still but was mostly dead. I made up for it by showing her how to grasp the base of the white convolvulus flower where it goes into the green bit. If you press it gently with your thumb and finger the white flower pops out and flies up into the air and floats gently down like a parachute. I was surprised she'd never done that; as kids in Yorkshire we'd always done it. She tried to get me to talk about my childhood in Yorkshire and I felt very bashful, but when we sat on a bank between two large gorse bushes and were together in a world of our own, I found myself telling her about my dad and mam, and the way he wanted to be a foreman, about the house near Golcar where we would have had a garden and perhaps I could have learned the names of the flowers. When I told her about the way they found my dad floating in the millpond, she squeezed my hand and I was surprised to discover I'd been holding her hand for some time.

'You've had a rotten life,' she said.

'Compared to some I've had a good life. Friend of mine, his dad ran away with the girl from the butcher's shop and his mother broke up, and we used to joke that he had a new uncle every weekend, cruel as kids can be. Mick Foster, who was run over by a tramcar, spent most of his schooldays in and out of hospital without much success. Sammy's mother was a klepto and in and out of Armley Gaol for it. His dad used to get drunk and beat the hell out of him, because his dad really hated it when they put his missis inside. Sammy had five sisters, and last I heard they'd all gone on the game.'

That was what I called a hard life, when you didn't have a home to go to, with a clean bed and food, and a mam who polished your boots before you went to school, and bought stockings for you to wear that weren't cheap ones made of shoddy that always went into holes and wouldn't stay up your leg and made you feel embarrassed in school.

'My mam really looked after me,' I said to Mary, and now her eyes were sad for herself and I could have bitten out my tongue because, of course, she'd never had a mam. I cursed myself for a clumsy fool.

She shook her head. I saw her eyes were moist. A wasp came buzzing round us, and although it wasn't the first one we both made a big point of chasing it away. But she wouldn't let me kill it with my forage cap. We set off walking

162

some more. The sun was very hot and I wanted to take off my battledress blouse but I wasn't wearing the uniform the camp tailor had altered for me and I had braces holding up my trousers. She was wearing a dark blue dress with white collar and cuffs; if my braces had been as clean and white as her collar and cuffs I wouldn't have minded taking my jacket off. Her dress looked as if it might have been some kind of uniform; I didn't like to ask her in case it wasn't and she would be offended. She'd pinned her hair back in a very severe style and as we were walking along the path her hair gradually shook loose and finally she said 'Oh bother,' and took the hairclips out of it. Her hair fell down round her face and on her shoulders and I remembered how it had felt when we'd been dancing. She had a long thin sort of face and usually looked rather serious when I was with her, but on this day in summer I could see she had decided to relax and now that her features were not so composed she radiated happiness and confidence.

You do the craziest things when you're happy, say the craziest things and everything becomes endowed with a special significance even though it may not be important. I remember we started quoting nursery rhymes to each other and I think I surprised her by the number I knew, because my mam was a great one for singing nursery rhymes when she was working about the house. 'Pussycat, pussycat where have you been, I've been with my grandmother over the green.' But the one Mary liked the best and insisted I teach her was 'Pussy can sit by the fire and sing, Pussy can climb a tree, Or play with the silly old ball of string, To amuse herself not me. But I like Bingo my dog because Bingo knows how to behave . . .'

I taught Mary the words and the tune and we walked together on that long summer's evening down the Pilgrims' Way, and even when it started to rain and we got wet through and I had to swear she was in the ATS to get her a lift on an army lorry, the day was not spoiled.

I think if she hadn't had to get home because her father

was giving a dinner party we would have gone dancing together that night. As it was I went alone to the dance in the camp, but I couldn't seem to settle and by nine o'clock was back in the barrack room reading a book. When Runty came in half pissed at a quarter past eleven he woke me up and asked me, 'Are you sick or something?'

'Fucking hot for June, isn't it?' Corky said. He was sweating in his uniform. My uniform was stiff with the salt water of the beach and I looked at Rainer and envied him his barathea. We used to turn out miles of that stuff in our mill, that and whipcord, and most of it went for officers' uniforms after the war started. I could remember the stink from the dye-house and the way the khaki dye fouled up the millpond.

Rainer didn't look hot. I could see he was thinking about something, deeply, intensely. He held out his left hand and made a motion for me to slow down a bit and gradually we reduced our pace and let Corky draw ahead. We were going down a track at the time with apple orchards on each side of us and many of the trees had been blasted by explosions.

When Corky was about ten paces ahead Rainer whispered to me, 'Quick, into this hedge and down.' He turned to the right where there was a gap, moving silently but rapidly. I followed him and Corky went on walking.

Rainer drew me to the ground. 'Corky has a knife in his hand,' he said.

'But why the hell . . .?'

I heard Corky run back down the path.

'Tom,' he shouted. 'Come away from him. He'll have you.'

I leaned forward in the ditch, pointed my rifle and took off the safety catch. It was already cocked and loaded. Rainer lay beside me, and I looked at him. Corky could be right, I thought.

Corky had gone to ground on the other side of the track about twenty feet away and I had his knee in my sights and if I pulled the trigger I'd put him out of action.

I gave the rifle to Rainer.

'He's in the hedge,' I said. 'Down there.'

'I'm coming out Corky,' I said, 'and I've left my rifle with the German.' I stepped out from behind the hedge and walked slowly up the track. Corky didn't move. Silly bugger. His arse was sticking up like a camel's hump; Runty would have hammered it black and blue. The buttons that should have connected his battledress blouse with his trousers were missing and I could even see his shirt below his big pack. I walked slowly forward, saw the end of his rifle waver.

'You must be out of your bloody mind,' he shouted, his voice muffled by the hedgerow.

'Come out of there, you silly prick,' I said. He got up, careful to use the shield I was providing.

'We're going to the paras,' I said, 'we're going to turn Rainer over to the paras. What they do with him is their business.'

I turned by head around. 'Come on, Rainer, you come out of there, too.' He sprang nimbly out of the hedgerow and walked towards where we were standing, holding the rifle in one hand. When he was about ten feet away I turned back to Corky and too late saw the gleam in his eye. He was holding his rifle in both hands and his knee came up and crashed between my legs. I felt a fierce red flash of agony run up into my stomach and bent over and tried to turn around. As I fell I grabbed at the butt of Corky's rifle, but the pain was too intense for me to move my hands forward quickly and I spun round as I went down and Corky started to squeeze his trigger, but the German must have fired one-handed from the hip and the shot hit Corky in the chest and his rifle exploded uselessly up into the air. He spiralled backwards and over with the impact of that shot at such a short range, dead before he hit the ground, and I hit the ground alongside him and felt the gravelly stones of the path smash my steel helmet backwards and scour my forehead. Rainer turned me over. He wiped my mouth with a hand-kerchief and unhooked my water bottle and poured a little of the whisky and tea onto my lips and wiped my face again. We sat for ten minutes, and didn't speak while the pain went from my balls.

'Come on, let's find the paras,' I said.

# 19

'What kind of a man are you?' Mary asked me. The dancing lesson had been going badly; she hadn't seemed to want to concentrate. I was feeling frustrated. I'd taught her the standard dances; the rumours of invasion were coming daily; I'd had a row that afternoon with Smithy who'd accused me, as he often did, of day dreaming and then made me look a charlie over a quick bit of 'gun stops'; I'd had a bad time at the weekend because I'd picked up a bird on the Saturday, promised to take her to a dance, but had let her down. When it came to it, I wasn't interested any more. I went to the dance on my own and she came in with a pal of Chalky's and made raspberries at me all evening, silly cow. When the time for the Tuesday lesson came, I found my best trousers had an oil stain on them, and was mad as hell.

I ought not to have taken it out on Mary Brassingham. None of it was her fault. I could see I was niggling at her, picking faults which normally I would have overlooked. It blew up when we were doing the sidewards chassis in the slow foxtrot and she picked her foot up because it was damned hard for her to slide her foot across in that movement. Normally I allowed for it when I did that step, but this time some devil in me made me push the step to its limit and my foot went under hers and she trod on my toe.

'There you go, clumsy again,' I said, and she said, 'I'm awfully sorry,' and maybe it was her accent that narked me but I flared up and said, 'It's no damn good being awfully sorry, you've got to learn to do it properly,' and she said in a voice that should have given me a clue, 'I will, I will. Give me time. Don't be so impatient.'

Like a fool I said, 'Well just how much time do you need,

clumsy?' She broke away from me with her eyes flaring, looking as if she could have strangled me, and that was when she said, 'Just what kind of a man are you, if you won't accept an apology?'

She turned and walked out of the room leaving me listening to Joe Loss. I said, 'Damn, damn, damn,' took off the needle, put the record in its sleeve on the top of the pile and thought to myself, You stupid bastard.

At that moment something important seemed to have gone out of my life and left a pretty big hole, and someone I'd been thinking of, perhaps, as a gentle kitten, had turned out to be a leopard with claws. The door opened again and I turned to it expectantly, but it was the major.

'Really put your foot in it this time, lad,' he said.

'I know, sir. I'm very sorry.'

'It's no good saying you're sorry to me. You have to make your peace with Mary, and that's not going to be easy. She may seem gentle, but once she's roused she's got the temper of a thoroughbred.' He chuckled and that helped a bit.

She was in the morning room. I went in with my knees shaking. I'd rather have faced the regimental sergeant major. She was sewing. She looked up at me and her eyes could have cut glass. 'Well?' she said. 'I thought you'd have been gone by now. I'm sure that girl of yours in the NAAFI doesn't pick up her feet.'

My dad always used to say to me, 'The ladies, God bless them, treat 'em right and you'll have them eating out of your hand.' My mam used to laugh at him because he always said that when he gave her the bottle of Mackeson's milk stout he sometimes brought her from the pub. I looked at Mary and wished I had a bottle of milk stout in my hand or even that I wasn't out of my depth and didn't know how to treat a lady right.

So I said, 'Look, I am a bad-tempered person to be teaching you anything and if you don't want to go on any more I understand, and I'm sorry, really more sorry than I can tell you, that I called you clumsy, because you're not

168

clumsy and considering the difficulty you have, honestly it's marvellous what you do, and I'm really sorry I said that.'

Her eyes were still icy, but she gave a smile and said, 'You don't need to say you're sorry three times. Once is quite sufficient.' Then she put down her sewing and said, 'I think it's time for supper.' I smiled, remembering what the major had said when he suggested I come into the morning room to make my peace, as he called it. Without knowing it he'd echoed the words of my father. 'You have to learn to be gentle with the ladies,' he said, 'and you'll find they'll be very gentle with you.'

We left the orchard field behind us and climbed a small hill. On the top was a German bunker. A parachute had been folded hastily and stuck in a niche in the stone wall.

The paratroops had been through the bunker with a flame-thrower and I didn't want to look at Rainer.

On the other side of the hill the field of battle was an arc in front of us and it seemed the Germans were holding the parachutists. I knew they couldn't hold them for very long because three more aeroplanes dropped their load of para-chutists overhead and a big bellied glider landed in a field and men poured from it and ran for cover.

The town we'd been told was Caen started on the extreme skyline and I knew that was a target for the paratroops. Other planes flying overhead were dropping heavy equipment and I even saw a jeep coming down under four enormous canopies. It hit the ground, bounced, and settled on its side. I saw the flashes of fire from German guns. The retaliation of the paratroops was quick and a group of them ran out of a wood through the fire and most of them made it to the jeep and turned it onto its wheels. One got into it while another filled it with petrol from a jerry can that had been strapped to the back. The jeep smoked when the engine fired but eight or nine paratroops hung on as the jeep raced across the field into the woods and was lost to sight.

A gun came down, awkwardly straddling the ditch of a

road, and men hauled it through the hedge and fired the first shot within a minute. Looking round I could see many such guns in operation pouring fire from close quarters into the German position and I could even see the Germans starting to back towards Caen and meeting the fire from the other paratroops. Canisters floated down and some broke on impact, but others were opened by the men in red berets who appeared from nowhere every time something landed. Below me at the foot of the small hill a long thin field was high with corn and a glider came down and started to land across the field, but the corn was false and full of spikes and the glider's nose crashed into the field. The glider was hit by an incendiary shell and burst into flames and no one came out of it. Another glider, which had been following closely behind and had been about to land, suddenly banked as the pilot tried to lift the nose and it went across the field at a crazy angle with the left wingtip scraping the ground and the wingtip must have caught one of the obstacles and the glider spun around like a crazy top and crashed. After a minute I saw the door open and five men came out. Two were limping badly. A third glider coming in to land was more lucky; the pilot managed to keep it level and must have pulled the nose up with superhuman effort and caught a rising thermal, like we used to do with kites, that brought him over the hill where we were squatting and carried him over a wood on the far side of the hill and we didn't see or hear him land.

Suddenly there was flurry in the air above us almost as if someone had shaken a giant tin of talcum powder into the sky above our heads, and hundreds of men were swinging on the end of their ropes in the sky about us and landing and rolling and bouncing down and rolling and tumbling forward and sidewards and backwards but always rolling and coming up. The ground all about us was covered by parachutists and mostly the men unclipped themselves and left the parachutes where they were and ran for cover, but some pulled their parachutes towards them and rolled them up and ran with them into the hedgebottom, and of all the men who landed I didn't see one who stayed on the ground.

It was three o'clock in the afternoon of D-Day, and a brilliant sun shone and we were in France in June and the air about us was heavy with the smell of crops, things growing, ripening, absorbing the sun. I was lying in a ditch with Rainer beside me and the nearest parachutist's position was only two hundred and fifty yards away, but I didn't stand up and show myself.

'What do I do?' I asked Rainer. 'You're the officer.'

'Leave me here,' he said, 'and find the nearest unit. Speak to the officer in charge and tell him where I am. Tell him I'm unarmed and want to be taken prisoner.'

'And if somebody stumbles on you while I'm away . . .'

'That is not your responsibility.'

I had a sudden thought. 'Officers carry pistols, not guns,' I said. He was wearing a leather belt and I could see where his holster should have been hanging from it. 'Where is your pistol?'

He looked at me and I knew he was wondering if he could or should lie to me. 'It's in my pack,' he said. 'A pistol is useless except at close range.' Now I knew why he'd been able to get Corky firing single-handed and from the hip. That was the way he'd trained to fire.

I didn't want to leave him. He *had* become my responsibility. He was an officer – the major all over again. The major had been like a father to me. The major had opened his home and his life, but more importantly his heart, to me, and in some curious way I felt that if I let this man be butchered I would be letting the major down. I would be denying everything the major had come to mean to me, the symbol of a new existence, a new life for myself. My dad would have understood. We lived the life of very ordinary people. We never had enough money to be able to forget the rules of survival. We'd never had enough money to be able to look at the life which exists outside the struggle for existence. My dad had gone to the public library, had borrowed books about all sorts of things and he had talked to me about them, and my mam had kept me more clean, more tidy, better nourished than any of the lads who went to school and to work with me. I knew damn well that we lived our life only just above the level of animals and the major's quiet reasoning and philosophy had opened a new world to me. I knew instinctively that Rainer was such a man and that the challenge of the war for me was not to turn my back on him, not to go forward to save my own skin, and leave him to be devoured.

'I'll be all right,' he said. I looked over that landscape and said, 'They're not taking prisoners. They haven't time to take prisoners. They can't cope with them.'

I was right of course. The battle for Caen was developing. Even I who knew nothing about warfare, any grand plan or master strategy, who didn't even know the names of any of the units involved, didn't even know what mob Rainer came from, could see the men below had only one purpose − to blast a way through that countryside and take that town. To do that I knew they would kill everyone in their path.

'Tell you something bloody silly,' I said. 'They told it to us before we left, but now I've forgotten it.'

'Forgotten what . . .?'

'The password. I don't know what the password is.'

Everyone below me was wearing either a red beret or a parachutist helmet. I was wearing a tin hat. I would stick out like a sore thumb. I could take a chance and go in there singing 'It's a Long Way to Tipperary' or shouting 'I'm English, don't shoot', but I'd have a German with me and he would be wearing a German uniform and even if he stripped to his underwear we'd still be taking a chance.

So I said, 'Come on, let's piss off out of here,' and he started to argue with me and I said, '*Come on*, let's piss off' and he could see his arguing would do no good; and I crawled back over and round the side of the bunker and I remembered everything Runty had ever taught me and my ass was never higher off the ground than a gnat's knackers and I kept watching the parachutists all the way in case they spotted us. Rainer too was crawling backwards and I saw

172

that he too was good and Runty would have approved of him because you could hardly see him move.

And that's when I crawled onto a landmine that had been put down to protect the bunker. The parachutists had missed it. I heard the sound first, a roaring sound as if someone had just opened the door of the furnace at the mill, and I saw the dust flecked with red that blew around my head and I felt the pain in my leg and the numbness that followed it. In the last moment of my consciousness I saw I had been pushed past where Rainer had been crawling and the blast had flattened him to the ground and my mind exploded and I saw again the patterns in that mirrored kaleidoscope of my childhood only this time the fragments were all blood red.

# 20

I was thinking about that song 'I'll see you again' and that night at the theatre with the major and Mary, when the nurse, Beth, came back into the room with tea and her private chocolate biscuits. She took a swab of what felt like cotton wool and wiped my eyes. That was the first I knew I had been crying lying there in that bed in the hospital.

Though no one had said anything directly to me I knew the next day they were going to operate and take off the remains of my left leg, the one you lead with when you're dancing, and the thought of dancing took me back to the nights I'd spent with Mary in the drawing room of the major's house, and especially the last days of that long summer when the newspapers were screaming for a Second Front.

After our row over me calling her clumsy, Mary had settled down again and we'd got on much better. I could feel the new strength in her. She was no longer the timid creature I'd always thought. I could see the strong relationship the two of them shared, each with an individual strength, each relying on the other but not dependent. And in a curious way I can't explain very well, I felt myself becoming a part of that arrangement, another leg of a tripod if you like. Once or twice, I even went to the house for supper on a night we didn't have a dancing class, and Runty pulled my leg and said I was hobnobbing with high society. Which, of course, I was, I suppose, since I was invited as myself and not as a dancing teacher.

When they finally put us on active service alert, the major took me into his study, and poured me a whisky.

'I want to tell you, Tom, how much it's meant to me and

Mary, you coming here like this to teach her dancing. And not only that; sharing our simple meals with us.'

I was mortally embarrassed. I mean, the thanks should have been coming from me. I'd begun to feel very bad each Thursday night when, regular as clockwork, he slipped an envelope into my hand with a pound in it. Damn it, he'd even been paying me the half a crown an hour during the time I'd been eating his food; but I didn't know how to refuse it without causing offence, and my dad had always said that was the worst thing you could do. So I said, 'It's been a great pleasure for me, sir, and I hope you're satisfied with the progress Mary has made,' and he said, 'My God, Tom, it's made a new gel of her,' and I said I was glad. Then he looked at me, stood up in front of the fireplace, looked at me as if he was guessing my weight. Assessing me for something, anyway.

'You have a lot of life ahead of you, Tom.'

I didn't know how to answer that.

'I get the feeling, Tom, you could do anything you wanted with your life. I feel that strength inside you.'

And again, what do you say?

'But you've got no sense of direction. Nobody's ever pointed you in a positive direction.'

Keep your nose clean, don't cause offence, stay out of trouble, these were the only pointers from my way of life. I knew they were all negative, but what the hell could I do about that? We are as we are made in my way of life. All right, I had ambition. I didn't intend ever to go back to the mill, for example. After the war, if I survived, I intended to better myself. He'd shown me that other ways of life existed, other standards of value. Of course, I'd never see the inside of the Savoy again, but there had to be something somewhere I could reach. And certainly, he'd fired me with the desire to do that.

'I don't rightly know how to say this, sir, but the best part of coming here for me has been the chance I've had to see the way life can be, if you know what I mean. And that's

175

given me an ambition to make a bit of something of myself if I can.'

'Good man, good man,' he said. His face wrinkled with real pleasure. 'Let me put you in for War Office Selection Board,' he said, rushing ahead. 'I'll take you off the battalion strength and you can join the cadre here until they make up their minds whether they want you at Officer Cadet Training Unit or not. How does that sound?'

It sounded marvellous and lousy, all at the same time. It sounded marvellous because of course I didn't want to go and be part of the Invasion. I was shit scared to start with. Being on the cadre would mean no guard duties; they'd probably make me up to lance corporal and I'd teach something, probably shooting which I loved. Later, if they accepted me, I'd go and train to be an officer. Me, an officer? Mam would bust a gut rushing to the darts club.

But then I could see the look on Runty's face, and Cutler, and possibly even the sergeant major, when they knew I'd fiddled my way off the draft, using the major. And I *would* be using him, wouldn't I? Using him to my personal advantage. I'd been two years with them, and with Chalky and Hargreaves and all the rest, and those two years of being together had to mean something. That long summer together had to have a purpose – not just to enable me to piss off when things started to get rough, but perhaps to teach me to take whatever was coming with the rest of them. Because if I ran away from that, half of me said I would never have a chance of being anything. If I let the major talk me into staying, then all I would become would be an improved version of what I already was, whereas if I stuck it out with the lads, then maybe I could even hope to become somebody else entirely. In practical terms, accepting the draft to go with the lads to the Invasion would make a new man of me. And somewhere inside, I wanted to try to be that new man, not just a different shade of the old one. Not just to repeat the pattern that had been formed somewhere back in the days of my great-great-grandparents, but to break the line, and start again.

When I looked at the major's happy face, and him going on about the WOSB and the OCTU, I knew I couldn't accept. I couldn't do it this way. 'No, sir,' I said, 'I don't want to do it that way. I want to stay with the section until this lot's over. Then I'd like to try to make something of myself.'

His face saddened. He sat down, thinking about it, trying to understand my point of view. But I don't think he could. He had nothing to go by. He'd offered me his help to improve my situation in life and I'd turned it down. He was too much a gentleman to argue, but all the same I'd turned him down.

When Mary came into the room she looked at her father first in an enquiring sort of way, and I knew she'd deliberately stayed out of the room while her father had talked to me, and I realized she was a party to it, but still I didn't cotton on to why. Or if I did, I wouldn't accept it.

'You're going away!' she said. Her voice was light, but I could feel the intensity in it. I know now that at that moment she wanted me to say, wanted her father to say, 'No, that's all been changed.' But neither of us could.

'Yes, I'm going with the battalion.'

She was wearing a dress I hadn't seen before, and she'd done her hair differently, and was wearing a strong perfume, and her father got up and excused himself and went out of the room without looking back, and though he hadn't used any words, I knew he'd said his goodbye to me. As an individual. From now on, I was 4732849 Private Wilkins, T., and I was in Number 1 Platoon of Number 3 Company of the First Battalion, and I was being posted.

She poured a glass of dry sherry for herself. Then sat in the chair her father had occupied. 'We shall miss you,' she said.

'I shall miss you, too.'

'You *two*, or you, *too*?'

'You two also.' I thought she was making fun of the way I

177

speak, of my strong Yorkshire accent which I'd always tried to hide but which comes out sometimes. Of course, I don't say 'tha' and 'thee' but you couldn't mistake where I come from. And she had such a pure and refined voice. 'I hope you'll go on with your dancing,' I said.

'It would be a pity to waste all those lessons.'

'Yes, it would.'

'Not to take advantage of all you've taught me.'

'I suppose it would.'

She couldn't let it be, sat worrying at it like a bone. 'Did my father say anything to you about War Office Selection Board?'

'Yes, we talked about it.'

'You didn't care for the idea?'

'It would be a good chance for somebody like me.'

'Somebody *like* you? What does that mean. You shouldn't put yourself down in that way, and you do, you know, all the time. Just because your people were in poor circumstances. I think it's marvellous what you've done, with yourself I mean . . .' There, it was out, it was said.

'I'll bet none of your friends is a private.'

'You're impossible,' she said. She got up from the chair and came rapidly and sat on the arm of my chair, and she reached out her hand and touched my face. 'Friends? Do you mean boyfriends? I don't have any boyfriends. I know, oh Lord, umpteen eligible young men, but you couldn't call them boyfriends.'

There was a card on the mantelpiece. I'd looked at it while I'd been waiting for the major to pour my drink. It was an invitation to a Regimental Ball. The Hussars. Captain Sir Roger Smythe requests the honour of Miss Mary Brassingham . . . A boyfriend?

She bent down and kissed me on the lips. I was too surprised to respond. When she withdrew her face from mine she looked at me anxiously. On impulse I reached my head forward and my lips met hers and I kissed her, chastely, lips together. Her lips were moist, mine felt dry

178

as kippers. She slid off the arm of the chair and sat in my lap, awkwardly, crushing the coins in my trouser pocket against my parts. I reached up my arm and tried to put it round her but her breast was in the way and to circle her body would have meant me touching her breast and I daren't do it. Me the gay Lothario of every ballroom, scared to touch a girl's breast in case I should offend her. So I put my arm round the outside of her arm trying to get it round her body to embrace her. I hadn't realized she was supporting herself on that arm against the arm of the chair, and I tightened and she fell away from me clumsily and her lips left mine, and it was awful. I tried to bend my neck forward to kiss her again, but I couldn't get my head low enough and she was struggling to get up and her forehead crashed hard against my nose and brought tears to my eyes.

She burst out laughing, a nervous tittering laugh, and looked up at me, and I felt the coins nipping my balls, and the tears in my eyes from the bang on my nose and needing to use my handkerchief, but not daring to pull it out even if I could get at it because I wasn't too sure if I'd got a clean one with me; and, oh bugger it, I heaved myself up out of the chair and went to the fireplace and got out my hankie where she couldn't see it and I was glad she couldn't see it because it was filthy, but I used a corner of it to dab the tears from my eyes and blew my nose and when I turned round she was sitting upright in the chair, looking for all the world as if she'd never moved.

She reached out to the table at the side of the chair and picked up a small black box and opened it, and offered it to me. 'Father and I wanted to give you a present,' she said. 'It might as well be a going away present.' And it was a silver chain, and on it a disc with my name and number. 'It's to hang your identity discs on. If you'll give them to me I'll put them on for you.'

'I can do it,' I said. My discs were hanging on a piece of very sweaty string. I unclipped the collar of my battle dress tunic and reached inside and took out the discs. I undid the knot on the string while she watched and then handed the discs to her. She slipped them onto the chain, then showed me how to unfasten the clasp and fasten it. I put them round my neck and let them hang out, not wanting to get any closer because it had all gone so wrong the last time.

'Thank you very much,' I said, touched by the gift. I turned the disc over and looked at it. On the back was engaved a dancing couple. When she saw me looking at it, she smiled.

'A little personal touch from me,' she said.

'They dance well together.'

'So do we.'

'When I stop bullying you.'

'That's all part of learning.'

'I've been a bit severe sometimes.'

'Only when you had to be.'

'Mary . . . I've really enjoyed myself, with you and the dancing.'

'With me, *and* the dancing?'

'You know what I mean.'

'Yes, I know.' She looked at me for a long time, but I, who'd talked my way into and out of a hundred pairs of of arms, could find nothing to say, no way of crossing this barrier I'd put between us.

'When do you actually go?' she asked.

'We're not allowed out after tonight. They say we'll get a forty-eight sometime but they can't say when.'

'Do you know where you go?'

'No. That's secret.'

'Father will know . . .'

'I wouldn't ask him. It wouldn't be right.'

'Where will you go for your forty-eight?'

'I don't know yet.'

'Will you go home to see your mother?'

'It would take too long to get there. Anyway, it would

only upset her to have me home for such a short time.'

She coloured slightly. 'I could meet you somewhere, if you wanted. London, or somewhere in the country.'

I was amazed. Nobody had ever invited *me* before. Certainly not to spend a forty-eight with them. For a moment I was tempted. What a wonderful thing to hold such a girl in my arms, and not for dancing, but for loving and being with and understanding.

'I'm afraid I promised a couple of the boys I'd spend the last leave with them,' I said. It sounded lame even to me and her face blanched as if I'd struck her, and she tucked her bad leg back behind the other as if that most probably was the real reason, and I wanted to tell her the reason wasn't to do with anything being lacking in her, but in me. Anyway, I probably didn't have the money. What does it cost to stay in a hotel? Two of you? Must cost a bomb. And I didn't have any money and they didn't give you extra pay when you went on a forty-eight.

So I said what I did about having promised the boys, and as soon as I could I got up to go.

And that was the last time I saw Mary Brassingham.

# 21

They brought me some lunch, Beth and two men. It was bread, soaked in hot milk, and a cup of what tasted like Oxo. Tea with it. Beth took the tray off the trolley the men were wheeling around, thanked them, and placed it on a table she'd trundled across my bed. She sat on the bed beside me to feed me.

'I could help myself,' I said, but she said, 'Don't be grumpy,' and so I let her feed me like I was a baby.

When I knew she didn't want me to pick up the cup and feed myself I brought my hand off the edge of the bed-table and went to let it lie on the bed, but it touched her leg above the knee, well, her uniform, and I took it away as if it had been scalded, but she gave that laugh and put it back there, and I could feel her warm beneath my hand.

When she'd fed me, she wiped my face, first with a dry cloth, and then with a face flannel that smelled of toilet water, nice and fresh, like the witch hazel my mam used to buy in twopenny bottles from the greengrocer's shop and dab her forehead with. And sometimes I'd sneak a bit and rub it on my hands because it smelled nice.

'You're very good to me,' I said. 'Are you like this with all the patients? Or just the handsome ones . . .'

She laughed. My type of girl. I could chat her very easily. I bet, if I'd wanted, I could have had her in that bed beside me.

'Only the handsome ones,' she said.

'Don't let them make any mistakes tomorrow. Don't let them take the wrong thing off.'

'Oh, I wouldn't let them do that. And I have news for you. You've got a visitor. I'll give you your bath after he's gone.'

'Promise . . .?'

She let her fingers briefly touch my lips. 'Yes,' she said, 'I promise. Now, let's get you sorted out.' She lifted my head from the pillow and I could sense her breasts in front of my lips, and she plumped my pillow, and straightened the sheet, and I felt sorted out.

'I would have brought you some grapes,' Runty said, 'but the dog ate 'em. I suppose you're going to tell me not to get him all excited,' he said.

Beth laughed. 'He's excited enough,' she said, 'just having a visitor.'

Runty. I could hardly believe my ears. 'Runty,' I said. 'I thought you were dead.'

'That's a bloody cheerful way to be greeted.'

'But I saw them, I saw them shoot you and the other two lads and you went down and you were dead.'

'Well if I'm dead and a bloody ghost,' he said, 'there's a certain bird in the NAAFI who's going to get a shock tonight.'

I laughed out loud. 'Oh you immortal bastard,' I said. Like all the others he put his hand on my cheek.

'It'd take more than a German bullet to get old Runty,' he said. 'But I see from all these bandages you've been biting your toenails again. I've had a hell of a job to find you.'

'Thanks for looking.'

'I had to find you. Remember, I lent you half a quid that night before we sailed. You never gave it back to me.'

I reached up my hand and grabbed his and we had a long silent moment together. 'Why don't you take the weight off your feet?'

He scraped a chair across the linoleum and sat down beside the bed. 'I'm too bloody low sitting down here,' he said, and must have got a stool or something. 'That's better.' I put out my hand and he found it with his and squeezed it. 'How have you been, then, you young bugger?'

183

'Have they confirmed you as sergeant?'

'Have they bollocks.'

'Oh, I'm sorry. Dropped you back to corporal, eh?'

'No, the bleeders haven't. They've made me up to sergeant major, that's what they've done, and they've given me the bloody Military Medal.'

'What for?'

'I got fed up. Of looking at that bloody gun. So I dropped a couple of grenades in through the slit.'

'I never knew you throw a grenade close enough to hit anything . . .'

'I didn't throw it. Bloody well crawled up there, didn't I, and dropped a couple through. Piece of cake.'

Piece of cake . . . Dammit, I'd seen that ground. Nobody could 'crawl' up there and not be seen, and fired at.

'You ran up there?'

'Sort of. Anyway, enough of that bugger. That's all done with, isn't it. We got rid of the gun, and that was all that was needed. And they brought a landing craft to the shore and we put the wounded on board, and came back to Blighty.'

'And you came with them?'

'Had to, hadn't I? Like a pepper pot by the time they'd finished with me. But nothing damaged.'

'And the rest of 'em. The sergeant major . . .?'

'All gone – the sergeant major, Chalky, Cutler, Lieutenant Soames. There was only twelve of us on that landing craft when it came back. That was all a big mistake, that bloody beach,' he said. 'They ought to castrate that bugger in the navy who was supposed to be directing the fire. For a start off, we ought never to have gone in until they'd pounded that effing pillbox flat as Morecambe Sands. They could have done it from two miles away, with Lieutenant Soames telling 'em where the shots went. We ought never to have got out of that landing craft until the guns on that pillbox had been stopped. But that's the way with the military mind and the infantry. Send the foot soldiers in, let them do the cleaning

184

up. Well, we cleaned up all right. Twelve men left out of the entire company, and the company commander never even set foot ashore. And when the bloody guns were knocked out, what then? The beach was useless, wasn't it? They couldn't land men there, couldn't land supplies there. I heard they're using it as a parking place and repair shop for small boats. Makes you puke, doesn't it.'

But then he fell silent, no doubt looking at me and thinking. Because they hadn't finished with me, yet. And all to make a parking place for small boats.

'You made a big mistake, lad,' he said, and his voice was very kindly, but full of regret. 'You forgot the one thing I tried to drum into you, over and over again. Look out for number one. We were all right, you and me, behind that gully. We were all right so long as we kept our heads down, and only moved when they'd switched the gun. You shouldn't have pissed about looking for that mortar, or running to help the sergeant major. Old Arthur was all right. Even if he wasn't, there was nothing you could do to help him. And then, on the road you ought to have stayed with me, instead of pissing about looking for the paras.'

'I got caught up in it all.'

'I know you did. I've seen it so many times. Lads who are normally sensible. Once the bullets start to fly they lose all sense. They want to become heroes, for King and fucking country. Well, let me tell you this, although it's too late now to start preaching, and I'm not a religious man as you know, but somebody makes us, and does a bloody good job of it, and it was not intended that we should throw it all away for somebody else. We're all made one at a time. We're not made in sections, or platoons, or companies. We're made one at a time, and that's the way we've got to live. Number fucking one.'

It was the longest speech I'd ever heard Runty make, except when he was talking to us on training. He reached out again and held my hand. 'But it's too late to be telling you that now, old lad, isn't it?'

185

'I suppose it is.'

He was quiet for a moment, his hand holding mine. Then he gave a bit of a cough. 'I've got a place,' he said. 'Not much. In Castleford, in Yorkshire. Belonged to my uncle and auntie. Well, they've both popped off at last, and left it to me. I used to go up there sometimes for holidays. It backs on to a farm, real nice. There's a room you can have. I thought I might go live there when this lot's over. Keep a few chickens, something like that. Get a job, local. Not down the mines. I'd look after you. They're bound to give you a bit of a pension, for baccy money and a pint or two.'

I was that choked I couldn't talk. Not right then. The tears must have started again, running down my cheeks, and I felt him scrubbing at them with his hankie. But then he found the cotton wool and he patted them and leaned close to me and I could smell the half pint of beer he'd had before he came, but I didn't blame him for that.

'That nurse,' he said. 'That nurse looking after you. By God.'

I gripped his hand, tight. 'Thanks for the offer of the house. I might take you up on that.'

'I should bloody well hope so, too,' he said, and more than anything else I was warmed by knowing he meant it.

'I'll tell you one thing,' he said, 'might make you feel better. They had a bit of a tunnel leading to that bunker where they had them guns. When we got in there, there were three stiffs in the place behind the bunker. You must have got them. That's your score, that is.'

And then I told Runty about Rainer and Corky and the paras and the landmine and he listened in silence till I'd finished and this time he didn't reprimand me and I knew he understood about Rainer and the major and all those things we'd never been able to talk about, him and me, like wanting to get out of the mines and the mills and starting a new life that had a bit of something in it other than working to earn enough money to live on, and I thought of my dad with his library books and Runty's dad with his

**186**

pigeons and so I told him something I hadn't told anybody else.

I recovered consciousness for a while after that mine exploded, and though the lower part of my body felt numb and I couldn't see I felt Rainer's hands, and they were the first of many hands I was to feel on my face, and I felt his handkerchief wiping my face again and he said, 'You'll be all right, Tom, I'll go and get the paras for you,' and I heard the scratch of a piece of paper and felt it being thrust into my battledress pocket and I heard him get up and start to shout, 'Here, wounded Englishman, here, here,' and then I heard the ratatatat of a parachutist's fire before I lost consciousness again.

I'd kept that note all this time, the note he'd stuck in my pocket, and now I felt in the drawer beside my bed and Runty said, 'Here, let me get it for you,' and I said, 'No,' and got it out and gave it to Runty and said, 'Read it to me.' There was a silence.

'It says "thank you",' Runty said, 'and it's signed by someone called Rainer von Bachenhausen. Does that make sense to you?'

'Yes,' I said, 'it makes a lot of sense to me.'

Runty went shortly afterwards, and I lay back listening to the music on the headphones.

Beth came back in, gave me the bath, but that was all. We talked all the time, but it wasn't like it had been before. Somehow she knew, I suppose, that my mood had changed, or maybe Runty had taken her into a linen closet on his way out. I wouldn't put it past him.

When Mary Brassingham came, I knew it was her as soon as the door opened and closed again. She stood there, and when she walked across the floor I heard her limp, slow quick, slow quick, slow quick. Before I could make any stupid remarks or protests, she bent over and kissed me and this time neither my lips nor hers were dry and our noses didn't get in the way, and this time there was no pain, no awkwardness, no misunderstanding.

187

'I've been invited to live in Castleford,' I said, 'nice house near a farm. Runty's going to keep chickens.'

'If that's what you want.'

'It's not if it's what *I* want, it's what *we* want.'

'You're sure?'

'Yes, I'm sure.'

Of course there was a lot to be talked about, a lot of understanding to be done. But I could learn. They had special schools, didn't they, to teach people.

'We could live with my father,' she said.

'Let's try it with Runty first of all. You understand? Not that I don't like your father because I do. But first of all, I want to learn a few things on my own, and then later, perhaps, your father can really help me.'

'And you won't be proud or foolish?'

'Of course I will. I'll be proud and foolish, and happy and sad, and irritable and moody, but I'll be alive and we'll be together and that's what counts.'

She'd written me a letter. I got it the night before we embarked for France. It crossed a letter I'd written to her.

Her letter said, 'I don't know how to tell you this, but while you've been teaching me to dance I've been falling in love with you,' and my letter to her had said, 'I don't know how to tell you this, but while I've been teaching you to dance, I've been falling in love with you . . .'

Mary's gone now. Beth's been in and sorted me out again, and the bed feels cool and comfortable. Beth has a wristwatch, not a stop-watch. No more dancing for a while, because tomorrow they're going to take off my leg. Beth says it's amazing what you can learn to do on a tin leg and there's even a man who flies an aeroplane with two of them.

I'm writing this on a pad, and if I hold the pad with my left hand, as I've learned to do, I can guide my right hand across the page, and Beth says it's easy to read.

I've got used to being blind

Sailor Moon® the novel #2

THE POWER OF LOVE

D1360598

Written by
Stuart J. Levy
and
Lianne Sentar

Created by
NAOKO TAKEUCHI

=) SMILE books

Published by Mixx Entertainment, Inc.
Los Angeles · Tokyo
www.mixxonline.com

RL 4, 008-012

Mixx Entertainment presents
Sailor Moon the novel #2 · *The Power of Love*
Published on the SMILE Books imprint
ISBN: 1-892-21313-3

Printed in the United States

First printing July 1999

10  9  8  7  6  5  4  3

Mixx products are available online at:

## www.tokyopop.com

or ask for them at your local retailer.

# Chapter 1
# Weight Up

Soft white bubbles floated from left to right, then back again.  The warm water lapped up and down the ceramic tile, the bubbles flowing over the edge of the tub.

"Ahhhh," Serena Tsukino sighed, completely relaxed.

There was nothing like a bubble bath after a long, hard Sunday, Serena thought.  Of course, her entire day consisted of three naps, three complete meals plus three major snacks, a good hour or two of PlayStation, and a bit of chatting on the Net.  Still, oh how good it felt to kick back in a luxurious bath of eucalyptus, peppermint and Siberian pine bath crystals.

"Luna, you don't know what you're missing," Serena yelled out, teasing.

Like any cat, Luna stayed as far away from water as she could. Serena could see Luna stretching her little black body in the bedroom. Approaching the doorway to the bathroom, Luna sat down and stared at Serena.

"If you keep soaking your body for so long like that, you're going to end up looking like a prune," little Luna scolded.

Serena stuck out her tongue at Luna, although she couldn't cover up a big smile. Sometimes it just cracked her up to see Luna, this little black cat, talking like a person. Sure, Luna wasn't an average cat, and since Serena had first met Luna, her experiences fighting evil as Sailor Moon gave her a new perspective. Even so, it was cute seeing the little furry feline chattering away.

"You're just a big baby, scared of the water and all." Serena flicked a few drops of water towards Luna, who promptly jumped back to dodge getting wet.

## the power of love

Getting out of the tub, Serena threw a towel over her soaking wet body. As she walked over to the mirror, the sound of water dripping in the tub echoed throughout the bathroom.

"Agggggghhh!" Serena screamed at the top of her lungs.

Luna dashed into the bathroom, and Serena's entire family ran to her bedroom, worried. Clutching her towel, Serena turned towards Luna, her eyes bloodshot red.

"Luna!" Serena struggled with tears as she caught her breath from the shock. "I'm getting fat!!!"

Luna stopped dead in her tracks. "That's it?"

"What do you mean, 'That's it?'!" Serena cried, desperate in her panic. "This is a major deal!"

Serena's parents came rushing in the room with her little brother Sammy.

"Serena, you're going to give Mom and Dad a heart attack!" Sammy yelled, seeing that Serena was perfectly fine.

"What's wrong, honey?" Kind as always,

Serena's dad looked concerned.

"Daddy—" Serena begged for some sympathy. "Look how fat I'm getting!"

"Honey, being fat isn't a bad thing," her dad responded. That was not quite the sympathy Serena was hoping for.

"Daddy, how can I become popular and," Serena paused, "get boys to like me if I'm fat?"

Serena felt a little guilty about ragging so hard on being fat. After all, some girls were fat, but were still popular, funny and had lots of friends. So, it wasn't being fat that was a bad thing. It was *Serena* being fat that was a bad thing. Being fat just wouldn't look right on her, Serena reasoned.

"That's what you get for pigging out all the time!" Sammy stuck his thumbs in his ears and waved his hands back and forth, teasing Serena.

"Shut up, you jerk!" Serena snapped at him.

"Sammy has a point." This time it was Serena's mother. "After all, you don't exercise and you eat between meals. Not to mention the fact that you never do your homework."

"Mom, what does not doing my homework have to do with getting fat?"

4

# the power of love

"See, you don't even realize it, do you?" Serena's mom scolded. "If you were doing your homework like you should every day, you wouldn't be spending so much time in the kitchen raiding the refrigerator."

That was it, Serena decided. She wasn't going to put up with this any longer. It was time she did something about her weight problem so no one could tease her anymore. That meant only one thing, spelled with four little letters.

D...I...E...T...

Serena would show everyone!

At school the following day, Serena barely made it to fourth period. Feeling weak, she put her head on her desk and prayed for class to end. Having skipped breakfast and her usual snack at recess, Serena's stomach was rumbling like thunder.

The bell rang, and everyone stormed out of the classroom for lunch. Only Serena did not budge.

"Come on, Serena!" Molly Brown noticed her blond friend slumped over in her seat. "Are you feeling sick?"

Serena just stared at Molly's moving lips. Her energy level was too low to even respond.

"Serena, what's wrong with you?!"

"Molly..." Serena struggled to get up, but was somehow able to lift her body from the desk. "I...need...food..."

"Serena, it's lunch time," Molly said, reassuringly. "If it's just food you want, no need to stress. Let's go!"

"Molly, you don't understand." Serena struggled up and made her way outside with Molly at her side. "I can't eat. If I don't starve myself, I'll never lose weight."

"You...on a diet?!" Molly had to hold her side from laughing so hard.

"What's so funny?" Serena protested.

"Serena, you're the grub queen," Molly said, shaking her head. "You on a diet is just wrong."

Serena could hear Molly's words, but nothing was computing in her brain. All she could do was home in on the food being eaten all around her. Joe Pestone was in the corner with his buddies Bill and Zach, all three of them munching on

## the power of love

Burger King take-out. Jill, Tina, and June were in the middle of the courtyard eating home-made sandwiches. Just then, Serena started to smell the most delicious aroma in the world.

"Hey Serena!"

The voice called out from behind her. Serena spun around to see Melvin holding a plate of sushi up to her face.

"Here, have some." Melvin offered her the entire plate of succulent California rolls. "I brought way too much for just me."

Serena felt her jaw drop down to the floor. Her saliva started drooling out of the corner of her mouth. She could not take her eyes of the gleaming white rice and shredded crab. Sushi was her favorite! Sure, it was one of the most expensive meals around, but that only made it more romantic. Her dream date was a fashionable, charming stud taking her to the most intimate sushi bar in town.

"Serena, don't do it!" Kim Matthews was yelling for Serena to stop while shaking her by the shoulders. "Molly just told me you're starving yourself to lose weight. You've got to stop. I went through this anorexic period last year, and it almost killed me."

"Kim's right, Serena," Molly agreed. "There are much healthier ways to lose weight."

"Really?" Serena was easily convinced. Snatching the plate of sushi up from Melvin's outstretched arms, Serena started gobbling down the fancy fish treats. With her mouth full of rice, Serena looked over at Molly. "What...other... ways?"

"First of all, they say that exercise is key," Molly explained.

"It's true," Kim chimed in. "A properly balanced diet with regular exercise is the best way to lose weight."

Wishing Serena luck, Kim excused herself since she had to meet another friend in the library. The girls waved goodbye to Kim and carried on their conversation.

"Actually, have you noticed Miss Haruna?" Molly asked, referring to their homeroom teacher, Patricia Haruna. "She's been on a new health kick and lost like 15 pounds in less than a week."

"Really?" Serena asked, surprised. "I didn't

# the power of love

notice."

"Look here." Melvin pulled out two Polaroid photos of Miss Haruna. "The one on the left here is Miss Haruna when she first joined her new club. This one on the right is what she looked like four days after joining. Amazing, isn't it?"

Serena could not believe it. How could Miss Haruna lose so much weight in less than a week? Was it some special diet that her new club had her on? Or was it just because she was exercising? Either way, Serena had to join this club. If starving herself was not the answer, this club was the key to losing weight.

"Melvin, did you take those photos?" Serena asked, hoping to find out the club's location.

"Yeah, Melvin," Molly joined in. "What are you doing with photos of Miss Haruna in her aerobics outfit?!"

Serena sensed Molly's accusatory tone and knew Molly was ready for a classic nerd-roasting session.

"Don't you know that's a crime—invading privacy?" Molly started to turn up the heat.

"And just think," Serena couldn't help it. "She's your teacher! You'd probably get suspended if Donan the Dreaded knew." Everyone at Crossroads called their principal "Donan the Dreaded" because Principal Donan was so mean.

"Come on you guys," Melvin pleaded. "It wasn't like that." The school's biggest geek started to back away from the tormenting girls.

"Let us have those photos," Molly insisted, closing in on him.

"Hand them here, Melvin." Serena moved in on the left, with Molly on the right.

"Please," Melvin begged. "Leave me alone!"

Ducking in between Serena and Molly, Melvin dodged the girls and ran past the courtyard. The girls wasted no time in pursuit.

"Get back here, you little dweeb," Serena called out, while Molly giggled.

Little Melvin proved no match for the girls, and his lack of athletic ability left him collapsed on the ground near the gym. Panting, Melvin looked up in protest.

"OK, you can have the photos," Melvin

cried. "But please don't hand me over to Donan the Dreaded."

Molly snatched up the photos, and Serena leaned down next to Melvin's face, so close she could easily touch Melvin's nose. Pointing her index finger right in front of Melvin's eyes, Serena played the part of the ruthless private investigator.

"It's time for you to cough up some info, loser," Serena feigned an Italian accent. "Where's this so-called club where you shot your peeping Tom photos?"

Trapped, Melvin had no choice but to spill the beans. Melvin told the girls how he followed Miss Haruna after school, and watched her go into the fitness club named the "Shape Salon." With a contented smile on her face, Serena turned to Molly and continued her Italian undercover routine.

"Molly, baby, forget about this loser." Serena's voice was husky Pacino. "It's time for a rendezvous at the Shape Salon."

# Chapter 2
# Shape Salon

After school, Kim, Serena, Molly and Lisa Brownridge gathered outside the three-story, round building made with sheer glass windows. From the street, the girls could see rows of fitness equipment. The glass was mainly reflective, so the equipment was barely visible, but it seemed that the club was crowded with people working out.

"Well, let's give it a shot," said Kim, looking over at her friends.

"It can't be any worse than not eating." Serena shuddered at the memory of that morning, and the girls entered the lobby.

## the power of love

On a huge video screen hanging from the ceiling in the lobby, a beautiful model clutched a towel and smiled.

"Girls, welcome to the Shape Salon!" The model's voice blared out of the video screen, as if someone knew the four girls had just walked in.

"Hey, look, you guys," Molly squealed, excited. "It's Pamela Ooh Sanderson from Bayswatch. She's talking to us!"

"In just one day," the model explained, "you can lose two pounds. In two days, you can lose eight pounds, and after three days, you can look gorgeous, like me!"

"Guys, I bet this place is totally pricey," Lisa commented, worried.

"Yeah, but no price is too high to become drop-dead gorgeous," Serena reasoned.

"I've spent too much money on clothes lately, though," Lisa explained.

"Good point," the other girls agreed.

"Best of all," the model continued. "This month's special campaign means you can join now for a free trial. There's no excuse not to become drop-dead gorgeous."

"It's like Pamela Ooh is reading our minds," Molly said.

"Yeah, it's a no-brainer now," Serena agreed. "Where do we sign up?"

The girls wandered over to the reception desk and rang the bell. Out came a tall, blond instructor, with tanned skin and very defined muscles. Gaga over the stud-muffin, Serena and her friends tried hard to contain themselves. If this is what losing weight was all about, Serena thought, she'd start shedding pounds like a snake sheds its skin.

"You're here for the free trial, right?" The blond instructor showed teeth so white they sparkled. "My name's Jed. Pleasure to meet you."

"Hi Jed," the girls recited, swooning.

"Come with me, and I'll give you the special VIP tour."

"Wow, he's treating us like VIPs," Molly whispered to Serena, giggling.

"Maybe all the instructors look like him," Kim added hopefully.

Jed, with his totally cut body, showed off brand-new exercise bikes, rowing machines, stairclimbers, and bizarre combo machines only found on late-night infomercials. In the back were pools, lockers, changing rooms, and the full-on steam room and Jacuzzi set. Besides the machines, there were racquetball courts, an aerobics studio, a juice bar, and a relaxation room with yoga and meditation classes.

"This place is amazing," commented Lisa, visibly impressed.

"Girls, I can tell you are some of the elite in Crossroads," Jed cooed. "The Space Salon features the most modern fitness equipment available today. I *know* we will be able to satisfy your discriminating tastes. However, I must warn you about one thing."

The girls looked at Jed's tanned body, wondering what he was about to say.

"Losing weight is something you must be completely committed to," Jed warned. "Not only do I want to see you here everyday, I want you to give yourselves completely to the process. Capiche?"

"Capiche," everyone except Serena yelled out, nodding earnestly. When they noticed Serena looked puzzled, they turned to face her.

Serena looked around. "Uh," she said, her face reddening. "Isn't Capiche that little Italian restaurant over near the Crossroads Mall?"

Molly, Lisa, and Kim exchanged glances and started busting up.

"Serena, *capiche* means *got it* in Italian," Molly explained, in between laughs. The blond god Jed just shook his head in disgust, while Serena slinked back, embarrassed.

After changing into their workout clothes, the four girls walked out into the main exercise room and looked around at the sophisticated fitness apparatus.

"Good thing I brought my Dolce & Gabbana lycra fitness clothes with me," Molly said, with a sense of relief.

"You're always so prepared." Serena was amazed that Molly always seemed to know what to do.

The girls split up and headed towards different areas of the work-out room. While Kim and Lisa hopped on exercise bikes, Molly gave the rowing machine a shot.

Serena walked over to the stair-climbing machine and inspected it. She had seen stair-climbing machines on TV before, but how in the world did they work? Serena stepped on one of the stairs carefully and stood up. Suddenly, the stair started dropping down, and Serena completely lost her balance.

"Help!" she yelled, as she fell off of the stair-climber onto the ground. "This thing's *dangerous*." Serena was really worried about messing up her clothes. She didn't have the beautiful Dolce & Gabbana that Molly was wearing, but her CK out-fit certainly wasn't worth ruining.

"Do you need some help there, honey?"

Serena looked up and saw Jed offering his hand to help her up. She blushed and took it. "Thanks. I'm not really used to exercising."

"That's okay," Jed said, reassuringly. "I'll help you out. Just step on the bottom stair here, and when you're balanced step up on top and keep repeating the pattern like you're walking up stairs."

Serena followed the blond hunk's instructions to a T and was soon climbing up stairs like a fireman in a burning office building. What a stupid exercise, Serena thought. After all, if she needed to go up, she would just take the elevator. What was the point of climbing all those stairs and stepping off exactly where she started?

After what seemed like four hours, Serena's body would not budge. She pressed the stop button and carefully exited the nasty machine. Looking at her watch, Serena realized that she had only been stair-climbing for five minutes! Losing weight was *really* a pain.

After all that work (even though it was only five minutes), Serena decided to reward herself with a dip in the Jacuzzi. Throwing her exercise clothes into the locker, Serena headed towards the ladies-only steam room.

In the main exercise room, Molly was taking a break from the rowing machine when the blond instructor Jed strolled by.

"Hey, you!" Jed snarled at Molly. "You can't afford to take a rest. Don't you want to become drop-dead gorgeous? After all, you're pretty cute, so if you try hard enough, I know you can do it."

Molly turned crimson red. "Do you really think so?"

"I know it," Jed reassured her, resting his muscle-laden arm on Molly's shoulder.

"You're right." Molly planted herself on the rowing machine again. "I can't give up until I'm drop-dead gorgeous."

"Good girl." Jed walked away, smiling to himself.

After about a half-hour of intense exercise, Molly's face turned completely pale, and she leaned off the rowing machine and literally dropped on the floor. Kim and Lisa stumbled up to her, both of their faces the same pale shade, and collapsed on the floor next to Molly.

Jed came strolling up to the exhausted girls. "You all worked so hard today, I have a special treat for you."

The three girls looked up at Jed, weak but interested.

"Usually this costs extra, but since this is our special campaign week, and you worked so hard today, there's no charge." Jed led the three lifeless girls by the hand to the tanning beds. "This is our special Shape Sun Salon. These aren't just regular tanning beds. The UV rays are treated to remove extra lipids from your body, so that you go home even thinner."

Molly looked at Kim and Lisa with an excited expression on her face. "This is what Miss Haruna must have used to lose so much weight in less than a week."

"These little pod-like capsules look kind of freaky to me, but if they help me lose a few extra pounds, I'm in." Lisa headed over to the black tanning beds.

"Wait up, Lisa," called out Kim. "I want to try it, too!"

"Me, too!" Molly ran behind the other two, limping but determined to shed a few more pounds.

The blond instructor watched the three girls enter the capsules and muttered to himself. "That's right, girls. Just let the rays sap up the rest of your energy." Jed chuckled under his breath.

When Molly, Lisa, and Kim finished their

## the power of love

Shape Sun Salon session, their faces were paler than Casper the Ghost.

"Girls, you look so beautiful," Jed complimented them. "It's amazing!"

"Cool!" The three girls high-fived each other, even though their bodies seemed ready to collapse.

"Remember, if you want to become drop-dead gorgeous, make sure you come here everyday," Jed reminded them.

"Okay." The girls nodded and headed off toward the showers.

Thousands of miles from the Shape Salon, pitch-black columns shaped like bones reflected only the glow of fireflies. Amongst the crawling worms and scrambling rats, Queen Beryl rubbed her black crystal ball. An image of the Shape Salon and its blond, studly instructor came into view.

"Jedite, report in at once!" Queen Beryl's booming voice echoed throughout the dark chambers.

"Queen Beryl, you will be pleased to hear that my strategy is working perfectly."

"Excellent!"

"The stupid girls here want to look beautiful so badly that they'll do anything to lose weight," Jedite explained. "My machines are sapping up all their energy."

"Perfect," Queen Beryl hissed. "Continue with your plan."

"As you wish, Your Majesty." As Jedite bowed, his eyes flickered with the same glow as the fireflies.

the power of love

# Chapter 3
# Nuts for Donuts

Finished drying off her body outside the Jacuzzi, Serena changed into her DKNY casual jeans and baby tee. Glancing around, she couldn't find Molly, Lisa or Kim anywhere. Confused, Serena approached the picture-perfect beef-stick instructor.

"Uh, Jed." Serena's innocent, baby-blue eyes were slightly red from the Jacuzzi. "Have you seen my friends?"

"Oh, you mean those three girls? They left about ten minutes ago."

They left without Serena? What were they

thinking?! Even though they tended to be a bit selfish at times, Serena found them leaving without saying anything to her a bit unusual.

Jed looked over at Serena with a twinkle in his eyes. "How about trying the relaxing Shape Sun Salon bed?"

"No thanks," Serena muttered, shaking her head. "I've really gotta head out."

"Well, make sure you come back tomorrow, sweetie." Jed flashed another pearly-white smile. "You look great in your work-out clothes."

Blushing, Serena ducked out and began walking home. All that sweating, she thought. Really, all the gym ended up doing was just making her hungrier. How could anyone lose weight if they just ate more food after their workout?

Crossing the street, Serena glanced to her right. Coming down the sidewalk was a little boy about four years old. His mother was strolling about fifteen feet behind him, window shopping. The boy's hands were covered with red goo, dripping down between his fingers. His hands grasped a white, creamy donut, with red goo dripping from the bottom. Stuffing the donut in his mouth, the boy cackled an excited laugh, as he gobbled the donut up, bite by bite.

Serena's eyes started bulging from her head. Stopped dead in her tracks, Serena stared at the boy walking right towards her. With saliva beginning to dribble down her chin, Serena stood in front of the boy.

"Do...nut..." Serena's voice sounded desperate. "Donut!" The tone raised and the boy looked up, finally noticing her. Serena towered over the boy, staring at his donut with zombie eyes and canine salivation.

"M..." The boy started backing up, eyes full of fright. "Mommy?" The boy's mother was still a few shops back. "Mommy!!" The boy yelled out, spinning around and running off towards his mother.

Serena felt pretty guilty. After all, harassing toddlers was a bit extreme. Still, the pang in her empty gut wouldn't stop. That donut looked so scrumptious! Without food, she might just pass out. Stumbling over to the Crown Arcade, Serena barely made it through the automatic sliding door inside.

Weak from hunger, Serena suddenly felt faint. Dropping her Prada bag, she began falling backwards. Too weak to stop herself from falling, she closed her eyes, braced for the smash onto the floor. Instead, she felt soft arms catch her and hold her up. Opening her eyes, she saw an attractive male face. It was Andrew Foreman, the part-time guy at Crown!

"Serena!" Andrew's face showed worry, on the verge of panic. "What's wrong? Do you feel sick? Do you want me to take you to the hospital?"

"Hospital?" Serena looked up at Andrew. "Can you take me to a nice restaurant?"

"A restaurant?" Andrew looked perplexed. "Why would that help?"

"Because I haven't had anything to eat all day long *and* I worked out," Serena whined. "Thank you, Andrew, for saving me." With that, Serena faded out again.

"Serena, snap out of it!"

She could barely hear Andrew's words as she slipped into dream mode. "Andrew, baby," Serena whispered, deeply content in her day-dream.

## the power of love

"Serena, I know how to make you feel better." Andrew stroked her hair while talking to her in his deep, husky voice. "If you just feel the power of my love for you, your energy will flow right back into your body."

Serena smiled at the handsome face in front of her. "Oh, Andrew, that's so *romantic*."

Her dream fading away, Serena felt hot chicken broth on her lips. Opening her eyes, she could see Andrew's concerned face, with his hands holding a cup of instant soup up to her mouth.

"Serena, I'm glad to see you conscious again," Andrew said, relieved. "You had me worried. Here drink the rest of this soup."

"Andrew, you're so sweet." Serena smiled, thinking of the dream she had a second before. "I feel much better now."

"So, why haven't you eaten anything today?" Andrew looked at her, curious.

"Well," Serena began, slightly embarrassed. "I just started this diet."

Andrew started cracking up at the mention of diet. Serena just stared at him, shocked.

"What is so funny about that?" Serena's

face had turned bright red.

"It's just..." Andrew tried to contain his laughs. "It's just that you're so skinny, if you start a diet you'll end up skin and bones."

"You're just saying that!"

"No, no," Andrew insisted. "If anything, you need to gain a few pounds. I prefer a girl with some meat on her over those anorexic-looking types."

Serena was definitely pleased to finally hear someone tell her she was *too* skinny. With that kind of encouragement, Serena easily recovered and headed over to the donut shop to pick up a bag of fresh jelly-filled. With a mouth full of rasberry-flavored jelly, humming as she walked down the street, Serena could not have been happier.

"Blondie, is that jelly-covered T-shirt the new junior high look nowadays?"

Serena turned to confront the sarcastic male voice. To her disgust, it was the same tall, dark-haired, Oakley-shaded guy with the sky-high ego problem.

"It's my new look, OK?" Serena pouted. "Anyway, it's none of your business what's on my

T-shirt!"

"Well, if you keep piggin' out on donuts like that, you really might end up looking like one."

That did it! Who did this guy think he was? After all, Serena didn't even *know* him. Someone needed to stick a pin in that over-inflated ego of his.

Serena reached into her bag of donuts and grabbed one. Hurling it with all her might at the guy, she shouted. "Here's one for you, jerk!"

The guy lifted his Oakleys up a bit with his right hand, and with his left hand he easily grabbed the donut in mid-air. Chomping on the fresh jelly-filled, he looked over at Serena, grinning.

"Blueberry—my favorite kind. This is four hundred calories that won't go straight to your thighs," the guy commented, adding insult to injury. With that, he disappeared around the corner.

What a real jerk, Serena thought, completely frustrated. Luna looked up at Serena, snickering.

"With just one donut, you can gain two pounds." Luna started to tease Serena. "With two donuts, you can gain eight pounds. After three donuts, you can look just like a donut!"

"Ha, ha, ha." Serena rolled her eyes. "Luna, to show you how much you know, Andrew actually likes chubby girls. So there."

"No, Serena," Luna countered. "He said he likes a girl with *some* meat on her. That's quite different from *chubby*."

My god, Serena thought. Luna was right! Maybe she shouldn't have eaten so many donuts. How many did she eat?

"By the way, Serena, we have a serious situation going on," Luna said.

"Tell me about it, Luna," Serena cried. "I ate more than six donuts! This is definitely a serious situation."

"Look," Luna interjected. "Miss Haruna looks like a twig, and so do all the girls working out at the Shape Salon. We've got to get back there and check it out!"

"Shape Salon, that's it!" Serena was on a totally different plane. "I've got to get back to Shape Salon and lose some weight once and for all."

## the power of love

Without even thinking about Luna or her words, Serena dashed off towards Shape Salon. This time she was determined to *really* get in some exercise.

# Chapter 4
# Killer Workout

Serena ran through the glitzy entrance to Shape Salon, flashing her ID card on the way in. Without slowing down, she headed straight for the lockers and quickly changed into her work-out clothes. Almost knocking down two girls on the way out of the locker room, Serena hurried over to the exercise bikes and hopped on one.

"Hey, there!" A muscle-clad instructor came up to Serena and flashed a smile.

Serena was too busy pumping away on the bike to even notice the instructor. Her arms were locked in front of her, clutching the handlebars, and her head was down, watching her feet push the pedals over and over, faster than the speed of light.

"You know, you really should pace yourself a bit more," the instructor warned. "The most effective workout is a series of repetitions over a long period of time. That way, your endurance is built. If you knock yourself out all at once, you'll just over-exert yourself and run out of energy."

Serena looked over at the instructor, furiously pedaling all along. "I...can't...help...it..." Serena was working so hard she could barely spit out the words. "I've...got...to...work...off... those...donuts..." Serena actually sped up her pedaling to the point where she looked like a crazed Tour de France cyclist.

Everyone in the exercise room momentarily stopped their workouts and stared at Serena's hyper-cycling. Mouth agape, even the instructor backed away from Serena, leaving her on her own.

Serena didn't care. "This time, I've gotta get in a good workout. There's no way I'm going to let that jerk guy and Luna convince me that I'm fat. I'll prove it to them. I'll prove it to everyone!!"

Pedaling as fast as she could, Serena tried to keep herself going without feeling the pain. "I'm going downhill," Serena mumbled to herself. "This is easy. There's no pain at all. No pain. I'm going downhill." Serena kept trying to psyche herself out of feeling the pain that was working its way into her legs.

Out of the corner of her eye, she noticed Luna outside the window. Luna was looking at Serena making a disgusted face. This really annoyed Serena, who kept cycling as fast as she could. Luna was being so uncool. They used to have so much fun hanging out together, but now Luna was acting like every little thing Serena did was wrong. Don't eat this, don't eat that, don't play video games, don't sleep in, don't go shopping. Was her mom paying Luna off, or what?

Serena noticed that Luna was glancing towards another part of the club, distracted. Luna's eyes started to open wide as she jumped up, dashing away from the window at top speed.

Shaking her head, Serena went back to pumping the pedals on the bike. Little by little, she started to run out of power. First, she felt the pain

## the power of love

creep in to her side. Her side? Out of all places, why did the pain start there? Pain is a weird thing. Serena did her best to ignore it, but she couldn't keep cycling. Pausing for a moment to catch her breath, Serena stared at the pedals, sitting on the bike, panting.

Just then, Luna darted into the room like a black comet. Heading right for Serena, Luna let out a long and furious meow. Serena couldn't believe her eyes as Luna dove for the exercise bike, hitting Serena like a torpedo and knocking her off the bike.

That did it. Serena had no idea what had gotten into Luna, but there was no excuse for this. Maybe Serena did eat too much. Maybe she did play too many video games. Maybe she didn't complete her homework on time. But Serena was fed up with Luna's rude attitude!

After knocking Serena off the bike, Luna looked right at her and meowed. In front of people, Serena knew Luna wouldn't let them know she could talk. After meowing one more time, Luna stuck her tongue out at Serena and dashed towards the door of the gym.

Ooooh, that cat, Serena thought. Wait until she got her hands on the black furball. She'd squeeze Luna until her face turned blue, Serena was so mad! Running outside to chase down Luna, Serena stormed out of the Shape Salon's glitzy entrance. Spotting Luna down the street on the left, Serena ran after her. Luna dashed into a park and stopped on the grass near some trees. When Serena finally caught up, she noticed that no one else was around.

"What are you thinking, knocking me over the bike?!" Serena was livid. "After exercising like that, I was in a state of semi-consciousness. That could have been the end of me!"

"Serena, you don't understand. We have a major problem." Luna spoke calmly yet firmly. "For once, you've got to stop thinking about yourself and listen to me. Miss Haruna is going to die!"

The words went right through Serena. Between not eating almost anything but donuts, exercising like the bionic woman, and being in a state of fury, Serena couldn't think straight.

"You want to know who's going to die?" Serena went on, hands on hip. "You, Luna! Once I

## the power of love

get my hands on you, I'm going to kill you!"

Serena dove for Luna, who dodged out of the way at the last minute. Of course, Serena wouldn't really kill Luna, but she *was* fed up, and wanted to teach her a lesson. Before Serena could turn around, Luna jumped onto Serena from behind, knocking her down again. This time, before Serena could even move, Luna pinned her arms down and hissed.

"That's it, Serena," Luna snapped, eyes on fire. Serena started to shake with fear. "I've had it with you! You've got to transform into Sailor Moon and get back to that Shape Salon. The Enemy is running that place! I saw that blond instructor Jed from the window carrying Miss Haruna's body. He just dumped her in the other room, laughing the whole way! Before it's too late, you've *got* to turn into Sailor Moon and go save those poor girls! Don't you understand?"

Serena couldn't believe what she was hearing. How could this be true? She was in the Shape Salon, even talking to Jed and the other instructors. They were perfectly nice. More importantly, they were major hotties. How could *they* be the Enemy?

Well, Serena knew she *had* been acting pretty lame lately. It must have been all those donuts. Or maybe that jerk she bumped into who she threw a donut at. No matter what, she had to believe Luna.

"MOON PRISM POWER MAKE-UP!!"

Serena instinctively lifted her arms in the air and she spun around. With a flash of light, Serena no longer wore her funky CK work-out clothes. Instead, she sported a shiny sailor-styled bodysuit with long white gloves, a red bow, a sparkling tiara and red boots. This was her Sailor Moon uniform. Move over, Batman!

"OK, Luna, let's go!"

This was only the fourth time Serena had ever had to transform into Sailor Moon to battle evil. Although it was really a pain in the butt, she was starting to get used to it. After all, *someone* had to fight evil, even though it would have been nice if it didn't have to be her.

Serena didn't waste any time storming back into Shape Salon and looking for the blond instructor Jed.

"Serena, they've got Haruna downstairs!"

## the power of love

Luna dashed left and headed down the hidden staircase. Serena quickly followed, and they burst open the closed door.

The blond instructor looked up to see Serena ready to fight.

"You! I knew you'd show up eventually. This time, I, Jedite, won't let you win!"

Serena saw that the good-looking instructor Jed really was the same Enemy, Jedite, whom she had encountered in her last battle. She remembered how she was fooled by his radio DJ disguise, Jay Dight. For some reason, he always looks like such a stud. How could she be attracted to a bad guy? Except, now she was totally unattracted since evil wasn't really what she looked for in a guy.

"So you remember me?" Serena remarked. "Just in case, I'll remind you again. I'm Sailor Moon, Champion of Love and Justice, and on behalf of the Moon, you're punished!"

"That's exactly what you said last time," Jedite scowled. "Can't you be more original?"

"Look who's talking, Mr. Creative," Serena snapped back. "Last time, your disguise name was JAY DIGHT instead of your normal bad-guy name of JEDITE. This time it's JED instead of JEDITE. What are you going to choose next time, JEDD HEIGHT?"

Jedite's face started to turn flush red. "That's easy for you to say now, but it worked on you!"

He did have a point, Serena thought. "Yeah, but not for too long. See, I figured you out!"

Luna looked up at Serena and stuck her tongue out. OK, so maybe it *was* Luna who had figured it out, but Jedite didn't need to know that.

Jedite called over his three instructor assistants. "Get her!" he barked.

Each of the three assistants looked like they were cover models for *Muscle & Fitness* magazine. With biceps bigger than Luna, the three instructors surrounded Serena.

"Uh-oh." Serena gulped. The three instructors had her cornered and came in to attack. Why did Serena always get herself surrounded like this? Looking up at the three muscle-men, Serena started to sniffle.

"Destroy her for good," Jedite ordered. With an evil smile on his face, Jedite disappeared into the darkness.

One instructor picked up a weight and hurled it towards Serena.

"Agghhh!" Serena dodged it at the last minute, and the weight came crashing into the floor, cracking the wood.

"Luna, help!"

"Sailor Moon, see those rings over their heads?" Luna pointed to the instructors. Sure enough, there were glowing rings almost hidden over the three instructors heads. "Those rings control their actions. If you break the rings with your tiara, they'll turn back to regular men."

"You mean regular beefcake, right?" Serena smiled, enjoying the thought.

One of the instructors picked up another weight and hurled it at her again. Serena dodged it, but this time the last instructor grabbed her.

"Luna, they've got me!" Serena cried.

"Fight, Sailor Moon!"

"What can I do?" Serena began to panic. "This jerk's got me in a lock. I can't move!!"

"Sailor Moon, just fight hard! If you do, you might actually lose some weight," Luna said, sarcastically.

Lose weight? Just the thought of actually shedding a few pounds gave her inspiration. With a kick into the instructor's groin, Serena broke free of his hold.

"That's it, now use your tiara!" Luna yelled.

"MOON TIARA ACTION!!" Serena wasted no time flinging her Frisbee-like tiara over to the instructors. Like a boomerang, the tiara nailed all three rings and flew back into Serena's hand. Not bad, Serena thought.

The instructors looked around, dazed and confused.

"Luna, do you think I lost a few pounds?" Serena's hopes were high.

Back at home, Serena soaked in her hot bath. This time she really deserved the relaxation of eucalyptus, peppermint and Siberian pine bath crystals.

"Luna, I'm so glad we were able to get Miss Haruna to the hospital in time for her to recover," Serena said.

"It's true," Luna agreed. "Another hour or

two and she wouldn't have had enough nutrition left in her to make it. You did well, Serena."

Pleased, Serena got out of the tub and headed over to the sink. Casually stepping on the round, white, digital scale in front of the sink, Serena weighed herself.

"Agghhhh!!" Serena's face turned pale.

From the other room, Luna called out. "Serena, what happened?!"

"Luna, Luna!" Serena started to panic. "After all that exercise, I actually *gained* a pound!!"

Luna couldn't help but burst out laughing while Serena chased the little black furball around the room.

# Chapter 5
## Who's Afraid of the Big Bad Luna?

Serena was standing in the darkness. As far as the eye could see was a black abyss, and the air felt stale and cold.

"Where am I?" she whispered, then covered her mouth as her voice echoed loudly in the shadows. When finally the noise died down, she looked around.

What was going on? How did she get to this awful place? She took a step forward, and her shoe clicked on an invisible floor. Serena rubbed her arms and shivered as she walked quietly through the nothingness. How creepy, she thought. She felt lost—a stranger in a strange land.

## the power of love

Suddenly, Luna's face popped up in front of her. Serena jumped back, wincing. Luna had told her more than once that daydreaming was going to get her hopelessly lost some day.

Yeah, well, Luna was too strict with her anyway. What was a girl without dreams? Bored and lifeless, that's what. Serena sniffed and thrust her chin into the air. Luna just didn't understand what being a truly modern and dynamic female was all about.

Just then, Serena could hear a loud growling from behind her. She whipped her head around, then choked back a scream.

A huge female wolf-creature was crouched in the darkness. She looked like a woman who had grown fur and pointed ears. Her eyes were long and pointed.

Serena began to shake. This time it's personal, she thought. Could Serena really fight her? That wolf-lady looked hungry!

The creature snarled, and charged.

"Aaaghhhh!!!"

Serena ran for her life, her shoes slapping the ground madly as the creature's roars rang in her ears. As fast as she ran, she still heard the wolf-lady closing in behind her.

"No!" Serena screamed, pumping her legs faster. "Leave me alone! Help!!!"

Light suddenly flashed in front of her, and a white-gloved hand clutched her own.

"Jump, Serena!" a familiar voice cried.

Serena's heart nearly stopped. Could it be...Tuxedo Mask?!

Serena held her breath and jumped as high as she could. Strong arms caught her, and she was pulled into an embrace. She leaned her cheek on Tuxedo Mask's chest as the two of them floated into the air, well out of the reach of the wolf-lady. The creature roared in anger.

Serena breathed heavily, looking up into Tuxedo Mask's face. "You...you can fly?" she whispered, unbelievably.

"There's much you don't know about me," he replied, his voice gentle. One gloved finger gently touched her cheek.

Serena blushed. "Th...thank you for saving me," she stuttered.

Tuxedo Mask brushed some hair from her

flushed face. "I'll always be here for you," he whispered.

Serena stared up at his eyes, blocked by his white mask. So close, she thought. I'm so close to him; I can feel how warm he is. So close, I could just...take off that mask...

Serena swallowed, then gently, carefully, reached her fingers up towards his goggles.

Tuxedo Mask just smiled.

"Aggggghhhhh!!!"

Serena's eyes popped open.

"Aggggghhhhh!!!"

She shot up in bed, grabbing her ears. "Hey! Who's screaming?"

"Get away from me! Get away!!!"

Serena's eyes narrowed angrily. "Sammy? Arrrgh! How dare he wake me up from such a perfect dream," she muttered, realizing that Tuxedo Mask had been a dream. "Aww, it's no *fair*!"

"Get away!!" Sammy's voice shrieked from the other room. "Get away!! Get away!! Serena!!!"

"Geez, Sammy, I'm coming!" Serena mumbled angrily as she pushed aside her covers and slipped her feet in her bunny slippers. She yawned as she opened her bedroom door and went down the hall to her little brother Sammy's room.

Luna was on the end of his bed, violently awakened by Sammy's screams. Sammy was curled up against his headboard, eyes wide with terror, a pillow hugged against his chest. His huge blue eyes flicked to Serena as soon as she stood in the doorway.

"Serena!" he screamed. "Save me! Get that *thing* off my bed!"

Serena blinked. "Luna? You're screaming because of Luna?" She rolled her eyes. "Sammy, you are such a baby. Luna's a *cat*. She won't hurt you. You ruined my beautiful dream for *that*?" she complained with another yawn.

Luna looked up at Sammy with curious red-orange eyes. Sammy shrieked.

"It keeps looking at me," he cried, throwing his pillow at Luna. Luna dove out of the way of it, and the pillow whacked Serena in the face instead.

"Sammy," Serena roared, her eyes red. "That hurt!"

A frightened Luna jumped into Serena's arms, and Sammy covered his head. "Keep it

## the power of love

away, Serena!"

Serena frowned. What was wrong with him, anyway? Who'd be scared of little old Luna? Well, she thought, when Luna got in one of her I'm-mad-and-gonna-yell-at-you-for-a-good-half-hour moods, she could get pretty scary.

Then Serena remembered—Sammy hated cats.

"Here, Sammy," Serena murmured wickedly as she held up Luna. "Wanna kiss?" She waved Luna up near Sammy's face.

Sammy cringed and squeezed his eyes shut.

"No! Serena, stop it!"

"Serves you right." Serena hissed, pushing Luna closer to him. "You have to learn that you can't just throw things at animals."

Just then, their mother's voice drifted in from downstairs.

"Serena, Sammy! Pancakes!"

Serena suddenly froze, her eyes wide.

"Food!" she squealed. "Better yet, pancakes!"

Ditching her taunting of panic-stricken Sammy, Serena dashed from the room, leaving only a cloud of dust behind her.

At the breakfast table, Serena happily crammed pancakes in her mouth as Luna quietly ate cat food by her feet. Sammy, across the table, crossed his arms angrily.

"Mom," he whined as his mother placed a dish of pancakes before him. "Tell Serena to get rid of that ugly, little cat!"

"I wouldn't tawk abou being ugy," Serena snapped back through a mouthful of pancake. "You have no wight to—"

"Don't talk with your mouth full, dear."

Serena swallowed. "Leave poor Luna alone, Sammy," she said with a glare. "She's my pet, so don't you touch her!"

"Dad," Sammy said, pleading to his father sitting beside him. "Can't you make Serena get rid of it?"

Serena's father shrugged, turning the page of his newspaper. "It's up to you kids, really," he said as he picked up his coffee mug. "Reach an agreement between you, though. Whether the cat stays or goes, I don't want to hear any more arguments."

Serena pushed back her chair and stood up. "Well," she said as she bent and picked up Luna. "I have to go to school. My lovely and *harmless* cat will escort me." With one final glare at Sammy that practically said *you're gonna lose this war*, Serena picked up her lunch and walked out the door.

The sun was bright outside, and Serena stretched her arms above her head as she stepped onto the sidewalk. Brushing her long ponytails over her shoulders, she sighed.

"Luna," Serena said as soon as she and the black cat had started walking. "Why on Earth did you try to sleep at the foot of Sammy's bed last night? Do you have a death wish or something?"

Luna shrugged—at least, made as much of a shrug as a walking cat can. "I've been very tired lately, searching for the Moon Princess all day while you're at school. Despite the many times I've asked for your help," Luna said, throwing a glare towards Serena, "you seem to not be interested in helping my search. So I'm doing it all myself."

"Well, excuse me for dealing with nerve-wracking school by day and ghouls and ghosts by night. Forgive me for not finding time for your princess-hunt in my wide-open schedule." Serena let out a breath angrily. It wasn't like she asked for this added responsibility.

School was bad enough, but trying to find some princess, hidden off who-knows-where? Yeah, right. Fighting monsters as Champion of Justice was bad enough. Although, Serena would gladly trade school in for helping Luna find the princess. Her parents would have a little trouble with that one, though.

"Besides," Serena added. "If you're so tired, why don't you just sleep at the foot of my bed?"

"You kick, Serena. I'd call *that* a death wish."

Serena scowled. "With Sammy looking to give you the boot, I'd kiss up a bit more to your only ally. Considering I stood up for you today, you aren't acting very grateful."

Luna's face fell. "I guess... I just want Sammy to like me," she said quietly. "What should I do?"

Serena flipped her backpack over her shoulder to carry it more comfortably. "Well, considering he's gotta agree for you to stay at our house, I'd suggest becoming his friend." She waved a hand. "Though I don't know what would get him to like you. He's really scared to death of cats."

Luna sighed, her eyes wandering over to a cat on the other side of the street. It was running to a little girl. The cat jumped on the girl and licked her face. The girl, squealing with pleasure, hugged the cat and giggled.

"Maybe," Luna whispered. "Maybe, something like that would work."

"Man," Serena mumbled, completely off-subject. "I could go for a croissant ham and egg sandwich right now. Those pancakes didn't fill me up."

Luna rolled her eyes. "*Pancakes* didn't fill you up? Serena, how did you get to be such a pig?"

"Pig?" Serena slapped a hand to her mouth. "Does that mean I look fat? Oh, tell me I don't look fat!" She quickly turned around, scanning her figure in a store window, with panicked eyes.

Luna moaned. "Not again. We just finished the diet chapter."

Jedite stepped from the shadows, bowing on one knee. Darkness, thick and hot, swirled through the air in the stone kingdom. "You called, my Queen?"

"Yes," Queen Beryl answered, her voice low. Her long finger nails trailed down her floating crystal ball. "Do you have your next plan ready, Jedite? I am tired of waiting."

Jedite's lips curled in a smile. "Yes, Your Majesty. My plan is ready to be put into play at your command."

"Then proceed."

Jedite looked up, and cold blue eyes flashed. His smile was wicked. "With pleasure, my Queen."

# Chapter 6
# Sinister Scents

"Really?" Molly blinked. "Your brother's so scared of your cat he won't look at her?"

Serena dug into her lunchbag and pulled out a sandwich. Flipping open the top piece of bread, she grinned. "Mmm, tuna."

"Serena, are you paying attention?"

Serena looked up. "Huh? Oh, of course I am." She bit into her sandwich. "So, what were you saying?"

Molly rolled her eyes and leaned back against the tree in the center of the school court-yard. The sun filtered through the leaves and speckled the grass with yellow light.

"I was just saying it's hard to believe Sammy is so scared of your cat. Why does he hate cats so much?"

Serena crammed a few Pringles in her mouth. "I fink it's becawse—"

"Don't talk with your mouth full, Serena."

Serena wiped her mouth with the back of her hand and finished chewing. Everyone was always so concerned with talking and eating at the same time. All she really wanted to do was eat.

"Sammy was bitten on the nose by a cat when he was a baby," Serena explained as she picked up her juice. "So now he's scared of all cats."

"Hi ladies!" Melvin shouted as he suddenly appeared by Molly's side. "Mind if I join in?"

"Eeeek!" Serena screamed and threw her juice, splattering it all over Melvin. She grabbed her chest and glared at him.

"Melvin, you big dork! Don't scare me by popping up like that!"

Melvin looked down at his juice-stained shirt. "Oh, man!" he squeaked. "Now my mom will use that special Tide With Bleach stuff, and that always makes me itch."

"Melvin, gross. Don't you have anybody else to bother?" Molly asked.

Melvin frowned and tried to wipe the juice off him with his handkerchief.

Only a real dork would carry a handkerchief around, Serena thought. Besides, every time Melvin popped up, there was some type of trouble. Not to mention the fact that no cute guys would come over if Melvin was there with them.

"I heard you say your little brother was bitten by a cat as a child, and now he's scared of them," Melvin commented. "Something like that happened to me, too."

"A cat bit you?" Molly shrugged and stretched her arms out. "Can't say I blame it."

Melvin shook his head. "Not cats. I'm just allergic to them. But I have a real fear of alligators."

Serena and Molly exchanged glances.

"We *all* have a fear of alligators, Melvin." Serena wasn't impressed.

"So what happened, an alligator chomped on your face when you were a kid and that's why you're so ugly?" Molly twisted the knife.

Melvin frowned. "Actually, it was an alligator skin purse, and it didn't bite me—it just sort of bonked me on the head. But it had the same effect."

The girls counted to three and dumped their lunches right on top of Melvin's head. "Melvin, you're such a dweeb!"

Later that day, Serena and Luna stood outside of Crossroads Elementary School waiting for Sammy. Serena wasn't daydreaming as she usually did when she was standing around and the sun was out. Instead, she was holding her stomach and moaning.

"I'm dying of hunger." Serena's stomach rumbled. "Luna, you don't happen to have any food on you, do you?"

Luna sighed. "What do I look like, Meals on Paws?"

Serena shot her a look. "Very funny."

"Serena, your mother packed you a huge lunch today. How could you possibly still be hungry?"

## the power of love

"I didn't get to eat that huge lunch FYI," Serena complained. "I dumped it all on Melvin because he was being a dork."

Luna did not show Serena any sympathy. "Then it's your own fault, so don't come whining to me."

"You can at least feel sorry for your starving Champion of Justice, you cruel feline." Serena's face turned red. "Considering I had to give up a normal life once you came to me, you owe me big for not bailing out on you. I could just as easily refuse to fight."

"Serena?" The voice of a boy came from behind her.

Serena froze. She whipped her head up, only to see Sammy looking at her strangely. His hands gripped the straps of his blue backpack.

"Talking to yourself again?" he asked with a shake of his head. "Geez, Serena. You're such a loser."

"Quiet, brat!" Serena snapped. "Mom said you were getting out late today, so I have to walk you home."

"What?" Sammy made a face. "I'm going

shopping with Mika today. Not that I'd wanna walk home with you if I was going home anyway. Man, what was Mom thinking when she sent you? I'm surprised you didn't get lost coming here."

Serena's mouth dropped. She had come all that way for nothing?! All that walking just to be rejected and insulted by her own brother. It would have been much easier just to have headed straight for the Crown Arcade. At least the Sailor V video game wouldn't reject her. And maybe she would have even had a chance to talk to Andrew!

Sammy hadn't yet noticed Luna was there. Before Serena could get back to yelling at her little brother, Luna suddenly jumped in his arms and began to lick his face and purr, just like she had seen another cat do that day.

"Yaagggghhh!!!!" Sammy screamed as he frantically tried to pull Luna off. "Serena, get this nasty thing off me!"

Luna sniffed and jumped back down to the pavement. Sammy breathed heavily, covering his head with his arms. "No!" he shrieked. "Get it away! Get it away!"

Serena couldn't stop laughing. Her annoying little brother, screaming bloody murder because of Luna? It served him right. Serena suddenly wondered if keeping Luna around her would keep him in line. Now that was an idea!

Luna ran off, as Serena watched her go. "Aw, Sammy," Serena said as soon as she could control her laughter. "You hurt Luna's feelings."

Sammy had taken his backpack off and was shielding himself with it. He glared over the top zipper. "You...you keep that thing away from me," he shouted. "I want that creature out of the house, Serena. Get rid of it!"

Serena put her hands on her hips and narrowed her eyes. "When pigs fly," she taunted.

"Fine, I'll be looking for *you* up in the sky," Sammy muttered angrily as he put on his backpack. He ran a shaky hand through his hair. "I'm going with Mika," he said flatly. "Tell Mom I'll be back by dinner."

As he walked away, Serena scowled. Little brat, she thought. Not only does he insul my cat and me, but he leaves me stranded thirty minutes from home.

Serena froze.

Home. Food.

A half a second later, Serena had disappeared, leaving only a huge cloud of dust behind her.

A small girl stood outside the arcade. Her hair was red-brown, and fell past her shoulders, framing a small, button-nosed face. As soon as she saw Sammy in the distance, she jumped up and waved.

"Hi Sammy," she called cheerfully.

Sammy brightened, and ran the rest of the way.

"Mika!" He panted when he reached her. "Sorry I'm late—my stupid sister held me up."

Mika laughed. "Oh, it's ok." She took his hands; her eyes bright.

"There's the best new place that just opened," she said excitedly. "It's a pet shop with the cutest new pets there—you've gotta see!"

Sammy blinked. "A pet shop?"

"Yeah," Mika said, giggling and pulling him. "C'mon, let's go check it out!"

After a few minutes, Sammy began to sniff

the air.

"Something... smells nice," he commented. "What is that?"

Mika giggled, pointing to a large store. The words PERFUME PETS were printed over the door in shiny pink letters.

"This is the place." She tugged on his backpack. "C'mon, let's go in."

Sammy opened the door, and a wave of perfume-scented air flew at him. He blinked, then breathed deeply, smiling.

"Wow," he murmured. "It smells like... strawberries."

Mika led him in, and over to a long row of cages.

"See, Sammy," she said, pointing to something small and white in a cage. "This is the kind of pet this place has. They're called Shaneeras."

Sammy looked closely through the bars. The creature inside looked like a tiny, fluffy rabbit with small ears and big blue eyes. It shuffled slightly as he sniffed again.

"That's the smell," Sammy said, excitedly. "It's coming from the Shaneera."

"The Shaneeras give off perfume scents," Mika explained. "And each one has a different scent."

Sammy went from cage to cage, smelling each different Shaneera.

"This one is peppermint, and this one smells like violets." Sammy grinned as he put his face near another cage. "And what do you smell like, little guy?" he asked with a smile.

The Shaneera looked at him, and its big blue eyes caught his own. Sammy suddenly froze. The Shaneera's eyes narrowed and began to glow. Sammy's face fell as he gazed hypnotically at the Shaneera.

"Sammy..." Mika said in a zombie-like tone as she came up behind him. She was holding a Shaneera, staring into its eyes. Her pupils had gone fuzzy, and a big, dreamy smile was on her face. "I'm...getting...this...one..." she said fuzzily.

Sammy slowly opened the cage, then picked up the Shaneera and stared deep into its blue eyes. Sammy's pupils had also gone cloudy, and the same goofy grin was plastered on his lips. "This one," he chanted, his voice as hazy as Mika's.

**6 4**

## the power of love

"It...smells...like...spring..."

The clerk walked over to the two of them. She was a tall woman, with red hair and bright green eyes. She grinned and put her hands on Sammy's shoulders.

"So, you kids want those Shaneeras?" she asked, her voice sweet.

Sammy and Mika nodded, not taking their eyes off the creatures.

"You can take them home, then." The woman waved a hand. "Pay for them whenever you can—there's no rush!"

Sammy and Mika nodded again, walking towards the door with their Shaneeras held in front of their faces. "Yes..." they chanted, voices oddly robotic. "We'll...take...them...home..."

The woman smiled wickedly as soon as Sammy and Mika were gone. "Excellent," she purred.

She turned around to the Shaneeras and smiled. White fangs glinted in her mouth. "Good work, my pets," she whispered. "Jedite's plan is working perfectly."

# Chapter 7
# Furby Imposters

Back at home, Serena sat on her bed with Luna. The talking black furball was very upset.

"I don't get it," Luna said with a sad sigh. "I tried to get him to like me. Normal people like it when cats lick them."

Serena shrugged. "Yeah, but Sammy's my little brother, so he doesn't qualify as 'normal.'"

Luna covered her face with her paws. "I'm a failure," she moaned. "Now I'll never get to stay here!"

"You could stay in the alley behind our house," Serena suggested. Wait a minute, Serena thought. What was wrong with this picture?

Here's bossy, commanding, pushy Luna, giving up without a fight?

"Don't throw in the towel yet," Serena insisted. "I don't get you at all. You always tell me to fight until the end. You should take your own advice!"

Luna looked up at her, eyes hopeful. "You think I could really get him to like me?" she whispered.

Serena nodded with confidence. "Sure! Convince him with your cuteness, your charm, your prowess," she explained, waving her arms out. "Convince him with your beauty. Intrigue him with your savvy. Turn on your kitty charm and melt him so he wouldn't dare try to get you out of the house."

Serena put down her arms and shrugged. "Or, if all else fails, do what I always do." She slapped her fist into her palm and grinned wickedly. "Convince him with a knuckle sandwich."

Just then, Sammy walked in. He was still holding his Shaneera, eyes glued to the small, odd-looking creature.

"Serena," he said, his voice sickeningly sugary. "I..."

Before he could finish, Luna jumped from the bed and ran to him, meowing madly. She rubbed against his leg, batting her eyes at him and giving the sweetest little kitty smile she could give.

Serena winced. Geez, Luna. Talk about pouring it on. This was more like drenching it on.

Sammy momentarily moved his eyes from the Shaneera and glared darkly at Luna. He pulled back his leg and kicked at her.

"Myaaw," Luna cried, jumping out of the way just in time. She hopped back on Serena's bed, and Serena shrieked in anger.

"What on Earth do you think you're doing?!" She grabbed Sammy by the arm, her eyes blazing. "You never hit an animal! How dare you try to kick Luna. What has gotten—"

"Get rid of that thing," Sammy spat, breaking from Serena's hold. His eyes, normally an ocean blue, looked a murky, fuzzy brown.

"We don't need that worthless cat," he cried, holding up his Shaneera. "This will be our new pet. It's much better than that dumb feline."

Serena grabbed the Shaneera out of

Sammy's hold and looked it over. She made a face. "This?" Serena shoved it back into his awaiting hands. "It looks like a Furby, only uglier."

Sammy's eyes flashed with anger. "Don't you say that!" he screamed, holding his Shaneera close. "This Shaneera is the most wonderful pet anyone could ever have. No one could ever get bored with it."

Serena snorted. "That's what they said about Furbies."

"Serena, Sammy, snack time!" Mrs. Tsukino called out from downstairs.

Serena's eyes widened, and she started to drool. "Oooh! It's Wednesday, which means lemon pie day." She grabbed Luna and flicked narrowed eyes at Sammy.

"We'll talk about this later," she said sternly, then shot down the stairs like a lightning bolt. Nothing could get in the way of Serena and her lemon pie.

The next morning, Serena ran downstairs, late as usual.

"Aaaaggghhh! Where's my lunch?!" Serena

shoved a piece of toast in her mouth and ran around frantically. "Mom! Dad! Where's my lunch?!"

Serena's mother was washing the dishes. "By the door as always, dear," she called cheerfully. "Oh, before you go, could you run upstairs and make sure Sammy's awake? He's going to be late if he doesn't come down soon."

Serena stopped dead in her tracks. Sammy? Late? Sammy was *never* late.

"I'll check on him, Mom," Serena called as she dashed up the stairs. Luna had just awakened and was walking through the hall with a yawn.

"Serena," she asked as Serena ran to Sammy's door. "Are you ready to go?"

"Hang on a sec, Luna." Serena knocked on Sammy's door. "Sammy, are you awake?"

No answer. Luna sat down and curled her tail around her body. "He's not up yet?"

Serena shook her head, eyes wide with surprise. "This is weird," she muttered. "Sammy likes going to school. How could he sleep in this late?" A better question, Serena thought, is how could he actually like going to school?

## the power of love

Serena turned the doorknob and pushed the door open. "Sammy?" she called quietly as she poked her head into his room.

All of the lights were off. The shades on the windows had been pulled down and blocked the sunlight, turning the room frighteningly dark. Sammy was sitting on top of his bed, staring into the eyes of the Shaneera.

Serena gasped. "S...Sammy?" she spluttered. "What are you doing? You're gonna be late for school."

Sammy suddenly realized Serena was watching him. He grabbed the Shaneera and pushed back against his headboard. "Get out of here!" he shouted. "I'm not going to school. I'm...I'm sick!"

Serena sucked in a breath. Sammy looked skeleton-thin, and his cheekbones stood out sharply in his face. His wide eyes, which had looked brown the day before, now looked black. He almost looked malnourished.

"Sick?" Serena bit her lip. "Sammy, you better go see the..."

"Get out!" Sammy cut Serena off in mid-sentence, throwing a pillow at her. "Just get out and leave me alone!"

Serena swallowed hard and closed the door. Luna looked up at her with wide eyes. "Why is Sammy yelling at you?" the cat asked.

Serena bit on one of her fingernails. "I don't know," Serena mumbled, her voice concerned. "But I think something's wrong with Sammy."

By running faster than the speed of light (well, that's what it felt like to Serena), Serena managed to get to school before the second bell rang. She fell into her seat, exhausted.

"Hey, Serena." Molly hopped up to sit on Serena's desk. She patted Serena's head, lying on the desktop. "Good job. You made it without being late for once."

Serena was panting so hard she could hardly talk. "I think...I'm...going...to die."

Molly rolled her eyes. "You can't run yourself to death at age fourteen, Serena."

"Molly..." Serena weakly took Molly's hand. "Tell...my family...I love them."

Just then, Miss Haruna walked into the

room. Molly went back to her desk.

"Good morning, class," Miss Haruna called as she put down her bag. "How is everyone today?"

No answer. Ms. Haruna looked around the classroom, surprised. "Class? Why are you so quiet?"

Serena, surprised, looked around at her classmates. She gasped.

Nearly everyone had a Shaneera. Kim Matthews had hers on her desk and stared into its eyes. Lisa Brownridge did the same with her own Shaneera. Even Rica Kelton, even Tim House—it seemed that everyone except Serena and Molly was staring at a Shaneera.

Well, except for Melvin. He was in the back staring at a nerdy computer book, just like he did every day.

"Molly..." Serena leaned over towards her best friend. "What's with all the Shaneeras?"

Molly shrugged. "They're a big hit now," she whispered back. "I don't get it personally. I think they're ugly."

Serena looked around. "It's like everyone's

**7 3**

been brainwashed with them," she whispered. "Don't you think that's weird?"

Molly yawned. "Not really. Last year, it was Tamagotchis, then it was Furbies. Now it's Shaneeras."

Serena clasped her hands together. She wasn't buying it. Tamagotchis and Furbies were just toys that entertained people until they got annoyed. These Shaneeras were in a totally different league. Everyone who had a Shaneers didn't seem either entertained or annoyed—just hypnotized. Something was suspicious about this Shaneera thing.

Ms. Haruna crossed her arms. "All right, I want everyone to put those weird pets away," she barked. "I've heard about them from the administration at Crossroads Elementary. They're too distracting to have in class."

Nobody moved. Miss Haruna stomped over to Kim's desk and hovered over the girl. "Kim, didn't you hear me say put it away?"

Kim didn't look up from staring at the Shaneera. Miss Haruna's face grew red with anger. She reached for the Shaneera. Kim suddenly

## the power of love

jumped up and grabbed the creature away from Miss Haruna's hold. "Don't touch it!" Kim screamed, backing away. "Get your hands *off* my Shaneera."

Serena's jaw dropped. Kim was always such the model student. She would never yell at a teacher like that.

"Wh...wh..." Miss Haruna' face reddened beyond tomato crimson. "Young lady, you better turn that attitude around immediately."

Kim ignored Miss Haruna and walked out the door with her pet. All the other students picked up their own Shaneeras and followed her out the classroom door.

"Wait," Miss Haruna cried, running after them. "Where do you think you're going? You can't just leave class!"

As soon as Miss Haruna and all the students disappeared, Serena looked over at Molly with wide eyes.

"Did you see that?" Serena drew a breath. "Kim screamed at Miss Haruna!"

Melvin finally put down his computer book and frowned. "Those Shaneera things are making everyone real weird," he agreed. "Tim wouldn't even talk to me this morning."

Serena looked over at Melvin. "Big surprise. No one ever talks to you." Looking back over towards Molly, she mumbled, "I have a bad feeling about this. Where are those things sold?"

"A new store named PERFUME PETS," Molly answered. "It's down the street from the arcade. You're not going to get one, are you?"

"I'm just planning on doing a little window shopping," Serena said, reassuringly.

Luna was waiting for Serena when school got out. The cat looked worried. "Serena," she said quickly. "Your brother hasn't left his room all day. Your parents are concerned about him."

Serena picked up Luna and put her on her shoulder. "We're going to the pet store that sells those Shaneeras," Serena said as she began to walk. "We've gotta check those things out."

"Good thinking, Serena," Luna commented. "This all may be part of the Enemy's plot."

"Enemy or not," Serena said quietly, her face sad, "I've got to find out what's wrong with

## the power of love

Sammy. He's a brat and a dork and a pain and all, but he's still my brother and I love him. It's not like him to act like this."

"Yeah," Luna answered gently. "I know what you mean."

When Serena reached the arcade, she stopped.

"Ok," she murmured. "Molly said PER-FUME PETS was a little further down the street from here."

"Don't tell me you're getting one of those Furby things, too, blondie." The mocking male voice was annoyingly familiar.

Serena whipped around to see the same dark-haired, fashion-conscious dude she'd been bumping into lately. Today he wore a light yellow polo shirt with one hand in the pocket of his khakis.

Too bad this guy had as much attitude as he did style, Serena thought. She crossed her arms and snickered.

"Well, looks like someone fell into the Gap," Serena said, narrowing her eyes. "Though in your case, too bad it wasn't a ravine."

The pretty-boy gave a sarcastic smile and waved a hand through the air. "I should bump into you more often," he mused. "You amuse me."

"Get lost, jerk," Serena hissed.

"A bit cranky, are we?" As the young man walked past, he leaned near Serena's ear and whispered, "I wouldn't get a Shaneera if I were you. It might mistake you for its sister."

As he disappeared down the sidewalk, Serena's clenched her fists. What a major creep! Every time Serena saw that guy, he offended her. For some reason, though, Serena's heart was beating fast and her palms were sweaty.

"Serena?" Luna cocked her head. "Why are you blushing?"

Serena immediately turned away, biting her lip. "I...I'm not blushing," she spluttered, straightening her skirt. "C'mon, Luna! We've gotta, uh, get moving."

Serena quickly began walking down the sidewalk. Luna sighed, then followed.

PERFUME PETS was empty of customers when Serena walked inside. The cages lined along the back walls were oddly silent.

That's weird, she thought. Pet stores were usually really noisy. She shivered. Something about this store was strange.

"Can I help you?" the female clerk asked as she walked up to Serena. Luna, at Serena's feet, looked up at the woman with narrowed eyes.

"Uh, yeah," Serena said. "I'd like to see a Shaneera."

"Why, of course!" The woman led Serena to the cages. "That little cat near your ankles looks a little on the moody side," the woman drawled. "A Shaneera would make a much better pet."

Luna hissed, but Serena nudged her with her foot to stay silent. The woman opened a cage and pulled a Shaneera out.

"This one seems perfect for you," she beamed as she placed the Shaneera in Serena's arms. "If you'll notice, it smells like bubble gum."

Serena's eyes widened. "Really?" she squealed, forgetting her mission at the mention of food. "I love bubble gum!"

Someone else entered the store, and the clerk went to talk to him. Luna immediately jumped on Serena's shoulder.

"Serena, be careful," Luna warned. "Remember, it was Sammy staring at the Shaneera's eyes that—"

"Bubble...gum..." Serena's eyes got hazy, and she smiled dreamily. "Did I say these things were stupid? I love bubble gum..."

"No!" Luna's voice was terrified. "Serena, don't look into its eyes!"

But it was too late. Serena was already gazing straight into the Shaneera's big, blue eyes like a smiling zombie.

# Chapter 8
# Clerk-zilla

"Serena!" Luna ran down the sidewalk after Serena. "Serena, look at me!"

Serena wouldn't take her eyes from the small Shaneera in her hands. She giggled and petted it. "My beautiful little bubble gum baby," she cooed.

Luna yanked Serena's shoes with her teeth. "Serena, stop looking at that thing!"

Serena angrily pulled away from Luna's teeth and growled. "Get away from me, stupid cat," Serena spat. "I don't need you—my Shaneera is all I need now."

Luna winced. "It's like Sammy all over

again," she said, sighing.

Just then, a little girl on a tricycle came riding down the sidewalk. She fell off near the curb and started to cry.

Serena just walked right past the little girl, preening over her Shaneera.

"Oh, Serena," Luna mumbled as she ran to girl and started licking her cuts. When the little girl finally started sniffing and rubbing her tears away, Luna ran back to Serena and jumped on her head.

"This thing is evil!" Luna shouted angrily as she batted the Shaneera out of Serena's hands. The creature jumped to the ground to avoid falling, and angrily glared at Luna. Luna bared her teeth, and the Shaneera's eyes widened with fright. When Luna hissed, the owl-like creature dashed away in terror.

"Serena?" Luna quickly licked Serena's face. "Serena, are you ok?"

Serena blinked. "Huh?" She touched her face. "Where am I? What happened?"

"The Shaneera hypnotized you," Luna said as Serena gently put her cat back on the ground. "You looked into its eyes and couldn't look away."

## the power of love

"Really?" Serena's eyes widened. "It must be the Enemy's trick. Luna, we've gotta get rid of these Shaneeras before they take over everyone!"

"Quickly," Luna cried as she began to run down the sidewalk. "We've got to get to your brother!"

Serena nodded and ran after her. She swallowed. "Hang on, Sammy," Serena whispered. "Please, hang on..."

When Serena threw open Sammy's door, the room was still as pitch dark as it had been that morning, and Sammy was still staring at his Shaneera.

"Sammy!" Serena ran in and grabbed the pet from his hands. "Snap out of it!"

Sammy snarled, jumping up. His eyes were deep black vortexes, with yellow swirling within them. "What are you *doing*?" he screamed, grabbing the Shaneera back. "This Shaneera's mine!"

"Sammy, listen to me!" Serena yelled, grabbing his shoulders. "That thing's evil. If you don't get rid of it, you—"

"Get away from me!" Sammy shrieked,

pushing Serena away. "You don't know anything. I'll *never* give up my Shaneera." Clutching his pet close, he ran out of the room and down the stairs.

"He won't listen to me," Serena cried as she ran after him with Luna at her side. This time the Enemy had gone too far, trying to destroy her own brother. Serena was ready for vengeance.

"He's probably going to PERFUME PETS," Luna said quickly as they reached the sidewalk. "Serena, transform!"

"Gotcha." Serena looked around to make sure no one was watching, then reached up towards the heavens.

"MOON PRISM POWER MAKE-UP!!"

Serena closed her eyes as light washed over her, and, after the usual fancy 4th of July celebration style morph sequence, she ran off down the street again as Sailor Moon.

Upon reaching PERFUME PETS, Serena was horrified to see the place packed with children and teenagers, all holding Shaneeras. Their eyes were black and yellow vortexes, focused on the store clerk, who stood upon a countertop with her arms spread. Serena scanned the crowd and found

## the power of love

Sammy, Mika, as well as Serena's own classmates.

"Listen up!" the clerk commanded, a crazy smile on her face. "You pitiful humans—you are now my slaves. Spread the Shaneeras to all your friends. The Shaneeras are draining all your energy, but Jedite needs more energy. More! Give Shaneeras to all the moronic humans you know, and darkness will finally rule." The crazed clerk laughed maniacally.

"Yes..." chanted the crowd, their eyes wide but their faces blank like zombies. "We will obey..."

Obey? Oh, boy, Serena thought. Not another group of regular people-turned-zombies. Didn't the Enemy have any other creative tactics?

"Enough of your Shaneerantics," Serena yelled, jumping on top of another counter so she could point directly at the clerk. After all, eye contact was crucial to make a truly threatening superhero speech.

"How dare you brainwash innocent people with Furby wanna-bes! You've corrupted the young people of Crossroads long enough. Prepare to be thwarted!"

"Thwarted," Luna whispered from Serena's feet with an approving nod. "Nice vocab word."

"I looked up a few choice words in the dictionary after the last battle. That was the only one I could remember," Serena whispered in Luna's ear, proud of herself. Looking back at the whacked-out store clerk, Serena clenched her fist. "I am Sailor Moon, Champion of Justice and Defender against Evil, and on behalf of the Moon, you're punished!"

The clerk narrowed her eyes at Serena. "Sailor Moon, huh?" she hissed. "Well then, on behalf of evil, prepare to get eaten!" She roared and a great shadow melted over her, warping her form. When the darkness faded, she had turned into a green lizard with a woman's body.

Serena couldn't help but giggling.

"What's so funny?!" boomed the fire-breathing green lizard-woman.

Serena tried to contain her giggles. "Hee...nothing...hee. It's just that...you look like such a dorky version of Godzilla." Serena kept cracking up.

This only angered the lizard-lady more.

## the power of love

"Get her, you young fools!" Clerk-zilla snarled, pointing at Serena. "Take her down, and stop her from laughing!"

All the young zombies turned to Serena with dark eyes. With a cry, they started to grab at her legs.

"Hey," Serena screamed. "Let go of me!" She jumped and dove over the crowd, rolling along the floor to break her fall. Pushing open the door and running as fast as she could, Serena dashed outside with the mob in hot pursuit.

"What should I do?" Serena cried, her voice panicked. "Oh, Tuxedo Mask, where are you?"

"You can't depend on Tuxedo Mask or anyone else, for that matter," Luna yelled as the children approached. "You have to learn to fight on your own, Sailor Moon!"

Someone grabbed Serena's pigtail, and she screamed and fell. Somehow escaping from all the arms grabbing for her, she yanked her tiara off her head.

"I can't use the tiara on Sammy and all my friends!" Serena cried.

"You can use the tiara to de-brainwash

them," Luna advised. "Throw the tiara and cry MOON TIARA STARDUST!"

Serena bit her teeth, closed her eyes, and threw the tiara with all her might.

"MOON TIARA STARDUST!!!"

Serena's tiara soared through the air above the young zombies' heads. Glowing a golden light, the discus rained sparkles of gold, which glittered down over the brainwashed mob.

The youths immediately froze. As the gold sparkles fell on their heads and shoulders, their eyes changed from black and yellow vortexes to their normal colors. Slowly, everyone's eyelids drooped, and the mob collapsed to the sidewalk.

Noticing Serena's frightened expression, Luna shook her head and smiled. "They're fine, Sailor Moon, just sleeping. You did it!"

Serena let out a breath and put a hand over her heart. She saw Sammy's sleeping form, and her eyes softened.

Oh, Sammy, she thought with relief. You're finally okay. Now I can go back to teasing you again.

A long tail suddenly wrapped around

# the power of love

Serena's throat, choking her. Clerk-zilla snarled and pulled her tail tighter around Serena's neck.

"How dare you!" the lizard-lady screamed. "You think you can foil my plans and get away with it? You're history!"

Serena's face was turning blue. "Uh, Luna..." Serena eyed her black cat while gagging.

"Your tiara!" Luna cried. "Hit her at the base of the tail, Sailor Moon. That's her weak spot!"

Serena shakily reached to her forehead and pulled her tiara off. Fighting to breathe, she threw it.

"MOON...TIARA..." Serena choked trying to get the words out. "ACTION!!"

The tiara hit Clerk-zilla at the base of its tail, and Serena was immediately released. The lizard-lady screamed as gold light traveled up her green body and turned her to dust.

"Noooooo," she shrieked, fading away. "Someone, help—" Her screams were cut off, and sparkling light engulfed her. When it finally filtered away, her body was vaporized to a pile of moon dust on the concrete floor.

Serena caught her tiara and shakily put it back on. With a sigh she fell to the ground in relief, her arms spread on the sidewalk.

"Another easy day of fighting for justice." Serena stuck out her tongue at Luna, still catching her breath.

Luna smiled and walked over to Serena's face. She licked her fondly.

"Nice job, Sailor Moon."

Just then, the mob began to stir. Serena looked up, only to see Sammy sitting up among the other kids and holding his head.

"What happened?" he muttered vaguely. "I don't remember anything..." Looking up, he saw Sailor Moon, and his eyes widened.

Serena squeaked and dove behind a parked car. As she stumbled to her feet, she thought worriedly, I can't let him see me. He might recognize me!

"Hey!" Sammy ran up to her, eyes bright. "Sailor V! Wow, can I have your autograph? I'm a big fan!"

Serena scowled, and her shoulders slumped. Sailor V? After all that work, no respect.

## the power of love

A little bit of self-promotion couldn't hurt, Serena reasoned.

"I'm not Sailor V, I'm Sailor Moon," she corrected from behind the car.

Sammy shrugged. "You're still a super-hero, right? That's good enough for me. Can I have an autograph?"

Serena grinned. That was more like it. Serena wanted to tell Sammy who she really was, but Luna would get too upset. Speaking of Luna, Serena had an idea.

"If you're really a fan, listen up carefully," Serena called over the car. "Respect your fellow animals and treat them with kindness. Particularly cats!" she added, with a wink at Luna.

Sammy smiled and nodded. "Whatever you say, Sailor Moon," Sammy said, clutching the signed paper Serena had just given him. "Thanks!"

Serena picked up Luna and snuck away as Sammy went to go help Mika. "Maybe that'll do the trick, huh Luna?" Serena asked with a smile.

Luna scowled and crossed her arms. "I could've gotten him to like me on my own, you know," she grumbled.

Serena rolled her eyes. "Yeah, right, Luna. Sure you could've."

The next morning, Serena ran downstairs, late as usual.

"Aahhh! Where's my lunch?!" Serena shoved a piece of toast in her mouth, running around frantically. She ran to the breakfast table, then froze.

Sammy had Luna in his lap. He fed her some of his oatmeal from a spoon and patted her on the head. "Good kitty," he said with a smile.

"Sammy!" Serena ran to him, eyes wide. "You're actually getting along with Luna?"

Sammy shrugged, scratching Luna behind the ears. "Yeah, people should respect their fellow animals and treat them with kindness."

Sounds familiar, Serena thought.

"And Luna's pretty cool." He looked up at Serena and smirked. "Much cooler than you, Serena. I don't know why she hangs around you so much."

Serena snatched Luna from him. "If I wasn't in such a rush, you'd pay for that, brat," she said, snatching another piece of toast on her way out the door. "See you guys later!"

"You know, Serena," Luna said quietly as Serena dashed down the sidewalk. "Sammy knows how to pay proper attention to the feline race. You could learn a thing or two from him."

Serena jammed Luna on her shoulder and ran faster. "Well, you know who to thank for his change of heart," Serena said, grinning triumphantly. "Not bad, if I do say so myself. I guess even bratty Sammy can change."

Serena shoved the toast in her mouth and smiled. "An you know wha I awways say - wif Sawor Moo awwound, we haf nofin to feaw!"

Luna sighed and shook her head. "Don't talk with your mouth full, Serena."

# Chapter 9
# All That Jazz

The Crossroads Mall was bustling. Stores lining the many levels were jam-packed with people milling about, and lights glowed a rosy yellow in the high, domed ceiling. Serena, a lollipop in her mouth, skipped along next to Molly.

"Oh, Molly," Serena squealed. "There're so many people here today."

"Isn't it great?" Molly brushed the bright red bangs from her eyes and smiled. "I always love it on Saturdays because everyone shows up for the weekend sales."

"And don't forget all the cute guys," Serena pointed out, her eyes scanning the crowds. "Hmm,

## the power of love

let's see...there, and there, and over there..." If only Andrew and Tuxedo Mask were here, Serena thought. Then things would be perfect.

Molly nudged Serena playfully. "C'mon, Serena. If you guy-gaze all day, we won't get any shopping done."

Serena immediately turned back to her friend, taking her arm.

"You're right," Serena agreed. "What was I thinking?"

The air-conditioning of the mall was a nice change from the hot outdoors, and Serena breathed deeply. The weather report had said the heat wave they were in was going to end with a thunderstorm that day. Serena hoped it would be a mild storm. If there was one thing she hated, it was thunder.

The two passed a music store, and Molly stopped and grabbed Serena's sleeve.

"Hey, let's stop by Babel Records. I love this place."

"Babel?" Serena pouted. "Let's come back here later. I'm famished. How about some ice cream?"

Molly turned to her. "Serena, you're *always*

hungry. Just in the first two hours, we've had three slices of pepperoni pizza, a bag of choose-your-own candy, a can of cherry-flavored popcorn, and you're still eating that lollipop."

Serena pulled the white stick from her mouth. It was picked clean.

"Not anymore," she said with a giggle. "Ice cream is a mall must, Molly. Think about the famous Shakespearean poem: Ye scream, thee scream, we the people scream for ice cream."

Molly rolled her eyes. "You're really gonna make 'ye' scream," Molly muttered. "I'll make you a deal. Babel now, scream later. Cool?"

Serena sighed.

"Fine, fine," she said at last. "But as a fee for keeping me wait, Baskin Robbins is on you." She gave a peace sign. "And today I intend to scarf *all* 31 flavors."

Molly gave her a sideways glance as they walked in the store. "Why am I not surprised?"

Serena giggled and hugged her around the neck. "That's why I love you, Molly!" Serena knew she could always count on her best friend to put up with her demands.

## the power of love

Babel Music was huge. Tapes and CDs filled miles of display stands and shelves, and posters of bands plastered the walls.

"They have everything here," Molly declared. "There's so much music here. Just look at this selection."

"Here's Jewel's CD." Serena pulled down the CD and started singing. "Who will save your soul..." She glanced over at Molly. "What are you checkin' out, Molly?"

Molly flipped through the CDs she held.

"Bach's English Suites No. 2, 4, and 5, Miles Davis' *Highlights from the Plugged Nickel*, Louis Armstrong's *What a Wonderful World*, Mozart's *Le Nozza Di Figaro*...man, I want them all, but there's no way I could buy everything today."

Serena stood there completely dazed. Wasn't that all parent music Molly had in her hand?

"You listen to music like that, Molly?" she asked.

Molly nodded. "I love it."

Serena took a few of the CDs Molly was holding.

"I just got the new Brandy CD," Serena commented as she skimmed through Molly's choices. "But I've never heard of Duke Smellington."

"That's Duke Ellington," Molly corrected. "And that's because he's not hip-hop or alternative. He's jazz."

"Jazz?" Serena's eyes widened as she stared at the CDs. Molly had always been pretty sophisticated for her age. Even when Serena and Molly went camping together in third grade, Molly brought F. Scott Fitzgerald for reading material. All Serena had were three issues of YM. Even Molly's fashion tended to be more serious. While Serena would gleefully shop for the latest Hard Candy colors, Molly would stick with Dior and Chanel.

"No way, it's out!" Molly cried as she pulled down another CD. "This is the new Amade Yus."

"Who's he?" Serena asked as Molly gazed at the CD with starry eyes.

"He's my favorite jazz artist," Molly explained. "His music is perfect for a romantic, moonlit evening stroll. I think I have a major crush on Amade."

## the power of love

Serena glanced over at the CD and made a face. The CD jacket showed an abstract illustration with silver trim around the sides.

"Molly, the dude who makes this music is probably gray-bearded and almost 100 years old." Serena handed over the CD to her best friend. "How can you have a crush on someone so ancient?"

Molly simply smiled.

Serena shook her head. Geez, she thought. How could Molly even think of dating a guy so antique? With young studs like the Backstreet Boys around, what was Molly thinking? But, Serena remembered that Molly's dad was more than ten years older than her mom. Serena began to wonder if liking older guys was a genetic thing or something.

Queen Beryl sat upon her throne, thick shadows enveloping her snake-like body. Music was playing, billowing through the hot, musty air of her evil kingdom. She focused her cold orange eyes at the small plant on a table before her. "I do hope you're not wasting my time, Jedite," she warned, her voice a lizard's hiss.

Jedite smiled. "Please watch, my queen," he said softly as he moved his fingers and the music grew louder.

The plant began to quiver. As the music went on, the plant slowly shriveled until it became a sad, drooping clump of dead stem and leaves. Queen Beryl raised an eyebrow.

"What is this?"

"This is my new plan, Queen Beryl," Jedite answered, his eyes glowing in the darkness. "This music you have heard contains special wavelengths that steal energy from the listener. The energy from this plant was absorbed by the music." He smiled. "The same thing will happen to humans who hear it."

Queen Beryl's face lit up. "Excellent work, Jedite," she commended. "Those foolish humans love music. Set your plan into motion immediately."

Jedite bowed his head. "Of course, my Queen." Jedite straightened and snapped his fingers. "Slave, come to me," he commanded.

The thick air behind him began to tremble.

## the power of love

A beautiful woman with fiery red hair slowly appeared, the shadows melting from her form. A dozen bats appeared with her, and they flew off into the darkness, their screeches echoing in the stone kingdom.

"You called, master?" she asked quietly, bending down on one knee.

Jedite held up a small cassette tape. "This music will suck the energy we need from those humans on Earth. Take it, and make sure every human hears it."

The woman smiled. "Understood."

JAM, Crossroads' biggest recording studio, was quiet that night. Rain pattered outside the tall, shining skyscraper that towered in the navy sky. In the darkness of the rainy evening, no one saw Jedite's deathly beautiful servant slip into one of the recording rooms. She pushed the door shut behind her with long, red fingernails.

"Excellent," the woman murmured. "No one's here." She pulled Jedite's tape out of her dress pocket. "If I put this tape in the recording machines, all copies made from them will contain the evil waves that absorb energy, and soon enough the energy-sucking music will be all over the city!"

She flipped the eject button on the machine and inserted the tape. It clicked as it slid into place.

"Queen Beryl will be so pleased."

Behind her, the doorknob suddenly turned. The woman whipped around, then quickly hid behind a tall plant.

An attractive lady with short brown hair entered the room. She walked over to the recording machine, her high heels clicking on the tile floor.

"Phew," She let out a sigh. "Why does this room have to be on the top floor?"

Jedite's servant narrowed her eyes as the brown-haired woman pushed the eject button on the recorder. The evil tape popped out, and the woman pulled it out curiously.

"There's no label," she murmured. "I wonder why?" She shrugged. "Well, it must be Amade's tape. How silly of him to forget to label it."

"Akiko," someone called from outside the

**the power of love**

doorway. "Amade just called. He's waiting for you at Cafe Crossroads."

"Coming," Akiko called. She slipped the cassette into a case and quickly left the room.

Jedite's servant growled. "Curses! That's Queen Beryl's special tape. I must get it back."

She whipped her hand forward, and her nails shot out to ten times their length. They glinted in the darkness as her eyes flashed.

"I will get that tape back," she swore. "No matter what I have to do."

# Chapter 10
# Rain Fall

Akiko quickly stepped into Cafe Crossroads. It was raining hard outside, and her high-heels dragged water onto the tiled floor.

"My," she giggled as she shook out her umbrella. "It's pouring out there." She stomped her shoes to dry them, then looked around. "Amade! Where are you?"

A young man at a nearby table looked up. He saw Akiko, then quickly jumped up.

"Akiko," he called, waving. "Over here!"

## the power of love

Akiko spotted him and made her way towards the table. "Amade," she cried, running up to him. "You're soaked! What happened?"

Amade held a bouquet of roses. As Akiko ran up, he blushed and quickly hid the flowers behind his back. "Uh, nothing," he blurted as Akiko pulled napkins from the table. "I just forgot my umbrella."

"Oh, Amade." She began to wipe his drenched jacket. "You're so silly! How could you forget your umbrella on a rainy day like this?"

Amade looked down. "I've had a lot on my mind," he said quietly.

Akiko smiled, pulling off his sunglasses. "And don't wear these indoors, silly," she said with a click of her tongue. "Now why would you want to cover up those pretty blue eyes of yours?"

Amade blushed.

Akiko pulled the tape out of her purse. "Here," she said, pressing it into his hands. "I picked up your demo tape. I listened to it yesterday. It's wonderful!"

Amade smiled shyly. "Um, thanks..." He scratched his head. His fingers were long and smooth, a musician's fingers.

"Uh, Akiko," he said quietly. "Isn't it your birthday today?"

Akiko laughed. "Oh, Amade," she cried, spreading out her hands. "How'd you find out? I didn't want anyone to know."

Amade blinked. "Why wouldn't you want anyone to know?"

"Because I'm getting old!" Akiko laughed again. "Amade, I'm twenty-six today. I can't believe how fast time passes."

Amade gently touched her shoulder. "That's not old," he insisted. "I'm already twenty-four. You're only two years older than I am."

Akiko smiled, touching Amade's shoulder. "Amade, you are so great," she sighed. "You always make me feel better."

Amade looked down again. His hands trembled over the bouquet behind his back, but he still didn't pull it out.

"Now, onto business." Akiko brushed some hair behind her ear. "The demo's fabulous, Amade. Finish it up and we'll be doing great. And don't forget to come up with a title, too. What do

# the power of love

you want on the next album cover?"

Amade shook his head. "I haven't decided yet."

"That's fine," Akiko assured. "Come up with a title first, then think about the cover."

Just then, a man approached their table. "Akiko," he said. "We're having a problem at the recording studio. Could you come help us out?"

Akiko turned her head to him. "No problem." She smiled at Amade. "I guess I gotta go. See you later, ok? Keep my umbrella, or you'll catch a cold the next time you go out."

She pushed her umbrella at him and ran to the door. Just before she left, she blew Amade a kiss and winked.

She didn't notice he had turned bright red.

The door shut behind Akiko with a wet slapping sound, and Amade stood alone. He slowly pulled the bouquet of roses from behind his back and looked at them sadly.

"I'm such an idiot," he murmured. He flipped over the cassette Akiko had handed him.

"She didn't see the title I wrote on the case, *A Waltz for Akiko*." He sighed, and slipped the tape in his pocket.

Amade took Akiko's umbrella with him and stepped out into the rain, opening the umbrella over his head. He shivered as the cold seeped into his already-wet clothes. Letting out a breath, he began to walk down the sidewalk.

"Don't move!"

Amade froze. Slowly, he turned back his head.

"Who's there?" he called hesitantly.

Jedite's servant stepped from a back alley-way, her eyes dark. Her dagger-like nails glittered in the rain.

"You're not going anywhere," she hissed, clenching a fist.

"Who... who are you?" Amade was shaking.

The woman's body began to change. Her arms and legs got longer, her eyes got smaller, her ears flapped out, and great wings spread out from her back.

Amade choked. "M...M..." He dropped the umbrella, spun around, and ran for his life.

"Monster!!!"

# the power of love

"This rain sucks." Serena sighed as she stepped down Molly's front steps. "I can't believe it was sunny and blue-skied this morning."

Luna, on Serena's shoulder, cocked an eyebrow.

"If it wasn't for the rain, no one would appreciate the sun."

"Sure, we would," Serena countered, shaking her head in disagreement. "Also, think about all the added benefits—permanent tans, constant beach weather, endless good moods, and no baseball rain delays."

Luna hopped onto Serena's shoulder. "I don't think any of the farmers would be pleased without rain."

"Or the umbrella makers," Serena added. "By the way, did you realize that you weigh like two hundred pounds?" Serena complained as she nudged Luna. "You're heavier than steel. Maybe I should get you some diet cat food."

"Diet cat food?" Luna muttered. "That stuff tastes terrible."

Just my luck, Serena thought. I'm stuck

with a cat who's not only bossy, but finicky too. She picked up Luna and put her on the ground.

"Then at least try to exercise instead because if you don't lose weight soon you're gonna break my back." Serena side-stepped a mud puddle on the sidewalk.

"Hey!" she shouted. "I know! A rainy day is a great day to play video games." She giggled. "It's a perfect excuse to spend some quality time with Sailor V and Andrew."

"Serena." Luna's voice began to take on its familiar pseudo-parent tone. "Don't you have a math test to study for? It's almost six o'clock, you know."

"Don't be silly, Luna." Serena thrust her chin in the air. "I can't study when it's raining. It's called Serena's Law of Addition. Math homework plus precipitation equals vacation."

Luna rolled her eyes. "Yeah, your whole brain is on vacation, Serena. You can knock on the door all you want, but no one's home."

Suddenly, a screaming Amade ran down the sidewalk and crashed into Serena. The two fell to the wet and filthy concrete with a loud splat.

## the power of love

"Aaaagggghhh!" Serena screamed as she saw all the dirt spattered on her clothes. "Look at my Miu Miu blouse! It's gone from earthy beige to muddy brown." She jumped to her feet, fuming at the young man who still lay on the ground. "Why don't you watch where you're going?! Do you realize that interfering with a hip chick's style can get you arrested? At least a fashion arrest."

"There was a..." Amade could barely talk. "It was...a...monster!" He looked up, saw Serena glaring at him with flaring nostrils, and screamed louder.

"Agghh!" he cried, crawling away from her frantically. "Not another one! Don't hurt me!"

Serena blinked. She quickly shook her head and blushed. "Hey, no, I'm not a monster." Serena frowned. Great, she thought. Why do I keep scaring people I've never met? First the little boy with the donuts a few chapters back and now this dude.

Amade peeked his head out from beneath his arms. "Really?" he squeaked. "I'm...I'm sorry. You just looked so mad a second ago that I got scared."

Serena sighed and brushed some mud off

her blouse. She looked up at the guy and realized he was pretty cute. Kind of fragile and timid, but good-looking. "No, it's ok. You didn't mean to bump into me like that." She rubbed some water from her cheek. "Why don't you have an umbrella?"

Amade shakily got up, covering his eyes from the rain. "I dropped it somewhere," he answered. "I'm not really sure where it is."

Serena held up her umbrella over the two of them.

"You might as well share mine, then," she offered. "I'll walk you down the street. You'll get drenched otherwise."

Amade blinked, then smiled.

"Thanks," he said. "You're kind."

"No problem."

As the two of them walked down the street, the drops of rain made tapping noises on Serena's satellite-dish-sized Tommy Hilfiger umbrella. The navy fabric seemed to cover Serena and Amade in a faint blue glow.

Serena scratched her head. "So," she asked. "What were you screaming about, anyway?"

## the power of love

Serena sensed another potential excuse for skipping her homework.

Amade frowned. "I...I saw a monster," he explained, wringing his hands together. "I was leaving the cafe when a monster jumped from the shadows and tried to attack me!" He looked down. "You...probably don't believe me," he added quietly.

Serena stared at him, mouth open. A monster? An excuse to not do homework is one thing, but another face-off with some Wes Craven movie ghoul was going overboard. Why did Serena always get the gory super-hero action? What about simple crime-fighting. Things like pickpockets or shoplifters. She could deal with them. Even car thieves or bank robbers. But enough of this Twilight Zone stuff!

Amade saw her staring, and he quickly shook his head. "I...I dunno. Maybe I've been working too hard or something. F...forget it." He rubbed a hand across his eyes and looked up. They stopped in front of a small brick building.

"This is where I have to work tonight," Amade said wearily as he pulled a business card from his jacket. He handed it to Serena. "I'm really sorry about your blouse. Thanks for sharing your umbrella." With that, he stepped into the building and closed the door behind him.

"Great," Serena mumbled as she looked down at the card. "Another monster for me to—" Her eyes shot open when she saw the name *Amade Yus* written in small blue print.

"Amade Yus?" That name sounded familiar. Suddenly, Serena remembered Babel Records. "That guy's the jazz musician Molly's into!"

Luna looked up at the building seriously. "Serena," she said quickly. "I think the Enemy is up to something again."

Serena nodded in agreement, but kept thinking about Amade Yus. When Molly showed her the CD, Serena imagined someone totally different. Amade was so much younger than she had thought. No wonder Molly had such a crush on him, even though he was too wimpy for Serena's tastes.

"Serena, pay attention!" Luna snapped. "You can't sit around daydreaming all day again. We've got to start investigating this monster story."

## the power of love

Serena sighed, then nodded. "You're right, Luna." Amade had been really nice. Serena couldn't let the bad guys get him.

"But, why would the Enemy be after that guy, Luna?" Serena asked. "He didn't exactly seem threatening, if you know what I mean."

"I don't know." Luna's eyes narrowed. "But we have to find out."

Serena looked up at the brick building in front of her. The words ALL THAT JAZZ MUSIC CLUB were printed in large letters above the doorway.

"We better get inside this club," Serena said, clutching the brooch on her school uniform as the rain slapped against her umbrella.

Don't worry, Amade, she thought. I'll protect you.

# Chapter 11
# Gone Batty

Serena stepped under the rain roof of the music club and closed her umbrella. As she reached out to open the door, she suddenly caught sight of the sign on the wall. "Uh-oh," she mumbled, slapping a hand to her head.

"What is it?" Luna asked as she jumped from Serena's shoulder.

"Look," Serena said, pointing to the sign on the building. *"Private Club for Musicians. Members Only. 21 and Over.* Not only am I way too young and not a member, but I couldn't play an instrument to save my life." She looked over at Luna.

## the power of love

"What now?"

Luna sighed. "Serena, do I always have to direct you? You're the Champion of Justice. Have you forgotten about the Luna Pen?"

Serena's eyes lit up. That's right, she thought. With the magic pen Luna gave her in the last novel, she could easily transform into whatever or whomever she wanted.

She paused.

"Luna, what do I transform into, a saxophone?"

Luna looked over at Serena and shook her head in disgust.

"Serena, please tell me you're joking. All you need to do is fake being a musician with a membership card."

Serena's face brightened. Cool, she thought. Here was her chance to morph into a glamorous pop star. She began to imagine herself as one of the TLC girls or Jewel or Mariah Carey or—

"Serena!" Luna was losing her patience. "What are you waiting for? Morph into a plain studio musician so we can get in!"

Serena made a face. "A *plain* studio musi-

cian? A Champion of Justice can't settle for plain."
She thrust her pen into the sky.

"MOON POWER...TRANSFORM INTO A
SLAMMIN' CHICK STAR LIKE JENNIFER
LOPEZ!!"

The pen's jewel shot out its light, and when
the pink and orange smoke faded away Serena
looked down at herself. "Wicked," Serena cried
happily. "I am so rockin'!"

Serena's blouse and skirt had turned into
black leather pants, a white tee-shirt, a red leather
jacket and big silver hoop earrings. Her hair was
flashy green like a techno pop star and went well
beyond her shoulders.

Luna snickered. "It's you, Serena."

Serena scowled. "Just because you can't
keep up with the young generation. Maybe you
should try The Box or MTV instead of watching
VH-1 all the time." She grabbed Luna and draped
her over her shoulder. "Now play dead. No pets
are allowed, so you're my accessory."

"What?!"

"No other option, Luna," Serena whispered
as she opened the door. "Now play like a mink or

we'll blow our cover."

Luna covered her head with her paws. "How humiliating..."

The music club was brimming as Serena walked inside. The dozens of tables were filled with musicians who stared enthusiastically at the young man on stage. Hardly anyone was talking, their attention completely focused on him.

"Look," Serena whispered to Luna. "It's Amade."

Amade sat behind a huge piano, a single spotlight on him. His eyes were closed, and his fingers gently pressed the black and white keys in beautiful combinations. Music drifted through the air.

"Wow," Serena whispered as she found an empty booth and sat down. "He's really good."

A waiter came up as she rested her head on the back cushion.

"Would you like something to drink, miss?" he asked, bringing up his pad.

Serena grinned.

"Sure. I'll take, let's see, one extra-large

chocolate milkshake."

The waiter blinked, and Luna's jaw dropped. "Serena!" she hissed into her ear. "What are you doing?"

"Shut up, Luna." Serena growled as she covered Luna's face.

"I'm sorry, ma'am," the waiter said slowly. "This is a music club. We don't carry, uh, milkshakes."

"No?" Serena tapped her chin. "Well, how about some cookies, then?"

The waiter's eyes widened.

Serena frowned as Luna slapped a paw to her forehead.

"Fine," Serena said at last, waving a hand. "I don't want anything. Thanks anyway."

The waiter nodded slightly, then walked away. Serena noticed him shaking his head and muttering something as he left.

"Serena!" Luna yelled as soon as the waiter was gone. "What's wrong with you? Ordering a shake at a club? Are you trying to blow our cover?!"

"I wouldn't talk," Serena shot back. "You're

## the power of love

supposed to be a fashion accessory. Yelling at me and squirming like that is a recipe for disaster."

Luna shook her head angrily. "Just shape up. You're supposed to be twenty-one, so stop acting like a kid." Luna angrily settled herself back as Serena's shoulders. "I don't even know why I bother with this girl," she muttered.

Serena sighed. How was she supposed to know they don't serve milkshakes or cookies at clubs? Her older friends were into clubbing, but Serena was too young. At any rate, Serena vowed to keep drinking milkshakes until she was silver-haired and wearing dentures.

She flicked blue eyes at Amade as Luna got more comfortable on her shoulder. After a moment, Serena asked, "Luna?"

"Yeah?"

"Look at Amade's closed eyes, his quick, gentle fingers, the slight smile curving his lips. Doesn't he look really happy up there?"

Luna looked up at Amade.

"Yeah," Luna answered. "So?"

Serena smiled. "I dunno," she murmured. "He just looks so content. I wonder if he's thinking of somebody." Serena started to imagine Tuxedo Mask next to her, listening to the soothing jazz music.

A few minutes later, Amade finished his piece and took a bow. The audience clapped as he stepped off the stage.

"Come on," Luna whispered. "Now's our chance. We've got to follow him, Serena."

But Serena had fallen fast asleep with her head on the table. "Tuxedo Mask," she mumbled. "Thanks so much for the night of jazz music and chocolate milkshakes..."

"Serena!"

Serena shot up, eyes wide. "Huh? What?" She looked at the stage, and blinked. "Oh no! Where's Amade?"

"He left through that door," Luna whispered, pointing to the back. "That must lead to the parking garage in the basement."

"Let's hit it!" Serena quickly got up and snuck to the back. As soon as she was through the door, she ran as fast as she could down the stairs. She pointed her Luna Pen into the air.

"MOON POWER...DETRANSFORM!!"

## the power of love

Light flashed around her, and as she jumped down the stairs her disguise melted off and her clothes and hair were changed back to normal.

"Finally," Serena mumbled as her golden hair flew out behind her. "Those earrings were heavy. It must be tough being a famous celeb."

"Serena!" Luna shouted as she ran beside her. "Look out!"

"Huh?"

Serena screamed and covered her face as something dark flew at her. It screeched and flapped black leathery wings around her face.

"Eww, what is it?!" Serena cried. "That thing stinks!" She swung her arms madly, and her hand smacked into the flying thing full force. The creature fell to the floor, stunned, before flapping back into the air dizzily and flying away.

Serena tentatively peeked from between her fingers. "Is it gone?"

Luna panted, eyes wide. "Yeah. That was a nasty looking bat."

"A bat?" Serena blinked. "What's it doing here?"

She was cut off as someone suddenly

screamed.

Luna whipped her head around. "That came from down below!"

"Oh my God!" Serena slapped a hand to her mouth. "That was Amade!"

Serena jumped down the last few stairs with Luna right behind. As soon as they reached the parking lot, Serena gasped.

A beautiful woman stood above an unconscious Amade. She laughed wickedly, clicking her frighteningly long nails together as she clutched a small cassette tape in her other hand.

"Now, to kill this worthless human," she said with a snicker. She raised her claws.

"Don't you *dare* touch him,!" Serena screamed as she ran towards the villain. "You creepy, slimy, disgusting thing—get away from Amade!"

The woman flicked her head at Serena, then snarled. She jumped into the air, spread her leathery wings, and flew out of the parking garage and into the night sky.

Serena gasped. "She's *definitely* with the

## the power of love

Enemy." After all, Serena thought, even the smartest car-jackers don't know how to sprout wings.

"Serena," Luna cried as she ran to Amade. "Come over here and make sure he's all right."

Serena quickly bent to one knee and checked Amade's pulse. "He's fine," she said after a minute. "She just knocked him out, thank God."

Something on the ground beside her made her blink. "What's this?" Serena reached over and picked up the empty tape case that had fallen on the ground.

"*A Waltz for Akiko?*" Serena muttered, reading the case. "Who's Akiko?" A small picture fell out of the case, and Serena caught it. A pretty woman with short brown hair smiled at her from the glossy photo.

"He's...got a crush?" Serena mumbled. She giggled, covering her mouth. "This must be Akiko."

Luna took a step back, surprised. "How can you be so sure?"

Serena snorted. "Obviously, you've never had a crush, Luna." Serena waved the picture at

Luna. "He carries a picture of her around. He named a song after her. Come on, Luna, this guy's diggin' her."

Luna looked at the case. "That bat-witch had a tape in her hand," she observed. "It must've been the one in this case. But why would the Enemy want this tape?"

Just then, Amade began to moan. Serena quickly lifted his head up.

"Are you ok?" she asked. "You got hit pretty hard."

Amade's eyes slowly opened. "My tape..." he groaned. "My tape...where's...my tape?" He suddenly sat up, grabbing the empty case. "That beast took my tape!"

Serena shrugged. "I guess that bat-lady's a big jazz fan."

"You don't understand!" Amade's dark blue eyes were wide as he looked at Serena. "This tape...it's too important. I have to get it back."

How cute, Serena thought. He *really* likes that Akiko girl.

"Ok," Serena answered as she helped him up. "We'll go get it back."

## the power of love

Luna hopped on Serena's shoulder as Amade fumbled for his car keys. "Serena," Luna whispered. "How come you're so willing to go fight this time?"

"Because this fight is for love, Luna." Serena clenched her fist and smiled. "And I'm not letting some smelly freak-lady get in the way of a man and his heart!"

Luna rolled her eyes. "I think you've been watching too many soap operas, Serena," she mumbled with a sigh.

# Chapter 12
# Love Power

Serena squinted through the window and looked to the sky as Amade drove his BMW Z3 full speed. It had finally stopped raining, but it had gotten dark and hard to see.

"Can you see that beast, Serena?" he asked as he turned the car around a sharp turn.

"No, it's too...Wait, there she is!" Serena pointed up. "She's flying east."

"Right!" Amade jerked the steering wheel, and the car flew down an empty road.

"I'm getting that tape back," Amade muttered through clenched teeth. "I won't let anyone take it away from me, not even some bat-lady."

## the power of love

Serena looked at him out of the corner of her eye. Amade's eyes were narrowed, and his knuckles were white over the wheel. She tried not to giggle. Man, he must really like Akiko, Serena thought.

"So, Amade." Serena grinned and leaned closer to him. "That song you played in the music club was *A Waltz for Akiko*, wasn't it?"

Amade's eyes widened, and he blushed.

Serena could remember how happy Amade had looked playing the piano. His gentle fingers, his curved lips...

"It was, wasn't it?" Serena repeated.

Amade was quiet for a moment. "Yeah," he answered at last.

Serena smiled. "It's a beautiful song. I saw the picture of her in your tape case. She's really beautiful." She raised an eyebrow. "You really like her, don't you?"

Amade turned away.

Serena laughed. "Why are you so embarrassed? Hey, it's ok—I have a crush, too." She held her chin. "Well, two, actually. Or maybe three or four. Everybody likes somebody. Having crushes is completely normal."

"I don't like her," Amade muttered bitterly.

Serena blinked.

Amade's shoulders slowly relaxed, and his voice went very quiet. "I don't *like* her," he said again, his voice barely above a whisper. "I...I *love* her."

Serena froze. Amade was staring at the road blankly, his eyes half-closed, his lips pressed together weakly on his face—not good since he was driving. But Serena knew he was sincere. This wasn't a crush. This was love.

Serena couldn't move for a moment. Finally, slowly, she shook her head.

She put a hand on his shoulder. "Then, tell her."

"I can't," Amade mumbled. "There's no way."

"Why not?" Serena's eyebrows creased. "She's never going to know how you feel unless you tell her so. Tell her, Amade!"

"You don't understand," Amade moaned as he bit his teeth together. "I've...I've been in love with her for so long."

## the power of love

"Then what are you waiting for?" Serena slapped her fist into her palm. "Come on Amade, you can't—"

"Oh my God!" Amade's eyes widened as he pointed to the sky. "Serena, what building is that lady flying to?"

Serena brushed hair from her eyes, squinted, and replied, "The JAM recording studio."

"No," Amade cried, horrified. "Akiko's in there!"

"What?!"

Serena could hardly keep up with Amade as the two of them dashed up the stairs. Geez, Serena thought as she panted and Luna flew beside her. For being such a wimp, this guy certainly doesn't run like one.

Amade reached the top floor first. He threw open the door just as Serena, breathing heavily, caught up.

The red-haired bat-lady stood in the room, holding the cassette tape and laughing. All the workers in the room were unconscious, including the woman with short brown hair Serena had seen in the photo, Akiko.

"Excellent," the bat-lady hissed, her red eyes flashing. "Nothing can stop me now."

"Wanna bet?" Serena yelled, planting her feet apart. She thrust her arms out by her sides. "You've done your evil long enough, freak-face! I will not let you proceed with this wickedness, for I am Sailor...OW!!"

Luna released her teeth from Serena's arm and hissed into her ear, "You haven't transformed yet, Serena. Make that speech and everyone will know your identity!"

Serena blushed and rubbed the teeth marks now in her flesh. "Um, what I just said...just forget about it."

"What are you doing?" Amade yelled at the bat-lady. "Why did you take my tape? And what did you do to Akiko?!"

The woman narrowed her eyes. "This isn't your tape-it's Jedite's!" Saliva dripped from her mouth. "Once I put it into these recording machines, all the tapes made from here will spread energy-absorbing music throughout the ranks of you measly humans, and our kingdom shall rule

## the power of love

all!"

Serena laughed lightly, waving a hand. "Oh! So it's not your tape, Amade. See, it was all a misunderstanding. Let's go, you guys."

Luna clenched her teeth and hissed at Serena.

"What?" Serena made a pouty pose. "No one uses tapes anymore since everything is going digital. It's not worth a major nerve-wrecking fight."

Luna's glare pierced through Serena.

"OK, OK, Luna." Serena turned back to the bat-lady. "Ahem. Like I said, you won't get away with that evil plan!"

"Why won't I?!" the bat-lady demanded.

Hm, Serena thought. Good point. She had the tape, the recording equipment, and she could fly like a bat.

Without hesitating, Luna jumped up towards the bat-lady and grabbed the tape with her teeth. The woman screamed as Luna landed in Serena's arms.

"You cursed feline!" she roared. "Give that back!" The bat-lady suddenly threw up her arms, and a black shadow melted over her. The room rocked with thunder, and the shadows became a flurry of bats. The bat-lady had completely transformed. Her eyes were pink, and her ears had turned long and leathery. Large bat wings protruded from her back.

"Hey," Serena said with a giggle. "You're really Batman's evil twin sister, aren't you?"

"Silence!" the half-bat, half-lady roared. She grabbed Akiko from off the floor and pressed sharp claws against the slender throat.

"Give me my tape," she snarled, "or this woman dies!"

"Akiko!" Amade screamed. "Leave her alone! You can take me instead."

"Uhn..." Akiko's eyelashes fluttered as she woke up. She opened her eyes wide, then gasped at the claws pressing against her neck.

"What...what's going on?!" Her eyes wildly traveled across the room, and she sucked in a breath. "Amade!" she cried. "Help!!"

Serena scowled. "A hostage? That's low, batlady. Prepare to get swatted." Serena threw the tape at the creature. "Get her, Amade!"

## the power of love

As the tape flew through the air, Amade dove towards Akiko and grabbed her, rolling to safety. Luna jumped in the air and caught the tape before the demon's outstretched hand could reach it. With all her might, Luna crushed the tape with her teeth and slammed it onto the floor. The pieces scattered all over the floor.

"Nooooo!!" The bat woman fell to her knees, picking up the smashed remnants of the tape. "Jedite's tape!"

She whipped her head at Serena, snarled, and jumped out the window.

Serena cried out. "She's flying away!"

"Akiko!"

Serena blinked and turned around. Amade was holding a shocked Akiko in his arms. She was shaking as he frantically stroked her cheek.

"Akiko!" he cried. "Are you ok? Akiko!"

"A...Amade?" Akiko stared up at him with watery eyes. She grabbed his shirt, and buried her face in his chest. "Oh, Amade!" she sobbed, curling in his arms. "You...you saved me!"

Serena cocked her head. "Aww...how romantic."

"Serena, come on!" Luna jumped onto her shoulder. "You have to transform and go after the Enemy!"

Serena frowned. "Man, just when we were gettin' to the good stuff."

Serena ran out the door and back down the stairs. Once she reached the street and made sure no one was around, she thrust her hand to the sky. "MOON PRISM POWER MAKE-UP!!!"

After the mini laser show her transformation always created, Serena was fully costumed as Sailor Moon. She grinned, taking a deep breath as moonlight washed over her sparkling uniform.

"Ooh, I feel so energized!" She looked down at Luna. "All right, Luna. Let's go get our bat-friend. Holy Moon Power!"

"Enough corny Batman jokes, Sailor Moon. Quick, to the roof of that concert hall down the street!" Luna yelled out as she ran towards the stairs.

After running three blocks, up twelve floors, and through several hallways, Serena was completely pooped. When she finally opened the door to the roof, she was panting.

## the power of love

"Evil...witch," Serena wheezed. "Beware... I'm...Sailor Moon..."

The demon, desperately trying to piece Jedite's cassette back together, turned to Serena with a growl.

"Get lost, kid!" she yelled as she threw her arm in Serena's direction. A wave of sound roared through the air and smacked into Serena. The impact threw the Scout backward several yards.

"Aaaiii!!" Serena grabbed her head as she was tossed on the concrete floor of the roof.

"Sailor Moon," Luna cried, running to her. "Are you all right?"

"Uggg..." Serena rubbed her ears. "I guess Mom was right when she said playing my stereo so loud was bad for me. I didn't know sound could hurt so much."

"This isn't ordinary sound," Luna muttered as Serena stood up shakily. "She's turning sound waves into a blast attack!"

"Well, I've had just about enough of this." Serena scowled, putting a hand on her hip for her standard Sailor Moon pose.

"You came between an innocent man and

the woman he loves," Serena yelled, pointing a gloved finger at the witch. "And for that, you must pay! No one loves romance more than me. I'm Sailor Moon, Champion of Love and Justice, and on behalf of the Moon, you're punished!"

Out of the side of her mouth, she whispered. "Luna, come up with a plan quick. She's gonna attack me now that my speech's done!"

Luna sighed. "Sailor Moon, that's your job as a super hero. You've got to be a bit more creative." The cat looked around, then suddenly picked up a microphone in her teeth.

"Here," she cried as she tossed it Serena's way. "Use this!"

"Huh?" Serena stared at the microphone as the demon roared and sent another wave of painful sound.

"Yipe," Serena screeched. "What do I do, what do I-wait, that's it!" She flipped the microphone on and threw it at the oncoming sound wave. "Take this, you winged rodent!"

The sound hit the microphone, and the noise suddenly blasted out of the speakers that stood behind the bat woman. She shrieked as the sound

## the power of love

knocked her over.

"Now's my chance," Serena told herself as she pulled off her jeweled head piece. She gripped the shining disk in her fingers, then let it fly.

"MOON TIARA ACTION!!"

The tiara sped at the demon, whizzing through the air with a crackling noise. The bat woman shrieked as the glowing disk zapped her and sent electricity through her body. Her scream echoed through the night as she slowly turned into dust and sprinkled to the concrete.

Serena sighed. Her tiara came back to her, and she caught it and put it back on.

"Sailor Moon?" Luna walked up to her. "Are you all right?"

"Fine, Luna." She suddenly blinked. "I hope Amade and Akiko are okay!"

"Let's go check," Luna proposed as she ran back to the stairs.

Serena moaned. "The battle's over, Luna. Do we have to run again?" It just wasn't fair. All the other super heroes got to fly or at least have some fancy car or plane. Couldn't she at least be bionic?

Serena poked her head around the doorway. Akiko was tying a bandage around Amade's leg.

"I can't believe you risked yourself to save me," Akiko muttered as she shook her head. "You could've been hurt, Amade!"

"I don't care," Amade answered quietly.

"You should care! What if you'd hurt your hand? You wouldn't be able to play the piano anymore."

"Akiko!" Amade suddenly took her hands in his, and she stopped. His eyes were glowing. "I...I couldn't play the piano," he whispered, "if anything had happened to you."

Akiko froze. "Wh...what?" she whispered.

"I...I love you, Akiko." Amade's cheeks turned red, and he smiled. "I love you."

Akiko's eyes were wide. A moment passed, and her eyes welled with tears. "A...Amade..."

Watching the whole scene, Serena started balling. "That's so *sweet!*"

Looking up, Amade and Akiko noticed Serena and started giggling, slightly embarrassed.

Two weeks later, Serena and Molly were at

## the power of love

Babel Records in Crossroads Mall. Molly picked up the latest issue of Rolling Pebble magazine, and her face turned crimson.

"No way!" she cried. "Serena, look at this article—Amade Yus just got married!"

"Mmm," Serena hummed as she looked at the shelves of CDs.

"How could this happen?" Molly wailed. "Oh, Serena-why he didn't wait for me?!"

Serena sighed. "C'mon, Molly-he's too old for you. Besides, he seems really happy with his new bride." Her finger trailed down the shelf of CDs, and she smiled. "Here's his new CD."

Molly's eyebrows went up. "The brand-new one? I thought it was sold-out everywhere."

"This is the last copy." Serena pulled it down. "It's got amazing music, so everyone's buying it. But it's a little different from how he originally planned. He was going to name it after his wife, but they decided that the two of them would name it after someone they both appreciated."

"And who was that?"

Serena smiled, flipping the CD over and showing Molly the cover. On it was a picture of

Sailor Moon, standing on a crescent of yellow light.
The words MOONLIGHT LADY were printed
along the side.

"See." Serena winked. "He's got good taste,
don't you think?"